*Y*OU have behaved very foolishly, risking your reputation, your brother's life—I wonder at you," said Lord Arundell. "Your father speaks highly of your mind and your sensibilities, but you continue to act like a giddy schoolgirl who ought to be sent back to her governess."

Charlotte was furious at his scolding. "How dare you speak to me like this!" Her hands dropped, she stiffened and faced him proudly. "You have no right to scold me, no right at all. Only my father has that right."

"You do not listen to him. It will take a stronger hand than his to tame you," he said contemptuously.

"No doubt, sir," she said, without thinking of her rashness, "you would have me bullied and put upon, so that I should be too afraid and low-spirited to whisper in public!"

He took another step closer to her. In the dim garden, she could not see his face clearly, but as his hands closed over her shoulders, she felt the heat in his hands, in his body.

"By God, I would like the taming of you!" he said thickly, all pretense at politeness quite vanished. . . .

Fire Opals

Rebecca Danton

A FAWCETT CREST BOOK

Fawcett Publications, Inc., Greenwich, Connecticut

FIRE OPALS

A Fawcett Crest Original

Chapter 1

Hundreds of candles blazed in the crystal and gold chandeliers, shining on the golden heads or powdered heads or glossy dark heads of ladies. Setting alight the diamonds and emeralds and rubies about smooth white throats. Shadowing passion-lit eyes, glittering in laughing eyes, flickering with swinging full ballgowns. Catching fire in the red-gold curls of a laughing girl with green eyes.

More than one masculine gaze followed the progress of the green gauze gown, the silver-shod narrow feet, as the mill owner's daughter, Charlotte Mary Gordon, waltzed with the handsome host, the notorious rake, Fitzhugh Rockingham. He was blond, handsome as a Greek or Roman god, and vain, but with a redeeming sense of humor. Now he was murmuring in Charlotte's ear, "My dear, you are the most glorious creature alive! Say you will marry me. I have spoken to your father."

"Spoken to papa? Did he tell you to what lower depths to descend?" She flung back her beautiful head, with the hair like living flames, and laughed aloud joyously at his discomposed expression. "No, no, you would not suit papa.

He wishes a sober, decorous husband to tame me, sir. No, you would not do at all."

"I do not wish to marry papa," said Fitzhugh, a twitch at his handsome mouth. "I do wish to own his daughter."

"Own?" Charlotte's smile disappeared, inside herself she felt the familiar stiffening. Sometimes she could forget that when she married she would be the property of some strange man, who could beat her, kiss her, order her about, sleep with her, whatever he chose. And she would have less freedom than she had under the strict rule of her father.

She found herself quite relieved when the waltz was over. She refused another gentleman charmingly. "I would so much rather have a glass of ratafia, sir, if you will? I am so warm."

The man offered her his arm eagerly, and strutted proudly beside her to the line of gold chairs set about the ballroom.

She sat fanning herself composedly while her escort plunged into the group of gentlemen about the punch table. She glanced about, met the cold gaze of a dowager whose plain daughter sat docilely beside her mama. The dowager looked frigidly at Charlotte, then turned to whisper to another woman her age, who lifted her lorgnette to gaze critically at Charlotte's flaming hair and flashionably décolleté gown, her bare arms with only a golden bracelet at her wrist.

She could guess what they said. The mill owner's daughter, they had called her all her first London season. The girl whose father had been a mill boy, had fought his way up cunningly to foreman, then had bought out his employer, and gone on to become a wealthy man. Three years ago he had purchased a London town house, and last year, he had presented his only daughter Charlotte. She had been a success in spite of the tight disapproval of the ladies of Almacks, the jealous dowagers, the fashionable figures that clung to the coattails of the Prince Regent.

For Charlotte Mary Gordon had been a success with the gentlemen, the rakes who lingered about her, the lords and their ladies who called at the modest London town house. They enjoyed Charlotte's quick wit and joyous laughter, her splendid tables, her beauty and charm, and that of her younger brother Neville. The two Gordons soon became the hit of London, and the town house was crammed with guests, the candles flaming until early morning when they entertained.

However, she had not married, nor was she engaged. She had firmly refused several offers, and Fergus had not pressed her. In his strict fashion, the rough man was intensely fond of his two children and proud of them. They were well educated, for he had promised his wife before she died that even the girl should have a good governess and a fine education. He had married above himself, a frail gentle lady whom he still mourned in the silence of his bedroom. He had never taken another woman to wife.

Instead Fergus Gordon had taught his daughter and son to work in the mill offices with him. Charlotte had perched on a high stool at a counter and kept books for her father, and dealt with woolen merchants and foreign buyers, settled problems of the workers such as housing and food for their children. She had learned much of the work, such as how to blend the wools, to order the colors, to price the best stuffs. She had her father's shrewd brain, for all her beauty, and he had appreciated it. But it was time she married, so he had carried them all to London to survey the marriage market with as keen a gaze as he did the woolen markets. They came to London for the season, then back home to Leeds, to their simpler home and their work.

Charlotte had thought much that first season, and she

had determined she would not marry a man she did not respect. She was too shrewd to hope for romance and love, as some of her lady friends whispered about. But deep in her well-guarded heart, she did long for a fine husband and eventually children to love and cherish.

The gentleman brought a cool glass of ratafia to her, and she smiled and chatted with him as they drank. Then her brother Neville claimed her with a smile.

The two tall red-haired ones drew many more gazes as they circled the rooms in a decorous round. Neville was only seventeen, but already inches taller than his tall sister. He was handsome, gentler than his sharp-tongued sister, and would make a good match, they whispered. He would inherit from his father one day, and all London knew that Fergus Gordon was making money hand over fist. Money was not to be despised, especially for some who had lost much in the Napoleonic wars.

"How does it go, Lotta?" murmured Neville. "Was it worth risking father's wrath?"

She grimaced quickly. Fergus would be furious when he discovered—if he discovered—that his chicks had attended a ball at the home of the notorious rake whom he had forbidden them to see. "Oh, he'll soon be over it," she shrugged. "Fitz is enjoyable, is he not? He told me he had offered for me, and papa refused; I am glad of it, he is not a settled man."

"Is that what you want?" her brother murmured wickedly. "I know several men of middle age who will be happy to hear of it. Shall I spread the word?"

"Don't you dare, you wicked boy!" she shot at him, squeezing his hand affectionately. She knew he would do nothing ever to harm her, for they were very close.

"If father is furious over our coming, I shall douse the flame by telling him Lord Arundell came," murmured Neville presently. "Did you see him?"

"No—where?" Charlotte glanced about, meaning to

avoid the tall aloof Marquis of Arundell. "He is so cold and cynical. I wonder that he attends balls at all. He seems to find them an immense bore."

"Not with his light o' love on his arm," said her brother, significantly, in her ear. "Look—over there—near Fitz now—the lady in black."

Charlotte looked, and felt herself stiffening with dislike. Mrs. Iris Holt was a divorcée, of blond loveliness, stunningly attired in her favorite black as though she were a wistful widow. Her blue eyes were gazing up entranced at the darkly tanned face of Lord Darcy Saltash, Marquis of Arundell, as though she hung on his words as she also hung on his arm. They were a fascinating pair, she had to admit. He wore black velvet, with rubies on his intricately tied stock and at his wrists and on one lean dark hand. Mrs. Holt, in her delicate black chiffon, with a long string of pearls about her white throat, was like a wisp of wind beside his dark thunder and lightning. Her blond hair gleamed in the candlelit ballroom.

"He's welcome to her," said Charlotte with unusual malice. "She has no charity in her, no warmth. Come on, Neville, let's go the other way. I don't wish to meet either of them."

Nevertheless, the company was sufficiently small that Charlotte could not avoid them forever. Following an excellent collation at midnight, Lord Arundell sought her out.

"Good evening, Miss Gordon," he greeted her gravely, the cold blue eyes studying her. She always had the feeling, when he looked her over, that her petticoats must be showing, or locks of hair falling about in a hoydenish manner.

"Good evening, my lord," she said, clasping her golden fan with nervous fingers. "It is a splendid company, is it not?"

"Splendid," he agreed absently. "Will you dance this

waltz with me? I have not had the pleasure tonight."

She could not refuse him. He was close to the Prince Regent and was rumored to have fought in a company of several royal lords. To cut him would be to cut her own throat, she thought with wry humor.

He put his black-velvet-clad arm about her, and under the velvet it felt like steel. It closed about her slim waist, and he swept her away deftly in the waltz. He danced well, as he did all things, she decided, with a bored grace.

"May I compliment you on your beautiful gown, Miss Gordon?" he said presently, swinging her around the corner of the room, his body for a moment pressed close to hers, then away, correctly.

"Thank you, my lord. You are most kind." Her tone must have been stiff, for he peered down at her quizzically.

"Have I offended you in some manner, Miss Charlotte?" he asked in a more friendly manner. "I am busily thinking of all the sins I might have committed recently."

She could not repress a giggle. "Laws, sir, does it take long?" she asked pertly.

"Minx," he muttered under his breath. But he was smiling when she dared glance upward. "No, indeed, have I offended you, truly? You have sent me only frosty glances this evening."

"Not at all," she replied, more correctly. "You must have—must have misunderstood."

"No doubt," he replied drily. His arm tightened for a moment, and she felt the lean hardness of it cutting into her slim waist, as though he longed to crush her insolence out of her. "Ah—you attend the party at Vauxhall Gardens this Saturday, Miss Charlotte?"

"We plan to, sir. And you?"

"Yes. I shall take my little daughter, Pamela. She adores the puppets especially."

Charlotte could not control a start of surprise. It was rare that he mentioned his daughter, a child of nine, and

Charlotte had not met her. She had only seen a shy dark-haired girl, of about nine or ten, lanky and shrinking from people, on occasions when she went shopping and happened to see Darcy Saltash from a distance. The gentleness of his voice stunned her. She had thought him a cold, unfeeling father. His wife had died some five years before.

"I have not had the pleasure of meeting Lady Pamela," said Charlotte, then could have bit her tongue. It sounded like an invitation. The waltz stopped. He conducted her to a chair near the door where air could reach her, and she fanned herself vigorously, cursing her quick impulsive speech. If only she would learn to stop and think first!

"I should like above all things to introduce you to my daughter." Lord Arundell seated himself beside her after a slight hesitation. "You would care for something to drink?"

"No, I thank you, my lord."

He did not get up and leave her, but continued their conversation in a grave manner, sometimes glancing down at her. He was so tall he made her feel small, and she was five feet six in her stockings.

"I fear Pamela is sometimes lonely in London, yet I do not wish to leave her for long months during the season. She has recently lost her governess, who departed for another post with more—shall I say—docile children?" A flicker of a smile creased his lean cheek.

"I would have thought Lady Pamela docile," blurted out Charlotte. "Oh, I do beg your pardon. I have not cured myself of making personal remarks." She fanned her hot cheeks more vigorously, looking everywhere but at her partner.

"She generally is a good obedient girl. But she is also intelligent. Her governess was more stupid than I had thought. When Pamela challenged her on some facts, it was more than she could endure. So I willingly gave her up to another family, and am on the search for someone more suitable to teach my daughter."

"I do hope you find someone good and intelligent for her," said Charlotte earnestly. "I was extremely fortunate in my governess, my dear Miss Morris. She was the dearest creature in the world! She left only when I was sixteen, and began to work full-time with father in the mill office. She went to a school for young ladies. I still miss her. She laid the foundations for an excellent education for me, and I still write to her and ask her advice in my reading."

He seemed to be listening intently to her, completely absorbed in what she said, his keen blue eyes fixed on her. "So you have worked also for your father," he commented.

She flushed deeper than ever. "Yes, the mill owner's daughter," she said flippantly, to cover her discomposure. "I am sure everyone in London knows of this."

He half smiled. "And I too have a mill owner's daughter." He smiled more broadly at her wide-opened eyes. "Yes, it's Pamela. You see, one of my relatives left a woolen mill to me, in the town near where our castle is situated in the Cotswold hills. Arundell castle is near Newton, so I can oversee the work. Fortunately I have an excellent foreman, so I am able to look after my other business matters without concern."

"Oh—I did not know that," she said, inadequately. So he too was a mill owner. But he was also a marquis, and that made a great difference.

Her cousin, Kenneth Mackay, danced past with a lovely dark-haired lady. He raised his eyebrows comically at the sight of her seated with a man whom he knew she detested. She smiled back blandly.

"Your cousin is most popular, Miss Charlotte," said the hateful deep voice in her ear. "I believe his mother is sponsoring your season?"

"Yes, Aunt Lydia Mackay has been marvelous to us all. She has lived in London these many years," said Charlotte, again on the defensive. Aunt Lydia had been on the fringes of society, living on her tiny widow's pension, unable to afford the fine dresses and the dinners of a member of Society. Only with the generous sums Fergus Gordon gave her could she now entertain. She had given up her flat to come and live with them, and managed the household well, in spite of her fluttery ways.

"A charming lady," said Lord Arundell. She wished she knew whether or not he meant it. "May I call upon you and her tomorrow afternoon? I should like to introduce you to my daughter. She admires you—from a distance—especially as you ride in the park. She wishes she might achieve such a seat. At present, horses frighten her."

He had coupled his request with a gracious compliment. She could not refuse him; nor did she have any previous engagements. She found it difficult to lie on any occasion.

"I should be delighted to have you come, and your daughter with you," she said, formally.

"Shall we say, about four o'clock, then?"

It was agreed. Kenneth Mackay made his way to them, and Darcy Saltash stood up at once. Kenneth gave her a little wink as the man greeted him and turned away.

"What was Lord Arundell speaking of so long, Lotta?" he asked, with the familiarity of long friendship and close relationship. "I determined to rescue you."

"Thank goodness you did," she replied in a low tone. "He is now coming to call tomorrow afternoon with his daughter. Heaven knows what else he might have asked for. I wonder at his persistence. He knows I do not care for him, I made it plain last season."

Kenneth looked at her keenly, leaning idly against the wall as he stood beside her. "Did he offer for you?" he asked bluntly, a shadow on his handsome young face. He was older, quite twenty-six, but somehow he seemed the dear brother she wished him to appear. He was always ready with a prank, keen on adventure, loved to dance and ride, accompanied her patiently on her shopping, carried her parcels, joked with her when she was depressed, comforted her when she feared she might be swept into matrimony.

"Oh, I am sure he has not! Father would have spoken of it, and perhaps snatched him up. He is so set on my marrying a title. Oh, if only papa had not earned all that money—" She ended bitterly, thinking of how people fawned over her now.

"Oh, my Lord Darcy Amberly Saltash is probably trying to think how to marry his exquisite divorcée and still remain in Society," said Kenneth lightly. "Look at them now, how she hangs on him. But she is not received, you know. Her husband, cruel bastard though he was— oh, I say, forgive me, Lotta!"

"No, no mind! Do finish what you were saying—"

Kenneth had colored uncomfortably and now sat down beside her where they might whisper in comfort. "I forget sometimes you are not a boy," he said with a little laugh. "Not because you are not beautiful and a lady, but because you refuse to be shocked at my language and do not squeal!"

She smiled with him but urged him on. "Do tell me the gossip, Kenneth, you know I depend on you!"

"Well, Jeremiah Holt was a good thirty years older than Mrs. Iris," he whispered. "But he had the ear of the Prince Regent, who has his own marital troubles, as you know. Iris swore that Holt was cruel to her and struck her frequently. When at last she obtained the divorce, the Prince immediately ordered that she should not be received in his presence. That excluded her from many an occasion, you may be sure! And no one would offend

His Royal Highness by inviting her openly, so she feels quite cut off."

"So that is why he does not marry her," mused Charlotte. "I suppose he values his position in Society too highly."

"Lord Arundell? Yes, I suppose so—"

She was struck by something else. "All call him Lord Arundell. I thought he was Sir Darcy until I heard one address him a few weeks ago."

"No, no, a distant relative died last winter, making him Marquis of Arundell. He is now Lord Arundell." Kenneth had been strictly schooled by his mother in all the proprieties and niceties of Society, and had conscientiously coached Charlotte and Neville, his cousins.

She was silent, digesting all this, when she saw that her host was again coming up to her. Kenneth said hurriedly, "I say, Lotta, don't you think we should go home soon? Uncle Fergus will be properly furious at us as it is."

"Oh, he always recovers from it," she said lightly, smiling as the handsome Rockingham came directly to her.

"Yes, but you know how he kicked up the dust the last time—" Kenneth was left talking to himself as Charlotte rose lightly and gracefully to her feet and took Fitzhugh's proffered hand. He watched them gloomily as they swept out onto the dance floor, the handsomest couple there.

She forgot all about Kenneth's warning. Fitz had invited her to join them in gaming in a private room. She won, lost, won again, and was shaking the dice and three in the morning, encouraged by Neville's laughter as Fitz's pretended gloom. They had drinks at their elbows. A footman constantly refilled her glass as soon as it emptied. It was not a mild punch, but a cool refreshing drink she did not recognize. The only trouble was, as soon as it hit her stomach, it made her feel hot and dizzy.

She finally rose from the table, staggered, and clutched the edge of it in embarrassment. Neville was in as bad shape, and Fitz laughed at them both. "There now, I am avenged that I have lost all those sums to you!" he cried merrily. "I have you dizzy and in my power." He was rising, and attempted to catch hold of Charlotte's bare arm.

Kenneth Mackay was ahead of him, a little the worse for drink himself, but able to move under his own steam. "I shall attend my cousin, I thank you, sir," he said formally. "Come, Charlotte, I will order our carriage."

When they went out into the ballroom, they were amazed to find it practically deserted. A footman was snuffing the candles in the chandeliers. The musicians were packing up their instruments. "Is it so late, then?" asked Charlotte, surprised to find her tongue feeling numb and her feet seeming a lost, long distance from her head. She swayed. Kenneth caught at her, and gently directed her toward the door.

"Quite late, my dear, and I can only hope your father and my mother have sought their respective beds a long time ago," he said rather anxiously.

Charlotte settled back in the carriage between her brother and cousin. Her head nodded strangely, she had never felt so woozy and peculiar. She must indeed have had too much to drink, and she was ashamed of herself. After this she must be more careful.

The London streets were dark and quiet. Kenneth kept watching uneasily for footpads, but they had two sturdy coachmen and a fast carriage.

They arrived home, Kenneth helped Charlotte to alight and put his arm about her waist to assist her up the steps of the modest town house. The early Georgian front was beautiful in its simplicity, with white marble pillars and balanced windows. The double doors led into a gracious hallway where a stairway of dark rosewood curved gracefully up to the first floor.

To the right of the hallway was a large parlor. The lamps were lit. Neville stifled a groan. The butler threw open the door and announced sonorously, "They have arrived, sir."

Fergus Gordon bounced out of his chair. He was small, tough, red-haired, shorter than his son and daughter, but full of rage and energy. "There you are, there you are!" he cried. "And where have you been, pray tell? Why out until four in the morning? Have I raised you myself to make you the ones to shame me?"

The more angry he became, the stronger his Scottish accent.

Charlotte swayed. Fergus stared at her.

"You are drunk," he said solemnly, fury dashed from him. "Oh, my God, that I should live to see the day. I thank God your poor darling mother is cold in her grave, and not a-living to see this shameful day! Her own wee small daughter, a-coming home drunken and wild—"

"Now, father, I am not wild," said Charlotte, precisely. Her tongue felt thick, her legs wooden. She caught hold of the back of a chair. Aunt Lydia, in her favorite stuffed armchair, began to weep softly into a handkerchief.

"We feared you had been set upon," she cried. "Oh, my darlings, why will you worry us like this? Kenneth, you promised to keep them safe. How can you act like this?"

"You see, we were gaming with Fitz," said Neville. "It was not really dangerous. We just forgot the time—" Then he realized what he had said, and went red.

"Fitz?" snapped his father. "You mean with that notorious fellow, that rake, Fitzhugh Rockingham? No good comes from him, I warned you of him! Where did you go, to his club? To his home?" Under the fury of his stare, they wilted.

"To his home, father. It was quite a respectable ball," offered Charlotte, hating her own weakness in the presence of her sturdy father. He would not beat them, he was not cruel. But she knew he was hurt and angry at their disobedience. "Lord Arundell was there," she added hopefully. "I mean very respectable people—"

"I told you I wished you never to associate with that rake! And you tell me you were in his very home," said Fergus, and put his hand to his head wearily. "We will speak of this tomorrow, my daughter. You are too drunken to make yourself understood tonight. Oh, that I should be so shamed. Woe on me, woe on me, that I should live to see it."

Charlotte gulped, her fingers pulling at her golden fan. What had started as a lark had ended in shame and drunkenness. She had to admit he was right. Fitz had deliberately drawn them into gaming, and the fact that she had won would not reconcile her father to it. That would have to be confessed tomorrow also.

Fergus shooed them all up to their rooms. Charlotte found her faithful maid waiting up for her, nodding in an easy chair. Noreen started up, rubbed her eyes.

"Oh, Noreen, you should not have waited up," sighed Charlotte, stumbling over a stool. Noreen put her hands to her hips, her graying reddish hair standing up in wiry locks.

"So, here you are, and it be four o'clock in the morning," said the Irish woman grimly. "And what did your good father have to say? Did he wish you a good morning and all?"

"Oh, my head aches," Charlotte moaned, and sank down on the bed. She would have lain there, letting her green gauze rumple and spoil, but Noreen pulled her up freely, with the skill of long dealing with her stubborn mistress.

She was perhaps the only maid who would have lasted

long with Charlotte. But she was a red-headed stubborn person herself, long in the service, and accustomed to dealing with ladies. She pulled Charlotte upright, abused her into letting her remove the fragile gown, and take off the little diamond ear drops, and the slender golden chain with the diamond on the end of it. The golden bracelet was removed, and placed carefully in the jewel box. Then she stripped Charlotte down, and put over her head the warm cotton nightdress that went to her ankles, just as though she were still the small child she had been when Noreen came to her many years ago.

She bundled Charlotte into bed, and shook her head. "We'll see tomorrow, yes, we shall certainly see what is what," said Noreen grimly. She drew the sheets and blanket up to Charlotte's chin, and patted the soft red curls. "Now, you'll sleep, me dear, you'll sleep," she said more gently. "I'll be by you, an you get sick."

"Won't get sick," muttered Charlotte, but she was wrong. About two hours later, she wakened, from the churning in her stomach, and Noreen wakened in time to get her to the bathroom where she gave up much of the liquor she had unwisely drunk that evening. "Oh, *ohhhhh*," she groaned.

"Serves you right, as I could have told you," said Noreen and tucked her into bed again.

Noreen settled down again in the small bed at the foot of Charlotte's bed. Charlotte muttered an apology. "I'm sorry I got you up, Noreen. Oh, I should never have had all that liquor—"

"Your good father will make you sorrier tomorrow, but that is another day," snapped Noreen, punching the pillow at her head.

Charlotte groaned, and closed her eyes. If she lived until tomorrow—she thought—feeling sick and weak still. Never again would she overimbibe. It was too horrible.

Chapter 2

Charlotte wakened about ten o'clock, but after gazing at her small golden clock, she rolled over and pretended sleep again. She knew she was in for a stiff lecture and worse. Fergus Gordon was as clever at dealing with his children as with his business affairs, and frequently he thought up splendid punishments that fit the crime, as he saw it.

It could wait. Charlotte drowsed again, drifted off to sleep, and only wakened fully when Noreen came in and rattled the draperies back from the windows. It was now twelve.

"You know you cannot put it off any longer, Miss Charlotte," said Noreen solemnly. "Fergus Gordon isn't one to wait forever. Your brother has gone down and taken his punishment like a man."

"Oh—what is it?" Charlotte forced herself upright, and pushed back her mass of tangled red hair. She might judge her own penalty by Neville's.

"You'll wait and see. Will ye wear your white muslin today, or the green?" Noreen was at the vast wardrobe, drawing out one gown and then another. Charlotte eyed them thoughtfully. Should she be young and innocent in white, or pretty in green, or subtle in cream? "I hear Lord Arundell calls upon you today, Miss Charlotte. You best wear white and look your nicest."

"Then I'll wear the cream with the gold trimming," said Charlotte, and giggled as Noreen gave her an outraged look. She slid out of bed, and her long legs reached for her slippers. She yawned widely. "Oh, I am sleepy," she mourned.

"Ye will stay out late, will ye?"

"Stop scolding me, Noreen. Papa will be bad enough," coaxed Charlotte, and gave her a hug as she passed her going to the bathroom. Her tub had been run, and she added lilac bath salts lavishly. She soaked in the tub as long as she dared, then climbed out, to snuggle into the warmed thick towels.

She thought of the cold house at Leeds, how the water must be carried up in kettles from the vast kitchens below, and how often the cold winter mornings had chilled her tub in front of the fireplace before she could finish washing. She shuddered at the thought. She would enjoy the luxuries here before they returned. They would go back in July probably, as soon as the London season was finished. Fergus was already impatient to return to his loved work. He endured Society rather than enjoying it.

Noreen had the cream tulle dress ready, and had laid out a simple gold bangle for her wrist, a golden chain with a pendant of a golden butterfly. Fergus did not believe in elaborate jewelry for his children. It seemed a foolish extravagance after his years as a mill child. Charlotte often felt the same way, and thought, as she observed society ladies in their diamonds, of little mill children in their shabby clothing struggling to reach the tall machines.

Noreen had set out a tray for her as soon as she had dressed. Charlotte sipped her hot tea gratefully as Noreen brushed the long red-gold curls, and contrived a beautiful arrangement *à la grecque*, the curls piled high, some escaping artfully to fall to the graceful white throat. She ate hungrily of the buttered rolls and jelly.

"There you are," said Noreen. "Now you'll go to your father's study. He sent word he was wondering where you was, and would you come to him at once."

"Oh, Noreen," said Charlotte, paling.

"Don't you 'oh, Noreen' me," said her maid. "It was you who said you could go to the ball at that Rockingham's and get away with it. And wasn't I telling you that you didn't get away with nothing in this world, that the Lord would catch up with you?"

"I wouldn't mind the Lord, it's father I'm worried about," said Charlotte, giggling with an abrupt reversal of feelings.

"There now! Blaspheming already today! You're a wicked girl, you are!" scolded Noreen, with a shake of her own red head. "You must learn to grow up and be wise, my dear," she said, more soberly. "You're nineteen, and you'll be married one of these days. And you must think of pleasing your husband, and advising your own children. You must not be a silly one."

The corners of Charlotte's generous red mouth went down. "I don't want to get married," she muttered rebelliously, shivering a little as she thought again of how hard and cruel a master could be. A husband, with complete control over her life, over her thoughts, over her body! Oh, she did not want that.

"Don't say that to your father, if you don't want a whipping," advised Noreen. "He thinks and talks of nothing so much as your marrying well—to one of the nobility if he can manage it. He would be so proud of you."

Charlotte went down soberly to her father's study, shoulders braced. She saw Neville's valet on the way, and paused. "What punishment has Neville?" she whispered.

The valet raised his shoulders, spread his hands. "He went to the booksellers, Miss Charlotte. He is to purchase a dozen books of history, of the heaviest sort, and to read and report on them all in the next two weeks."

Charlotte's brow lightened. "Oh, if I had that—" she mused. The valet shook his head as he watched her dance down the winding stairway. He figured Miss Charlotte loved reading too much, and her father would never punish her by giving her such a task to do.

Charlotte tapped on her father's study door. "Come in," he said evenly, and she went in with assumed meekness. Meeting his level look, her pretense went away as quickly as it had come. She lowered her head, and then took the chair opposite his desk.

"Good morning, Charlotte," said her father.

"Good morning, papa." She put her hands on the arms of the fine Queen Anne chair, nervously felt the carving. She had helped choose the furnishings of this house and was pleased with them. The study was a mellow brown, with glossy walnut desk and matching tables. The draperies were deep reddish brown, over trim white curtains. A bookcase was filled with books she had helped choose, and they would take them back to Leeds when they returned. The London bookstores were a never-ending source of delight to Charlotte.

The rug on which her slippered feet rested lightly was a fine Persian rug of reds, blues, golden browns. The lamps were of beautiful blue and white china. It was a comfortable room, though businesslike.

"You will tell me what you meant by defying me and going to the home of a notorious rake," said her father, after a minute of silence.

Charlotte stirred. "I am—sorry, papa. He was giving a ball, and I could not resist the invitation. And Neville and Kenneth were with me, and constantly in attendance."

"I have spoken with Neville. Your Aunt Lydia is attending to Kenneth. He has been scolded thoroughly. He is certainly old enough to know better, no matter how childish my own children are."

He went on in this vein for a time, not angry, but coldly set on making her understand the foolishness of her ways. She listened in silence, her head bent, her heart rebellious. Abruptly he changed his tone, observing her face keenly.

"But you do not listen to me, I think, Charlotte. You are only waiting to hear your punishment, and then you will escape with a light heart, eh? Well, it is not so easy. You are nineteen, and you continue to defy me. I think it was easier when we were in Leeds, and you had much work to occupy your mind. I have thought long and deeply about what I should do with you. I spoke with your Aunt Lydia, and she agrees with me. I think you are actually growing up, and restless to be settled in your own home. Yes, I think marriage is the answer for you."

Charlotte swallowed hard. This was worse than she had thought.

"Neville is yet seventeen, there is time for him to settle down. I think I shall send him to university next year. However, for you," said Fergus Gordon, his Scottish accent strong, "ye will be for marrying, and let your husband control ye. I am seriously considering several offers I have had for ye. Yes, flighty as you seem, I know there is a good mind and a sturdy heart beneath all that, and others know it also. I have some good offers, and soon it shall all be settled."

Charlotte could not keep her meek silence any longer. "Oh, papa, no, no, please, I do not wish to marry," she cried out. "Oh, please punish me in some other way. Do not force me to marry! I do not wish to!"

Fergus eyed his daughter in some exasperation and deep concern. "But Charlotte, me girl, marriage is the life for a female," he said gruffly, flushing a little. "Why, your mother and I were so happy together. You will be also, you have a warm heart, and you love children."

"I—I could not marry a man—whom I do not—respect," she blurted out. "Oh, papa, please wait. Maybe next season—"

"Next season! I shall be dead of fright by that time," roared Fergus. "What pranks you think up, and dragging your brother into them, and Kenneth along with you both—do you think I shall endure another season of this? No, no, I shall settle it all presently."

He went on in this vein until she felt quite ill with fright. Surely her beloved father, gruff and strict as he was, would not force her into marriage!

"Your reputation has suffered already," he was going on. "In the company of such notorious persons, how do you expect any respectable man to offer for you?"

"But papa, you admire the Marquis of Arundell," she offered eagerly. "He was there last night—" She bit her tongue to refrain from saying he was with a notorious divorcée. "He is quite respectable, and a friend of the Prince Regent. And—and he asked to call upon us today, at four o'clock."

Fergus stared at her, his green eyes thoughtful under the thick red eyebrows. "Ah—he did, did he? He comes today, and you said not a word? And no special cakes made, nor the housekeeper warned?"

"Oh, papa, I shall arrange all! He brings his small daughter, the Lady Pamela, with him, to introduce her. I—I'll make gingerbread cakes for her, in pretty shapes," she proffered eagerly. "And I shall be charming to them both, I really promise. Oh, please, papa, no more lectures today!"

He glanced at the clock on his desk. "Well, it is past two o'clock. You are dressed? Yes, you will do. Go and make something nice, and your apologies to your aunt for upsetting her, and make sure all is fine and pretty for the marquis, and we shall speak again another day!"

"Oh, yes, papa!" She jumped up with relief, and sped to her aunt, apologized prettily, told her hastily that the Marquis of Arundell was coming at four, and sent her into a flutter. Then she hurried to the kitchen, informed the cook of it, and set out to make something that would please small Pamela.

By four o'clock all was ready. The cook promised to take the last batch of gingerbread men out of the oven on time, and the smell of the ginger was rising through the house. Charlotte washed her hands, flew to her room to smooth her hair and make sure no flour remained on her face and arms. Then demurely she descended to the first floor drawing room, where she had arranged roses and violets in blue porcelain bowls.

The rumble of voices warned her that the marquis had arrived. She was fifteen minutes late. She hesitated in the doorway, then bravely entered.

"I do beg your pardon for my lateness," she smiled charmingly at the cynical face of the marquis. He bowed over her hand, not kissing it. "I decided to make some ginger cakes for our tea. Please do forgive me."

"That sounds quite lovely. You make pastries yourself, Miss Charlotte?" said Lord Arundell with suave accent. "There you are, Pamela, Miss Charlotte is also a cook. You shall tell cook that you are to have lessons with him."

Charlotte turned to the nervous small girl beside him. Pamela had straight brown hair, drawn back with a blue ribbon which did not suit her rather sallow complexion. Her wistful brown eyes gazed up from a white face with little color in it. The bright blue of her ruffled dress killed what color she had. Who had chosen such an appalling dress for a little girl? Charlotte blamed her father and could have shot him. He was so well-turned-out himself and to let his daughter appear like this! All fluffy ruffles suited to a curly haired blond, not a dark mouse of a girl. If Charlotte had the dressing of her, she would put her in a white dress with yellow ribbons, or a yellow chiffon, or a deep green.

Charlotte smiled down at the girl kindly, and put out her hand. She felt the cold fingers of the little hand. Why, the child was frightened of her! She drew her over to the green Louis XIV sofa and sat down with her. Darcy Saltash seated himself in a large armchair more suited to his height, and Fergus took the armchair across from him.

"I hear you go riding in the park also," said Charlotte softly. The small brown head nodded, and the frightened brown eyes looked down so Charlotte saw long dark lashes.

"Yes, I ride with papa, Miss Gordon," she whispered.

"And you would like to learn to cook?"

The girl nodded. "Yes, ma'am."

The conversation died. Fergus was talking with Darcy about the woolen business, and the men seemed absorbed in their conversation, as Fergus went on rather passionately about the foreign companies trying to flood the British markets with their stuffs.

Charlotte tried again. "When I was your age," she confided, "my papa made me a doll house. It is still in our home in Leeds. He made it just the way I wanted it. I had two small dolls, about two inches high. And he made everything to scale."

The brown eyes flashed upward to Charlotte's flushed face. "Oh—how big was it?" she whispered raptly. It seemed Charlotte had hit on a favorite topic.

Charlotte measured with her arms, about three feet apart. "This wide, and that tall. And he made three floors, with a cunning little kitchen, and a stove pipe and all. And the living room has a wee lamp, and two sofas. The rugs are made of woolen swatches—you know, samples from the mills. When I was a little older, I covered the sofas and chairs with silk and cotton fabrics. I made little sheets and blankets and pillows for the beds, and draperies and curtains for the windows."

Now she had all of Pamela's attention, and color rose in the sallow cheeks. The small hands clasped tightly together. "You—you made them all yourself? And the dolls lived in the house?"

"Oh, yes, and I played with them often. And I had other dolls. My favorite big doll was a baby doll, and I rocked her to sleep every night and put her in her cradle, which had been my brother Neville's."

"You have a brother?" murmured the girl wistfully.

Charlotte went hastily past that point. The girl's mother was dead, and Charlotte could not see the cold Mrs. Iris Holt producing a child for Darcy Saltash, even should he condescend to marry her. She probably valued her slim figure too much to risk it.

The teatray was wheeled in, and Charlotte asked Pamela to help her serve. The color came and went in the young cheeks. She walked very cautiously to her father, holding the teacup carefully in both small hands, and delivered it with an obvious sigh of relief. Charlotte wondered if someone had made her think she was clumsy. Actually, she was dainty and trim in her movements, but easily made to feel self-conscious and awkward.

The men took note of the teatray. "Ah, the famous gingerbread men," muttered Lord Arundell, his lips curling into a reluctant smile. "You are skillful indeed, Miss Charlotte."

"Thank you, my lord," she said, rather coldly, and turned back to Pamela. "Perhaps your father will prefer some of the coconut macaroons, or cream cakes. Will you serve him?"

Pamela said shyly, "Papa likes coconut macaroons the very best, Miss Charlotte." And she took him several of the sweets. He thanked her with a genuine smile.

"And my papa likes the cream cakes," said Charlotte, more cheerfully. She filled a plate, and Pamela took it to the fierce, red-haired man. Fergus patted her on the head, which seemed to startle her.

"Nice child," said Fergus Gordon. "I'll be bound she is not half the trouble my Charlotte was to me."

"Oh, papa!" Charlotte reproached, going scarlet. "I always tried very hard to please you. And I worked hard on my sums, so I could work in the mill office with you."

"Yes, yes, so you did," agreed her father, with a twitch of his lips. He turned back to Lord Arundell. "She was ever an intelligent girl, and helped with my books. Good housekeeper also. She takes care of our home in Leeds. Too busy in London, so I had to hire a housekeeper here. Flies about. You wouldn't think to see her gadding about in London, what a sober industrious girl she really is."

It was too outrageous. He sounded as though he were selling her to the highest bidder, and Charlotte choked over her gingerbread. She gave him a hard look, but he pretended not to notice, telling Lord Darcy Saltash cheerfully how much help Charlotte and Neville were to him.

"It'll be hard to manage meself, when Charlotte is married, and Neville in university," he said.

"Oh, indeed? And do they leave you soon?" inquired Darcy as he bit into a macaroon.

"As soon as may be. Neville will go to university this fall. I am entering him at once. He needs discipline if he is not to go wild, and he shall have the best tutor I can find. Oxford, I think," said Fergus complacently.

"And Miss Charlotte, is she yet engaged? I had not heard." Lord Arundell gave Charlotte a keen look. She gazed steadily at her gingerbread and bit off the head viciously. Pamela nibbled at the legs of hers.

"Not yet, not yet, but very soon," said Fergus, with

meaning. "I have had several offers. I wish her to marry happily, of course, with a man I can respect."

Fortunately Aunt Lydia came in at that moment, full of flurried apologies for her lateness. In the flutter, the topic of conversation was dropped and another taken up. Pamela whispered to Charlotte. "I always hate to finish my gingerbread man. I love them so."

"Then you must have another one—if your papa does not object." Pamela glanced shyly at her papa. He was not seeming to observe, so Charlotte set another one on her plate and gave her an encouraging smile.

They talked again of dolls, and Pamela told her of her dog who had not come to London, because he was always running off. "He is not wicked," she assured Charlotte gravely. "It is only that he is very young and loves to play. Papa said he must be left at Arundell, where there are fields to play in. London might be dangerous for him, with the horses and carriages."

The dog's name was Macduff, and he filled in the talk very nicely until finally my lord rose to depart. Pamela was reluctant to take leave of Charlotte, and there was a fine sparkle in her eyes as she shook hands.

For some reason Fergus was in a good humor after the marquis had left. Charlotte thought that, in spite of her dislike of the man, it had been a stroke of genius to invite him to the house that very day. It had taken the edge off Fergus's disapproval of his son and daughter.

Neville complained bitterly to Charlotte that she had gotten off with a scolding, while he must work hard for two weeks on the books. "Oh, I'll read half of them for you," she assured him. "I shan't mind."

His face lightened for a moment, then he shook his head dolefully. "Papa would find out, and it wouldn't be honest anyway."

Their father had brought them up to be honest, and

they kept trying, in spite of temptations which their high spirits and bright minds brought to them.

The next morning, Charlotte went out riding early with Neville and Kenneth. She loved the early morning best, before all of high society gathered in their carriages and cluttered up Rotten Row in Hyde Park, to wave languid hands, bow, lift high hats, flutter parasols, and all that nonsense. Charlotte wore her favorite riding habit, a severely cut black dress with full skirt, and a high black silk hat with a defiant green plume over her red hair which was secured in a black snood.

They had brought their favorite riding horses to London, in addition to the more sober carriage horses. She loved her Black Satin, a high-stepping stallion of some five years, whom she had had since a colt. She patted his neck now as he shied nervously at a carriage coming toward them. She drew him out into the grass to let the carriage pass, then set him prancing on the roadway again. The morning breeze fanned her warm cheeks. The main roads were lined with smooth grassy lawns, and there were lilacs and roses set about beautifully. The scent of fresh grass, the delicate purple French lilacs, and more heavily scented white lilacs, all was delicious to her. She drew great breaths of them.

Then across the park she sighted the tall arrogant figure of Lord Arundell, and beside him the slight form of Pamela. She seemed to be having trouble with her horse. Charlotte thought critically the horse was too large for her small hands. She impulsively left Kenneth and Neville, engaged in lazily arguing the respective merits of their mounts, and galloped toward the pair.

As she came toward them, she pulled up Black Satin so that he reared, and she balanced on him, laughing until he came down again. Pamela's eyes were huge, frightened brown pansies.

"I beg your pardon," Charlotte said at once. "I did

not mean to make a display. How are you this morning, Pamela?"

Pamela glanced up at her father. Charlotte suddenly realized she had forgotten to give the child her title, and also she had not addressed the lord first. She bit her lips and wished she had not come anywhere near them.

"We are fine, thank you, Miss Charlotte," said Lord Arundell, eying her with the cynical look she detested, as though he could look into her brain, and sense all the confusion about her. "We can see that you are in splendid health."

"Thank you, yes." She hesitated. She had dashed over to them impulsively, now she could not think how to leave them gracefully.

"You will ride with us?" asked Lord Arundell. "I see you have deserted your escorts. Or did they desert you? If a lady had left me so quickly, I should have galloped after her." His tone and words were subtly insulting, and she flushed quickly, and gave him a look of dislike.

"They will come up to me presently," she said curtly. "I must leave you—perhaps I had best ride back—"

"No, no, do not do that. We are proceeding more slowly, but we shall meet up with them in good time. Pamela is a little afraid of her horse this morning, so we are riding more slowly."

Charlotte blurted out, "The animal is too large for her. I had a pony at her age!"

"Indeed," said my lord, frigidly. "Permit me to decide what is best for my daughter."

Charlotte swallowed. "I do beg your pardon," she said hurriedly. "My tongue—it gets away from me at times. It is not my concern—" She was blundering on when she met his coldly amused blue eyes and went silent.

She turned her horse, and the reins must have been too tight. To her annoyance, he acted up at once, rearing again, so she had to calm him down and pat his glossy neck and whisper to him.

Pamela was watching her with fascinated gaze. "Oh, you do ride so beautifully," she murmured. "Miss Charlotte, aren't you afraid of your horse?"

"Black Satin? No, indeed, he is my pet," said Charlotte, more easily. "Why, I watched him being born. His sire was a great fierce black stallion only papa can ride. But Black Satin was always mine, and he knows me."

She chatted on to the girl, as Darcy Saltash chose to remain silent, riding beside them, his critical eye on his daughter's seat in the saddle. She wore a snuff-brown riding habit, which stifled what little coloring she had. The full skirt trailed over the saddle almost to the ground. It was much too long for her. She must surely stumble when she tried to walk, thought Charlotte, feeling intensely sorry for the girl.

It was all very well for men, but girls had to ride side-saddle, and sometimes they felt as though they would slip right off. Pamela had little confidence, and that animal *was* too big for her, thought Charlotte again.

Neville and Kenneth came up to them, lifted their hats, greeted Lord Arundell correctly, then Lady Pamela. If only she could remember her manners, mourned Charlotte, how much easier her life in London would be! As it was, she longed to return—unmarried—to Leeds, where she might gallop across the fields, and talk to whomever she pleased in the village or forest and not worry about etiquette.

The three men chatted together, drawing ahead a little. Charlotte took the opportunity to murmur to Pamela, "My dear, if you sit with your back more erect, it will be easier for you. Sit well back, then you won't slip." She showed her how to sit, and helped her move back in the saddle. Pamela gave her a shy grateful glance.

How awful it would be to have a man like Lord Arundell in charge of one's life, thought Charlotte. She was intensely glad that she herself was not in the power of that cold man. Fergus might get angry with her at times, but it was an honest relationship, and he never was cold and hard with her for long.

She was happy when they left the father and daughter, and galloped along the paths toward the stables. She could not help thinking of the blond Mrs. Holt and her devoted looks up at Darcy Saltash. The woman must be an excellent actress. No one could be half in love with such a man as he was! It could not be credited. She probably received jewels and her bills paid at the dressmaker, thought Charlotte. She would certainly have to be highly paid, to put on such an act with that man.

Then she forgot them both, and Pamela also, in teasing Neville about a girl three years older than himself, of whom he imagined himself enamored.

Chapter 3

Fergus Gordon did not utter the dread word "marriage" again that next week. Charlotte fondly imagined he had forgotten his fury. Neville was absorbed with his works of history.

Charlotte occupied herself with them also. She and Neville were always very close, only two years apart in age, and good friends. She sat in the drawing room with him in the morning, silently, and they read rapidly, then compared their impressions of the books. Neville began writing out his reports of them.

"I say, you are a good old thing, Lotta," he said, affectionately. "You could be running about with Kenneth and enjoying yourself."

"I would feel guilty," she replied, "knowing you are punished, and I got off with a scolding."

She felt very virtuous about this, and resolved to do better in the future. But before long she was in very hot water again.

It was Rockingham's fault, she said later, to herself. He would tease and torment her, and she could scarcely resist a dare. They met in the drawing room of a lady of quality who bored all of them. In a corner, they were conversing lightly, and Charlotte wondered if her father would learn they had met poor Fitz yet again.

"Has your father forbidden you to dine with me?" he teased her, his bright blue eyes shining wickedly at her. How warm and human he was, compared with the cold Darcy Saltash, thought Charlotte.

"Of course he has," she replied pertly, fluttering her fan to hide her laughing green eyes from the rest of the sedate company. Neville came up to them, to stand nearby, so that she was not alone with Fitz. She took Neville's arm, and squeezed it. "He does not trust you, dear sir. He fears you might lead me astray, and ruin my chances for a sober marriage."

"I wish I dared hope so!" murmured Rockingham, with a laugh. "A sober marriage, indeed! How terrible for you, a girl of your high spirits. I wonder that you were raised in a town such as Leeds, you seem London-born and bred to me, so brilliant of mind and of wit. And your taste in clothing is exquisite!"

It was praise indeed. Rockingham was noted as a beau par excellence. This evening he wore a brilliant blue velvet suit, a snowy white cravat tied in an intricate device of his own invention, a single blue sapphire set in the white folds. The sapphire on his hand perfectly matched the other. Charlotte gave Neville a little triumphant glance. She was wearing a creamed taffeta lined with green silk, with only her golden earrings to set off her red hair. And Rockingham approved of her, though other ladies were covered with diamonds and such.

"You have not gone riding these past mornings," Fitz reproached her presently. "I have gone every morning, earlier and earlier. Where have you been?"

"Oh, Neville and I have been—er—studying ancient Rome and Greece," said Charlotte, with a slight flush.

"Very fascinating. Papa wants him to go to university this autumn."

Rockingham raised his devilish eyebrows in mock reproach. "Miss Charlotte, my dearest girl, you must not admit to liking such heavy learning! I adore you for it, but I pray you, admit it not to London!"

They laughed together.

He persisted, "Why have you not been riding? I thought you enjoyed your riding. Surely your beautiful horse has not been injured?"

"Of course not!"

"I have it," said Rockingham. "You have grown bored! I'll wager you have. Come now, do come tomorrow morning, out to Hyde Park, and I'll guarantee you will not be bored. I'll bring my high-perch phaeton, you ride Black Satin—and I shall win!"

Black Satin was very fast. Charlotte hesitated. "Oh, that would not be fair," she said seriously. "My horse against a phaeton—I should be driving a carriage—and you also."

"Done!" said Rockingham. "You drive a carriage, any of your choosing, and so shall I. I'll meet you at eight o'clock at the entrance to Hyde Park. Our wager? Let me see—"

Too late Charlotte realized she had been drawn into a horse race. Fergus would be furious! But perhaps he would not hear of it. And she would dearly love to race Rockingham—and beat him! He was so arrogant about his ability to race. Her green eyes sparkled.

"What about a bottle of champagne?" she asked. "Neville shall bring mine—"

Rockingham drew down his mouth. "A bottle—my dear girl, how unimaginative!" he drawled. Two other gentlemen had drawn closer. He went on, "I had something else in mind for our wager. A kiss, for example, from those exquisite lips!"

The men insisted on knowing what was going on. Charlotte, her common sense finally roused, told them they must not repeat it, her father would be angry. And she insisted firmly on the wager of a bottle of champagne.

So it was set. Neville went to the stables early, and brought back his phaeton, with a fine gray hitched to it. The horse was one of their father's finest, and Charlotte eyed him dubiously. If aught happened to the gray, Fergus would be more than angry! But she had confidence in her ability to drive even two or four horses at a time.

They set out for the park before breakfast. Noreen had helped her into her black riding habit, innocently unaware of the impending race. "There, now, it's good for you to ride of a morning," said the maid. "You have a fine color in your cheeks."

Neville drove the phaeton to the park. The horse was nervous, side-stepping daintily when a gazette fluttered in its path. "I say, he is too fresh, Lotta," said Neville anxiously. "Let me do the racing, if you will. Surely Rockingham will agree. You know, I couldn't sleep last night, thinking what papa would say if you get into another scrape."

She patted his arm affectionately. "No fear, papa will not learn of it from us, nor from Rockingham. And no one else will be up this hour of the morning."

She was quite wrong. When they arrived, a small crowd of gentlemen surrounded Rockingham, elegant in black and silver, in his high-perch phaeton of yellow and black. He was laughing and they were grinning as they turned to welcome her. There was not a lady in the crowd, she saw with growing unease.

"It isn't too late to back down," Neville urged in a low tone. "No one will expect a lady to race—"

"There you are. You have the bottle of champagne for me?" cried Fitz, a devilish light in his blue eyes. "If you don't, I shall settle for the other prize I mentioned!"

The men laughed, great bellows of laughter. Charlotte began to realize how very unwise she had been to allow herself to be entangled in this race. It would be all over London. She hesitated. Neville waited beside her, shifting in his seat.

Neville said, quite clearly, "I think you are wrong to dare my sister into this, Rockingham. I disapprove of it. If you wish, I shall take her place and race you for any wager you care to name."

The men fell silent. Rockingham went from amusement to rage. His face flushed with fury. "Is she withdrawing?" he snapped. "I did not think her a coward!"

Both the Gordons stiffened. "How dare you, sir," said Charlotte, clearly. "Yes, I shall race you—and defeat you also!"

"Don't let him draw you into this," Neville urged her, his voice ringing over the park ground. "He is just deviling you. He knows father has forbidden us to see him."

"Are you challenging me, you little rooster?" drawled Rockingham. Charlotte caught her breath, and Neville's arm at once.

"No, no, Neville, leave it to me, I beg you!" she urged. Her blood ran cold when she thought of the secret duels, the deaths that had occurred, the race to the continent of the man who lived. Dueling was forbidden, the Prince Regent would be infuriated—to say nothing of Fergus Gordon! And if Neville should be injured or killed—it was said Rockingham was a deadly shot and his fencing very skillful—! "Of course I shall race you, Fitz," she said very slowly. "And I shall win. Shall we start? Who gives the word?"

"Do you answer for your little brother?" drawled Rockingham insultingly. She realized now that he had had something to drink already that morning. If he wished, he could draw her brother into a duel—and it would be much more deadly than any race of carriages.

"Your quarrel is with me, sir. Shall we not race now?" she answered, and smiled alluringly down at him. "Do get down, Neville, and watch how I can race him."

Neville, his face white under his tan, his lips compressed, climbed down from the carriage, giving her the reins. She lifted her chin, drove the phaeton carefully about, and set it at the beginning line.

Rockingham, his face like a cloud, jumped up into his phaeton. One of the men, his friends, came forward and gave the word to start. "Twice around the drive, and no one touches the grass," he said. "Back again to the beginning. All right, get set—and start!"

Charlotte had been waiting. Now she lightly touched her whip to the gray's back, and it went like the wind. The phaeton was high, she felt the wind whipping her hat. Some placid early riders on horseback hastily drew out of her path as she swept down the drive, Rockingham close behind her. She drove like an Amazon, her teeth clenched over her anger. If ever again she allowed herself to be drawn into a wager with Fitz—! He had done this deliberately. Her father was right about him.

Rockingham drew even with her, slowly, and he grinned at her, his lips tight, his eyes blazing blue. Then she saw him deliberately draw closer, as they swept around the end of the drive, out of sight of the gentlemen. He was driving too close—he would hit—

The wheels just hit, her phaeton swayed. She would go over! She drew back, pulling on the gray, furiously angry. Rockingham was a cheat, he would do anything to win. And he would have dueled her own dear brother!

Coldly she planned. She let him go ahead, sweeping down the drive to the cheers of his friends, their hats raised, saluting him. Neville stood a little apart, his hands in his pockets, his face drawn, red hair flaming in the early morning sunlight. He gave her an encouraging smile, his face seemed suddenly older.

Charlotte followed Rockingham, deliberately holding back the excited gray. They swept around the drive. Rockingham would not need to knock her over, she thought, he figured he was well ahead. He went into the final stretch yards ahead of her. Once in sight of the gentlemen, she let the gray out—encouraging him with cries, with a light touch of her whip. He stretched his long legs, his head up, and galloped forward.

She passed Rockingham. He gave her a startled look, furious. She gave him a sweet smile and went on. He jerked his reins, as though he would crash into her. But he would not dare now, not in their sight.

The gray was a fine one, she had handled him many times before. And Rockingham had been drinking, his touch was not so sure as hers. She wondered what would have been the outcome if he had been himself. But between the drinking and his anger, her rival was defeated.

She swept over the finish line, two lengths ahead of him. She drew up the phaeton. Neville was there before her, catching the head of the gray, soothing the excited animal.

"I say, magnificent driving, Miss Charlotte!" exclaimed one of the older men. The younger were silent, gazing at the angry Rockingham. He slipped down from his phaeton, tossed the reins to a friend.

"Beaten by a woman. I shall not live it down," he said, his smile false. He took the bottle of champagne from the bucket of ice and held it up. "Here you are, Charlotte, we'll drink to you from your prize."

"I have not yet breakfasted," she said sweetly, remaining in her seat. "Come up, Neville, we must get home before Aunt Lydia is furious with us. We'll drink another time, sir."

But not with you, was her silent addition. The man holding the ice bucket gave her a cheer. Rockingham handed the bottle up to her, his blue eyes as icy as the bottle.

"Another time, Miss Charlotte," he said significantly, and looked at Neville. "And to you, sir—" he added softly.

Charlotte drove away rapidly, a sick feeling in her stomach. Outside the park, she gave the reins to Neville. "Neville," she said, low, "he would have dueled you."

"I know that," he said dully. "And now—my reputation—I will be thought a very coward."

"A coward, not to fight with him? He is a bully, a cheat. He tried to upset my carriage on the first turn," she told him furiously. "He drove so close our wheels touched. If I had not drawn back, he would have had me over on the side."

Neville gave her a strange look. "Papa is right. Fitz is an outsider," he said quietly. "We shall not meet him again."

"No," she agreed, with a sigh of relief. "Let's not, Neville. I find I do not like him after all."

She was sorry about that. Rockingham could be amusing at times, his wit was caustic and his view of society enlightening. But he would have dueled Neville! A mere boy—against his experience.

She alighted at the door, and a coachman came to take the horse. They went in, to a silent house. It had been less than an hour since they had left. They went to change, and met again at breakfast. Fergus expressed his surprise at finding them up early, but he knew nothing of the meeting.

He soon found out. All London talked of nothing else for three days. Word came to Fergus Gordon that very afternoon. He stormed home from his club, and sent for his son and daughter.

In his study, he was wild. He stormed at them. "All my teachings—and you, Charlotte, will be off in the early morning, like some young rake, a-riding your carriage in a race! All my bringings up, your aunt's teachings, and you will disgrace me! My wild daughter, all London is talking of my wild red-haired daughter! You'll never marry anyone decent!"

She could not help but be glad about that. When he turned on Neville, however, she flew to his protection.

"It was not his fault, papa, he did try to make me cry off. But I would not. It was foolish of me," she told him quickly.

"Very foolish of you, miss," said her father grimly. "I have a mind to pack you both off to Leeds and put you to a seven-day week of work! That will occupy your mind and your reckless hands! The devil has work for idle hands—that is very true! I would send you at once, but all London would laugh at *me*! Not being able to control a couple of children!"

"I am very sorry, father," said Neville, in a controlled manner, new to him. "I think we both realize how foolish our friendship with Rockingham was. I watched him deliberately draw Charlotte into the wager—"

"Wager, was it? Over what? What was the prize?" he asked anxiously. "I had heard it was a kiss. You were not so very foolish, Charlotte?"

Rockingham had deliberately spread the story that she had wagered for a kiss! Fury burned in Charlotte.

"No, papa, it was a bottle of champagne. Neville has it," she assured him quickly. "And I shall never do anything of the like again, I promise you."

"I think not, I think not," said Fergus, and dismissed them both. Charlotte worried about his quiet dismissal of them for a time, then decided he realized how upset they both were.

The matter was not forgotten by Society. Kenneth asked them anxiously what had happened and shook his head over it. Aunt Lydia was frankly upset, weeping, and took to her room and hartshorn. What in the world she was to do with two such high-spirited children, she did not know. Her Kenneth had been a model of rectitude.

Neville and Charlotte had not the heart to tease Kenneth over her words. They stayed quietly at home, no one called for several days, except disagreeable gossips, no doubt sent by high-born ladies who wanted to know the inside story without committing themselves to calling on Charlotte and Neville.

There was a ball on Friday evening. Charlotte wore a demure white gown with a full-sweeping skirt covered with points of pearls. A single strand of pearls was at her throat, the gown was not so low-cut as some. There were single pearls at her ears, her hair was dressed demurely in a simple style, center parted, with sausage curls to each shoulder.

Fergus looked her over sharply before they set out. "I hope you will behave this evening, Charlotte," he growled. "You'll not dance with that Rockingham."

"No, papa, I will not, I promise," she said quietly. She did not tell him she had no intention of ever speaking to Rockingham again. He had frightened her with his deliberate provocation of Neville.

At the ball, she was intensely relieved to find that Rockingham had not come. From Kenneth, she learned he had gone shooting in the country for several days. "Oh, I'm glad," she murmured, and let her cousin lead her out in a quadrille.

However, she could not but notice that several recently attentive gentlemen turned a cold shoulder to her. And worse, some of the matrons raised their lorgnettes at her, and turned away without acknowledging her bows. Her cheeks burned. They did not mean to let her forget her escapade so soon.

She sat alone for a time, in a small gilt chair at the side of the ballroom. It was the main room of a fine town house, belonging to an earl. She had not met the gentleman yet, and now she thought she would not. He probably regretted the invitation to her. She watched another quadrille with set smile. Neville was dancing with a charmer in blue. Kenneth had disappeared for a time. Her father, she knew, had escaped from balls, which he detested, and was probably talking business over a glass in a study somewhere.

She sat out several dances, and from the catty triumphant looks of some young females, she realized the neglect of her was deliberate. She was beginning to plan to go home early. How quickly one's town friends deserted one, she thought, soberly. If she had been home, the rector would have approached her and spoken, or the squire's wife would have been sitting beside her. They knew her from childhood and would not let her be so humiliated.

The next dance was a waltz. From the corner of her eye she saw a gray silk suit approaching her. Whoever it was, she would dance with him, she resolved, and attempt to corner Neville and ask him to take her home. She could not endure this—this cold contempt, this unfriendliness. She wished she were home, well away from London, in her dear Leeds, or her childhood home in a village.

The gentleman bowed. "May I have the pleasure, Miss Charlotte?" and a white glove was held out to her. She put her hand automatically in his, allowed him to draw her to her feet. Then she looked up, far up, into the coldly handsome face of Lord Arundell.

She stiffened. "Good evening, my lord," she murmured.

He put his arm about her waist in silence, and drew her into the waltz. He did dance well, making the moves quite correctly, with a skill which once would have set her feet skimming in delight over the polished floors. Now her heart felt like lead.

The dance ended. He bowed, she curtsied. He offered

her his arm, and she put her fingers very lightly on it. Under his fine coat, she felt the muscles, like steel, she thought.

Instead of escorting her to a chair, he went toward the opened French windows leading to the wide veranda. "It is a warm evening," he murmured. "A breath of air—?"

She nodded politely. It would save her for a few minutes, then she would find Neville and escape.

"Our host has an excellent garden," said Lord Arundell and conducted her down the stairs into the first footpath. Behind them a round started up, with much laughter. Charlotte walked with him as far as the first fountain, splashing its merry little tune into a marble basin, then resolutely took her hand from his arm.

"This is far enough," she said coldly.

"You are very discreet with me, Miss Gordon," he said, as frigidly. "I could wish you were as discreet in your other associations. I am very distressed at your conduct. I have come to respect your good father, and I find he is overwhelmed with your escapades. This latest one— the race with Rockingham—was the outside of enough."

Her heart swelled with indignation. "It is none of your concern! You do not know the truth of the matter—"

"A friend of mine was there in Hyde Park. He reported the whole of it when I demanded it," said Arundell, gazing down at her pale face in the moonlight. "The wager, a kiss, I believe?"

"It was not!" she flashed indignantly. "That good friend of yours is a liar! It was a wager for a bottle of champagne!"

"I do not care for the way you speak of my friends. And you would risk your reputation, your father's high plans for you, all for a bottle of champagne! It is worse than I had thought! Do you have such little respect for yourself?"

Her temper made her incautious. She drew herself up,

faced him, eyes blazing at him. "You are not informed correctly, sir. No one could know the whole of it, for no one knows it but myself. Your good friend—who saw the episode of the bottle of champagne—should also have informed you that Rockingham was in his cups, and dared to try to challenge my brother Neville, for cowardice. It was only by drawing his attention to the race that I could divert him!"

"What?" asked Arundell sharply, drawing a step closer. She was too wrought up to guard her tongue.

"And furthermore, in the first turn, when we were out of sight of his *gentlemen friends*, he was so ungallant as to try to overturn me! I felt the wheel of his carriage touch mine, saw his face. I drew back—remained behind him until the final stretch, or he would have thought nothing of cheating and tipping me over!"

Arundell was silent for a long moment, long enough for a breeze to cool Charlotte's hot cheeks, and discretion to return belatedly to temper her sense.

"I see I shall have to speak to Rockingham myself," said Lord Arundell slowly, in a tone of voice which made her put her hand to her breast.

"Oh—no, sir, I pray you, do not!"

"You fear for my life? You need not," he said with soft irony.

"Not for yours, but for Neville's. You do not think Rockingham will challenge you, do you? No, he will insult my brother in public, and duel him—and Neville is but a boy—" Her voice ended in a sob, to her intense humiliation. She put her hands over her face.

"You should have had more regard for him, then, Miss Charlotte, than to allow yourself to be put in a place where your brother will have to defend you. You have behaved very foolishly, risking your reputation, your brother's life—I wonder at you. Your father speaks highly of your mind and your sensibilities, but you continue to act like a giddy schoolgirl who ought to be sent back to her governess."

She was furious at his scolding. "How dare you speak to me like this!" Her hands dropped, she stiffened and faced him proudly. "You have no right to scold me, no right at all. Only my father has that right."

"You do not listen to him. It will take a stronger hand than his to tame you," he said contemptuously. "One who is not foolishly fond of you, I think, could bring you under control in short order."

"No doubt, sir," she said, without thinking of her rashness, "you would have me as bullied and put upon as your daughter Pamela, so that I too should be too afraid and low-spirited to whisper in public!"

He took another step closer to her. In the dim garden, she could not see his face clearly, but as his hands closed over her shoulders, she felt the heat in his hands, in his body.

"By God, I would like the taming of you!" he said thickly, all pretense at politeness quite vanished. He pulled her to him, and she was too shocked to fight.

His mouth closed savagely on her parted lips. She felt the hot intimate pressure, she could not believe this was happening. The Marquis of Arundell, insulting her in a garden, making free of her person—

She struggled, too late. He had her close to him, one arm across her back like an iron bar, the other hand with fingers twined in her thick red hair, holding her head back. He tasted her lips deliberately, brushing his own across them, then he kissed her cheeks, her throat, the lobe of her ear. She wanted to scream, she had no breath. No man had touched her like this, even in a waltz, no one had ever dared hold her so intimately.

Her body was curved against his, off-balance, as he held her to his hard thighs, his wide chest. Her softness felt the lean strength of him as he held her violently close

to him. His mouth closed again over hers, forcing her
to accept his kisses.

She was so angry and frightened that she was close
to fainting. The blood had raced to her head, and her ear-
drums pounded. Her eyes closed, she felt as though she
could not remain upright. She went limp.

His arms continued to hold her, until she regained her
control, and pushed away from him with shaking hands.
He was speaking, saying something—she could not hear
him—

Her own voice was shrill with anger. "You seem to
be quite heated—my lord—" Her hands were gripping
the edge of the marble fountain, and the water cooled
them. "Perhaps—this will cool—you—"

With all her furious might, she splashed her hands in
the cool water of the fountain, up and at him—so that
water drenched his face, down over his fine gray silk
suit.

"Damn!" said Lord Arundell, his hands going to his
eyes.

Charlotte took to her heels. She fairly ran back to the
ballroom, her skirts held up in her wet hands. At the entrance to the room, she halted, looking about frantically
for Neville.

A hand closed over her wrist, she almost screamed, then
relaxed as Kenneth's voice said, low in her ears, "Charlotte, what is it? Has someone insulted you? You look—
so strange—"

"Take me home, Kenneth," she pleaded. "I must go
home."

He looked closely at her, then nodded, his fine face
darkened. "I'll see Neville and tell him we are going.
Get your cloak and meet me at the entrance."

In the carriage Kenneth tried to question her. She was
shrill with temper, close to tears of weakness. "I don't

want to discuss it, Kenneth! Let me alone—please, let me alone—"

"But if you were insulted—"

"I shall handle the matter! It was nothing—I have handled it," she ended, with more satisfaction, as she thought of the water splashing over his fine silk suit, over his face and eyes. He would be so angry he would never speak with her again, and nothing would please her more!

Men were beasts, thought Charlotte, and she wanted nothing more to do with them. Except Neville, of course. She was quite exhausted by her own temper and went meekly to bed, to the expressed concern of her maid.

Chapter 4

Charlotte felt quite weepy, unusual for her. Meekly she remained at home, reading before the fire. Neville was completing his reports, scratching away busily with a pen. She read over the reports, corrected his spelling—uncertain at best—and refused to consider calling on anyone.

"I wish we were home," she confided in her brother, somberly. "I think father is right. I would be better off with work to do. All this running about is bad for me."

Neville got up, came over in concern, and pressed his hand to her forehead. "You are ill, Lotta! You must have a fever!"

She grimaced and moved her head away sharply. "No, no, I am weary of running about all day, and the people here—they are not true friends of ours, Neville. I cannot forget—" Her voice lowered, quivered. "I cannot forget—how Rockingham challenged you—"

Neville's face sobered. "Yes, I cannot forget it either." He stood, feet apart, gazing down at the brisk fire in the fireplace. The cosy drawing room was quite warm and comfortable, the more so as wind and rain blew against

51

the windows and rattled the panes. His face was unusually pensive; she thought again how much older he seemed.

A footman tapped at the door, and came in. "Miss Charlotte, your father desires you in his study—at once, he said." His slight change in expression made her glance up alertly. The servants liked Miss Charlotte. Was she in trouble again?

Oh, that nasty Darcy Saltash! He must have complained to her father. She had held herself stiff the first days, thinking he would come calling on her father and tell what she had done. But my lord could not complain of what she had done without telling why she had splashed water on him! And he would scarcely do that!

Her mouth burned, remembering his hard, experienced kisses on her lips. He had a reputation in London, not so bad as some rakes, but he was not known for chastity! Charlotte thought wildly what she could have done if she had been a man, called him out, dueled him. But if she had been a man, he would not have dared to embrace her so brazenly, forced his caresses on her in such manner.

"You haven't done anything, have you, Lotta?" asked Neville anxiously, torn from his own brooding.

"Not recently," she winked slyly at him, and laughed as she left the room. She smoothed down her white muslin skirts, made sure her hair was demure, her ribbons in place before she went in to her father. The hall mirror echoed her face, the flash of green eyes, the fire in the red hair.

The footman opened the door and closed it softly after her. She advanced across the dark carpet toward her father's desk. He motioned her to a seat. She sank down, studying his face. He seemed, not angry, but very determined. Perhaps he had resolved to return to Leeds. Well, she would be glad of that.

He glanced at her, then down again at a folded letter

on the desk before him. It was a large white thick paper, with a dark scrawl on it, a black ink with dashing letters.

"Well, Charlotte, I have been thinking deeply," said Fergus Gordon slowly. "You have had several offers lately, and I have been turning them over in my mind. I have resolved on marriage for you, and I wish you to know my decision, and the reasons therefor."

Charlotte had stiffened at the first words. Her hands were clasped tightly together, her voice caught in her throat. "Papa—"

"No, hear me out." He moved several papers about, gave a gruff little cough that told her he was deeply moved. "That Rockingham has been brazen enough to offer for you. I have refused, of course. He is not the man for you."

She drew a deep breath of relief. "I don't think so either, papa," she said, relieved, with a smile.

"There were two other offers, I have rejected them out of hand. Fortune hunters, hungry for your money." And he tossed two pages aside with contempt. He picked up the thick white paper with the black scrawl on it. "Now, we come to Lord Arundell."

She put her hand to her throat. Had he been mean enough to complain?

"After thinking it over carefully, I called upon him yesterday. We had a long conversation, very satisfactory. He is a decent man, for all his airs. And he comprehends the situation exactly. I informed him that it is the London fops and rakes that have caused you to run wild. I told him I was certain that you are a decent girl and will settle down to be a good wife and mother. His girl needs a mother, he says, and his home a housewife. I am sure you will get along well together."

She kept on staring at him, her hand in a fist at her breast. Darcy Saltash had dared to offer for her, knowing how she hated him? And why would he? After that dash of cold water in his face?

Fergus Gordon kept on nervously, not looking at her. "He is coming this morning to speak to you himself. I have given my permission, Charlotte. You are not to refuse him, nor treat him ungraciously! He is a fine gentleman, with a title higher than I had dared hope. Ah, if your mother could see you now—" He sighed a little, more sentimental than he usually allowed himself to appear.

Charlotte managed to gasp, "But papa—I hate him!"

Fergus frowned, then glared at her. "None of that loose speech, Charlotte. You do not hate such a gentleman!"

"I do, I do, you do not know—" She choked. She could not tell him how the man had insulted her in the garden.

"I have allowed you too much license, Charlotte! Now you will listen to me! He agrees that I cannot longer control you. You require a husband, and he will school that recklessness and impulsiveness from you! You need to settle down and have children of your own. He is being generous. He will settle a large amount on you, and of course I shall also. You shall not go poor to him, I assured him of that!"

He was going on too fast. She heard him speak of a money settlement, bride-clothes, some jewelry. Darcy wished to remove at once to the country, to his estate in the Cotswolds. She would soon learn to manage his home there, and get Pamela settled with a new governess. Darcy had many concerns about the country and in France, he would be busy about them, and she must learn to manage by herself. He had assured Darcy Saltash that his girl was a good housekeeper and a fine manager, and it was up to Charlotte to prove herself.

"But papa—papa—please—I do not wish to marry him!" she pleaded. She darted from her chair, went to clutch his arm, tears in her eyes. "Please, papa, I do not wish it! You said you would listen to me about my marriage—oh, I do not wish this!"

"Nonsense! Nonsense, child." Fergus was more moved than he wished to appear. He stood up abruptly, and removed her hand from his arm. "He is a good man, he will be a good husband to you. You would put off marriage forever if I did not make up my mind about this! You are completing your second season—"

"I don't care about London! I'll go back to Leeds with you, I'll work hard, papa, oh, please, don't make me do this! Refuse his offer, oh, please. I don't know why he wants me," she ended resentfully, thinking of the exquisite Mrs. Iris Holt, delicate in her black lace, sparkling with *his* diamonds. Did he wish to marry so that he might carry on his affair with his mistress brazenly? He would please the Prince Regent by marriage to a proper wife, then carry on under her very nose. No, no, she would not endure that!

"I have made up my mind, I have given my consent," said Fergus curtly, turning his head away. "Now, you may go and inform your brother. You will await Lord Arundell in the drawing room, and I will inform your aunt she is to appear when he comes."

"Papa, I do not want to marry him!" Charlotte stood up straight and tall. "If you force me into this, we will both be very sorry. I warn you, papa—"

"Hold your tongue, girl!" he snapped, in a fury, because he was a bit unsure himself. "You have defied me too often! Arundell will take you to hand! Now, go to your brother!"

Rarely had her father refused to listen to her. She gave him one final wounded look and marched to the door, closing it with a slam behind her. In the hallway, the footman noted her brimming eyes, her quivering chin, and hastened to open the drawing room door for her.

Alone with Neville, Charlotte caught her breath. "I

say, what happened?" asked Neville, alarmed. He drew her to a chair. "What's going on? Are we removing to Leeds? I shan't be sorry—"

"Worse," she whispered. "He means to marry me to Lord Arundell! I despise him, I hate him! I tried to tell papa, he would not listen to me! He talks only of his title, the suitability, the way I shall make a fine house-keeper—oh, Neville!" She put her head in her hands and let a sob escape.

Neville was frantic. His courageous beloved sister, to be so overwrought! He held her to him, he patted her hair, he adjured her to be brave. Neville would talk to papa, they would call it off in a trice. What was wrong that papa was so stubborn today? A fine dinner would set him right in his temper.

Charlotte shook her head, drew back to wipe her eyes with her lace-trimmed handkerchief. "He is set in it, Neville. He—he called on—on Lord Arundell yesterday. They talked of me—as though—as though I were a horse! A horse to be bought and sold—he dared talk of—of—" She choked on the words, unable to say that her father had spoken freely of her having children and settling down. Yes, just like a mare!

There was a murmur of voices in the hall—deep voices. Charlotte was too overwrought to listen. She sobbed to Neville, "Oh, they are outside of enough! They would settle my future for me without my consent! And you know papa always said he would consult me—"

Neville murmured consoling words, patting her head as she sat on the sofa beside him. "It is too bad, Charlotte. I will talk to papa when he is more calm. He will see reason, I feel sure. He was ever fond of you—"

"He doesn't act like that! Ordering me to be ready to marry within weeks! Weeks, Neville! No time to think, or get out of it—"

"Never mind. Never mind, dearest. When the crunch

comes, I'll help you. If papa insists, I'll help you run away. That's it, you shall run away," he said more gaily, trying to make her smile. "We have plenty of funds, we'll just go off and hide——"

"Indeed," said a cold voice behind him. Both started to their feet. Around Neville, Charlotte's dismayed gaze met that of a furious tall man. The cold blue eyes surveyed her. She knew he had heard Neville's rash proposition. He came further into the room. Fergus Gordon turned from speaking to Lydia and followed him in.

"Ah, here we are, here we are," said Fergus excitedly. His red face was further flushed. Lydia was in a vast flutter of amazement. That Charlotte should be betrothed finally! Ah, she was so happy, it was amazing how matters worked out, she had thought Charlotte would never settle down——

Arundell was gazing with frigid composure at Charlotte's tear-stained face. Neville, unable to speak, was clasping his hands behind his back, clenching and unclenching them. Perhaps Arundell would cry off when he realized how reluctant she was, thought Charlotte. He could not suppose she longed to rush into his arms!

Surely he did not want such a bride! He could have Mrs. Iris Holt for the speaking, or the gift of a diamond! Let him have her, he was welcome to her, and she was welcome to him! Brute! Devil! That he should find such a punishment for her! All because she did not fall at his feet and swoon——

Angry thoughts were chasing about in her mind as Fergus came forward, took Charlotte's hand, with a frown at her tearful eyes. "Charlotte, it gives me great pleasure to give your hand into that of Lord Arundell. Darcy, your hand——" The big hand of the man met that of Charlotte's, as she tried to shrink back from him. The fingers closed cruelly tight about hers.

Was he a devil then? Did he delight in brutality? Did

he wish to marry her to command her and break her spirit? Oh, surely her father would not force her into such a cruel situation!

Arundell was speaking, coldly, politely. She forced herself to listen to his words. He would not let her release her hand, she only hurt her fingers trying to get free. Finally she let it lie passively in his.

"Your consent has made me very happy, Miss Charlotte," he was saying to her bent head. "I place upon your hand the ring of betrothal." And he thrust onto her finger a single huge emerald on a gold band. The weight of it was enough to depress her spirits, the glint was like that of a demon's eye, she thought morbidly.

"Ah, so it is settled, I'll ring for champagne," said Fergus, clapping his hands and beaming at them, studiedly ignoring Charlotte and Neville. Lydia was fluttering about.

"Where is Kenneth? Oh, he will be so upset at missing this beautiful moment! He is so fond of Charlotte!" babbled Lydia, her mob cap askew. "Do you plan an immediate wedding? Fergus said—"

"Practically at once." Finally Darcy Saltash released Charlotte and she rubbed her hand obviously. From the glint of his blue eyes, she knew he realized he had held her too tightly, too cruelly. "I find I must return to my estates soon, and settle some matters. Later I must go over to Paris—"

"Ah, Paris—you might honeymoon there?" asked Lydia.

The butler came in with a tray of glasses, the footman followed with an ice bucket and two champagne bottles hastily placed therein. From the curiosity of their looks, nothing was missed, not the brilliant emerald ring, the tall aloofness of the visitor, the tears on Miss Charlotte's cheeks. There would be much talk in the pantry tonight!

"Perhaps," said Darcy crisply. He accepted a glass of sparkling white champagne, Charlotte took a glass in her hand and it shook. "To my betrothed," said Darcy, raising his glass.

Charlotte did not drink, nor could she answer the toast. Not with that cold blue gaze on hers, the mocking light in his face. Neville drank, his anxious look on his sister. Fergus drank with relief, Lydia with a flutter.

Arundell turned to Lydia. "I would like to arrange all for the ceremony to take place within a month. Can this be done? I realize this may well be inconvenient for you, but business calls, and I have lingered too long in London as it is. Also my daughter should return to the country, she is not happy here."

Charlotte heard it all in a daze of pain. It could not be. Her father would not do this to her. He would not even meet her look of reproach. She must talk to him, she must, and urge him to give up this mad plan.

She felt weak. When they sat down, she sank nervously onto the sofa where she had sat with Neville only moments ago. Darcy sat down beside her and took her free hand in his. Under cover of Fergus's jovial remarks, he said in her ear, "And do not think of ways to escape from this, my dear Charlotte! I know you now, I think, and you shall not get out of this! If you try to run away, you will suffer for it, and your brother also! Be warned!"

"I cannot imagine," said Charlotte, the shock of his words bringing back her courage, "why you should want so unwilling a bride. With your money and your title, surely you can buy one that is willing?"

The fingers closed more tightly on hers, crushing them, before he released her hand abruptly. "You shall learn the lesson of that one day, I think," he said smoothly. He caught the anxious look of Fergus, and said more clearly, "My daughter wishes to call shortly and renew her acquaintance with you. She is in ecstasies about our wedding, you may imagine."

"How kind you are," said Charlotte. Pamela was the

one happy thought she had about this unwished-for
wedding. At least the child could be made happier and
would be a satisfaction to care for. "I shall await her with
eagerness, you may tell her. Perhaps tomorrow morning?"

He bowed. "I shall be happy to come with Pamela
tomorrow. We might also have more conversation about
the date, and plans for the reception. You have a prefer-
ence about the church?"

So he went coolly ahead with plans, and Lydia sparkled
at the thought of planning a beautiful wedding and a
grand reception. It did not sound as though he planned
to cry off. Charlotte sat in a daze, wondering what dreadful thing she could do to make him sorry and withdraw
quickly before the nightmare took place.

Presently Darcy rose, kissed his fiancée's hand with
outward devotion, and a glint in his cold eyes that told
her it was all an act. Charlotte endured her aunt's
babblings for a time, then escaped to her room.

She flung herself on the bed after locking the door.
She pressed her face into the pillow and sobbed tearlessly.
Oh, how she hated him! He was only having a revenge
on her for what she had done. He would withdraw
probably, having humiliated her, and be satisfied!

She wished she were home in Leeds. Surely Fergus
would take them home after that. She never wanted to
see London again. She thought of how everyone would
mock and scorn her.

Noreen knocked and knocked, and finally called her
sternly. Charlotte unlocked the door and let her in.

"Now, Miss Charlotte," said the Irish maid. "What is
this about? You never said you thought you might marry
the man! But Mr. Gordon is talking about bride-clothes,
and you must have fittings! Oooohh, the ring—" And
she picked up the slim hand and admired the emerald
on it.

"I can't marry him, I don't want to marry—" whispered

Charlotte, in despair. "Oh, Noreen, I must talk to papa—"

"Pooh, nonsense. You're upset, and nervy," said Noreen, with a quick look at her charge. "I'll bring you some tea, and we'll talk about the clothes you shall get. Your papa has gone off to his club to brag about his new son-in-law, and Neville has gone to the races with Kenneth."

"He cannot—cannot mean—to go through with this—" Charlotte muttered, her fist to her mouth.

Noreen thought she meant her father. "Laws, now, Miss Charlotte, don't carry on so," she said, sternly brisk. "You know your papa has meant to make a fine marriage for you! And what could be better? Arundell has offered for you and he means to have you."

She chattered on, as Charlotte sat numbly. He means to have you—he means to have you—oh, why, why, why? She wondered until her brain was numb, but could think of no reason for it. Unless he meant to make a conventional marriage, and so cover up his blatant affair with the lovely divorcée.

Chapter 5

The days flew past on wings of fear. Charlotte stood for fittings at the dressmaker's. Her father said proudly that she should have a completely new outfit to go to her husband, no one should say that he was shabby-spirited! She acquired new summer clothes for the wedding days, new winter garments for the winters in the Cotswold hills which were said to be cold.

Between fittings for muslin dresses, silk taffetas with fur hems and cuffs, thick woolen dresses and matching coats, adorable fur hats with tall feathers, gauze garments and frilly lingerie, satin nightdresses and matching negligees, Charlotte went to more teas and dances than she had all season. She had thought her former life hectic—this was much worse.

To all the evening affairs and some of the afternoon ones, she was accompanied by her new and seemingly devoted fiancé. His hand clasped her arm with cruel strength when she would have darted away from him to speak to a friend; he sat next to her, and shot warning looks when she grew sullen. He showered her with gifts she did not want, and looked amused when she forced herself to acknowledge them politely.

Aunt Lydia made up for Charlotte's coldness. She was quivering with excitement over the engagement. Her niece to marry a marquis! She looked forward to the day within a few weeks when she might speak of "my niece, the Marchioness of Arundell!"

Aunt Lydia accompanied Charlotte everywhere, her chaperon and guide. Charlotte finally realized this was deliberate. Neville and Kenneth were being kept from her! Out of mischief, she thought resentfully, catching the glint in her fiancé's eyes as the men were spoken of. Aunt Lydia took her to teas, sat with her over interminable gossips, sat on chairs at the dressmaker's, and cooed over bonnets and dear little gloves and the sheer night-dresses the woman recommended.

It was a nightmare. Charlotte moved in a daze, more and more resentful. She was being pushed about like a puppet! As though she had no will of her own! She tried to refuse her fiancé's gift of a set of enormous pearls, with the cool remark she thought they were not suited to her. "I do not care for such display, my lord," she said.

"They become you," he said smoothly and set the long double necklace about her throat. "Only one so tall and regal as you can wear them well." And he thrust on her fingers the immense pearl rings and the bracelets on her arms. He would have put on the earrings, but she backed away, and took them in her hand. "Look in the mirror," he told her, with amusement, "you will see how well you look."

She looked, saw a girl with flushed cheeks and bright, furious, green eyes. And the long heavy strands of pearls. Behind her the tall figure of her fiancé loomed like a threat. He put one hand on her shoulder; she moved away quickly. His hand fell to his side.

"I must have the family emeralds reset for you," he

said, as though not noticing her slight. "They will become you."

"Do not trouble, my lord. I dislike elaborate displays of jewelry. I think them in poor taste," she said, as Aunt Lydia gasped and looked anxiously at the marquis.

"You will like these, they are not in poor taste," he said firmly, and that was that.

She was ordered to like what he liked, to go where he would, to dance with whom he chose. At dinners, he sat next to her and directed the conversation. At dances, he looked over her eager escorts and chose only his close friends. Kenneth murmured to her one night that he himself was not sure he would get a dance with her!

"For my lord is jealous of you, they say," said Kenneth. "He has given orders that Rockingham is not to be invited to any event he deigns to attend! And of course everyone falls over himself to do as my lord wishes!" There was bitterness in his voice. She squeezed his hand.

"Oh, if only I could talk to papa—" she muttered. Her father refused to listen to any objections.

"I have my ears open," said Kenneth, mysteriously. "Perhaps he will change his mind. Keep up your spirits, my dear—"

"What is it? What have you heard?" she asked eagerly, gazing up with sparkling eyes. "Oh, dear Kenneth, do tell me—"

A hand touched her arm, and she knew that touch already. She stiffened, standing beside Kenneth at the side of the ballroom. My lord drawled, "My dance, I believe," and swept her away with him.

"What was he saying to you?" he demanded.

"My cousin Kenneth? What does it matter?" she asked in the cold manner she used to him. Oh, if only he would be so angry that he would cry off! She could endure any laughter, any mockery, any slights of the London society, if only she could escape this fate, this horrible marriage!

Lord Arundell gazed down at her, deliberately. He did not kiss her mouth, he was formal with her, only touching her fingers lightly with his lips on greeting or leaving her. But his gaze seemed to undress her, looking over her from head to foot, as though he had the right to stare and to surmise what lay beneath her garments. She cringed from that look, that calculating stare.

"A charming dress, my dear," he said, changing the subject after a pause. She wore a cream figured silk underdress, and over it a garment of sheerest green gauze which shimmered about her—as one admirer had dared to say—like sea water about a nymph. "It becomes you. Your hair is like fire tonight. A new mode, I believe?"

He noticed everything about a woman, she thought spitefully. Like a true rake. "Thank you, my lord."

Over his shoulder she had caught sight of someone who interested her. Her eyes narrowed. One did not usually see the beautiful Mrs. Iris Holt at the respectable gatherings of which Fergus Gordon approved. Yet there she was, elegant in black taffeta with diamonds sparkling at her wrists and in her shining blond hair. She glanced back at Darcy, to see him gazing keenly down at her.

"What is it?" he asked, then glanced across the room, saw the woman. His mouth tightened he frowned slightly.

"Are you not going to greet your—friend?" she murmured. This might be all she needed, for her father to see them together, with Iris Holt hanging like a willow on Darcy Saltash's sturdy arm! "I am sure she expects it!"

"Indeed? Why should you suppose it?" he said in his most frigid tones.

She shrugged lightly. "You have always been—so close," she murmured. "In fact, I have quite wondered that you did not propose to her."

It was out. A proper lady did not say such things, not

to her fiancé. Under fringed lashes, she watched his reaction. Except for a firmer line to his mouth, she got none.

"Ah, I believe supper is being served. I will seat you with your aunt, and bring a plate to you. Champagne, I believe, that is your favorite drink?" Lightly, he mocked her, recalling the race and the disastrous bet.

She required all her wits about her, if she were to win out against him. "Ratafia, if you please, sir. I am quite warm," she said. The late May evening was warm, and the doors to the ballroom stood open.

He bowed and left her sitting on a gilt chair beside her aunt. His broad shoulders managed a path through the crowd about the supper tables, and he soon returned, carrying glasses of champagne, while a footman followed him with plates of food. Charlotte said nothing, pointedly, but left her glass on the small table beside her and scarcely touched the food. Darcy did not seem to notice, he was laughing and chaffing with a friend of his from his old regiment, speaking of battles long past.

Charlotte burned with resentment. He did not wish her to enjoy herself, but he made sure that he did! She waited for him to claim Mrs. Holt after the supper, but he stuck close to Charlotte's side, and his behavior was impeccable. Mrs. Holt gazed at him wistfully from across the room, but aside from a bow in her direction he paid no attention to his former mistress. Oh, he would be certain to be correct! Charlotte wondered briefly if Lord Arundell was in the suds, and might have been promised a large dowry for her marriage, she could not think why else he would wish to marry her. But no, all London spoke of his estates, his management of several woolen mills, and the fortune in jewelry his family possessed.

Neville came around, and Charlotte begged him after their dance for a glass of ratafia, "for I am so warm, dearest."

"Did you have none with your supper?" he asked in concern.

She shrugged. "My lord brought only champagne, and I have a dislike of it now."

Neville's eyebrows raised, he went for the glass and returned with it as Darcy approached her. Lord Arundell looked on impassively as Charlotte sipped at the glass. She had scarcely set it down when he put his arm about her to lead her into the waltz that followed.

"You must have your own wilful way, I see," he murmured over her head.

"I beg your pardon?"

"You know very well what I mean," he said savagely. "Only you will not make scenes in public, I beg you! I dislike scenes!"

She bit her lip. "I cannot help it if I am thirsty, and you do not bring me what I desire!" she told him frigidly.

"You are more childish than Pamela," he said, unforgivably.

She stiffened, he jerked at her. "You are awkward tonight, also," he said rudely. "Too many late nights, I presume. You will find the quiet of the country more welcome!"

Did he mean to leave her there and go back to London without her? She thought he might, for Mrs. Iris Holt would be here to entertain him. The more she thought of it, the more she was convinced that was his intention.

He was in a savage temper when he took her home, though his manners were so excellent that Aunt Lydia did not seem to perceive it. Only on leaving, he said that he would bring Pamela to tea the next afternoon.

"Thank you, I shall be glad to see her," said Charlotte, more sincerely than she had spoken to him that evening.

He pressed her hand, raised it to his lips, brushed his mouth across her fingers. His lips seemed to burn them, she could practically feel his mouth on her fingers as she retired, and tossed restlessly for a long time before sleeping.

The following morning, she had more fittings at the dressmaker's, and twitched and fidgeted until Aunt Lydia reproved her. "I am weary of standing for this, I must have enough clothes for five years," she said savagely.

The little girls who helped the dressmaker looked at each other and giggled behind their hands. Aunt Lydia frowned, but finally suggested they leave early so that Charlotte could rest before the afternoon. In the carriage, she scolded her gently.

"My dear Charlotte, your father is being very generous with you. He is outfitting you gloriously, you should be most grateful!"

"Everyone gives me everything except what I wish, my freedom to move and go as I please," said Charlotte rebelliously, her mouth set in sullen lines.

"Charlotte, you are talking foolishness! A woman has no freedom, her will is her husband's. You should be happy that your father has made such a good match for you! All London envies you." And she went on in that vein until Charlotte could have screamed.

She rested after luncheon, and felt a little better when Darcy Saltash arrived punctually at three o'clock with Pamela. Charlotte was always glad to see Pamela, the little girl was shyly pleased about the approaching marriage, and they always had something to talk about.

Today Darcy, speaking in a more friendly manner, entered into the conversation, telling her about the family seat in the Cotswolds.

"It is my favorite of the houses," he said, crossing his legs easily. He was dressed in close-fitting pantaloons of blue satin, a matching tight coat which set off his broad shoulders and fine chest. Under the coat was a magnificent silver and white waistcoat finely embroidered, and his cravat of white lawn was tied in intricate folds about his deeply tanned throat. Set in the cravat was a single huge ruby, and on his right hand was a matching ruby cut in a signet.

Pamela was in sharp contrast, her thin frame in a snuff-brown dress, a little too large about the waist, her sallow cheeks glowing with excitement. Her hair was cut badly. Who had the dressing of her, Charlotte wondered again. Her father was so smart, she so dowdy.

"I am to have a new dress for the wedding, it is pink, with many ruffles," murmured Pamela confidingly, as she sat beside Charlotte on the sofa.

"Pink?" asked Charlotte, quite sharply, startling the girl. Darcy raised his eyebrows.

"You do not approve?"

"The color does not suit her. I should think a pale yellow, in a straight dress with ruffles at the hem and sleeves, might do well, and a matching yellow bonnet with yellow flowers."

Pamela's eyes opened wide in rapture. "Oh, I do love yellow, but Mrs. Holt does not think it suits me! Do you think I might have a yellow dress one day, papa?" She looked anxiously at her father.

A dull flush had stained his high cheekbones. Charlotte gazed at him with cold irony. So that was who dressed the child! His mistress!

"Perhaps. We will discuss it later, Pamela," he said curtly. He changed the subject abruptly. "We were going to tell your new mama about the Arundell castle and its grounds, were we not?"

"Oh, yes. It is a fine house, everyone says," said Pamela, curling her fingers confidingly in Charlotte's. "It is very large, and Mrs. Nettleton gets cross about how hard it is to keep good help! And the dusting is e-normous!"

Charlotte could not help it. At the discomfited expression on Darcy's face, she burst out laughing. After a minute, he joined her, in a gruff sort of laugh.

"Well, that was not what I had in mind. You will discourage her, Pamela! I meant for you to tell her the good points about the house," he said drily. He turned in more friendly fashion to Charlotte as Pamela hung her head. "It was built on the ruins of an abbey of the fifteenth century, and part of the stonework remains. First the center was built, the great hall reaching three stories, in which the battle flags are hung, and armor of our ancestors standing about. Rather grim! But we are accustomed to it."

"It sounds a—fine place," murmured Charlotte nervously. She had never lived with battle flags and armor. The house in Leeds had a comfortable quality, sometimes a squeeze, with chintz about and things getting shabby and dulled in the sunlight, but it was home, and she felt a vast longing to be there.

"The master suite has been redecorated recently," Darcy went on. He continued to describe the place, and Pamela chimed in about the beautiful gardens, and how her dog Macduff enjoyed a run around the fountains. But Charlotte's mind had stopped cold at the words "master suite." Would she be expected to live there with—with *him*?

"Before we depart from London, I should like to show you over the town house, to see if you wish changes made in that. We come here in season, and also I use it when I have business here. We keep a skeleton staff here on those occasions. Then there is the hunting lodge up near the Scottish border—"

Darcy went on, coolly enumerating the several places, adding that she must see them soon. Then he went on to speak of his various properties. As she sat silently listening, she wondered if he sought to persuade her to keep to the marriage by thinking of all he owned that she would share. Did he not realize that she cared little for large properties or boxes of jewelry, and that her father generously supplied her with more clothes than she could hope to wear in a year?

She did rouse when he spoke of his woolen mills. "You know that father worked many years as a mill child," she said, watching him under her lashes. "He worked his way up to foreman, and presently bought out his master, then expanded the works. You must get him to speak of it sometime."

She felt a malicious satisfaction at reminding him that she came of common parentage. Surely that must give him a twinge! But he was too much the gentleman to let any feelings show.

"We have spoken of it already," said Darcy. "He will come one day to visit us, and perhaps honor us by looking over the mill. He might be able to advise a better method of working. However, I have an excellent manager. He keeps the costs well down, by using orphan children from Wales and Scotland. He brings them in when they are quite small and trains them well. They are not much to house and feed, much less than adults. He tells me they are most teachable, and of course it is a way of keeping them from the poorhouses."

Charlotte's eyebrows met in a slight frown. Child labor? Using orphans? Many places did so, and so did her father, but he was careful to oversee the conditions of their labor, and had a house where the housekeeper made sure of the good condition of their bedding and food. Some of them had risen in the works and made excellent trainers and foremen. She must see to it when she went to Castle Arundell, she thought, biting her lips. She knew much about mill operations. Darcy spoke very dispassionately about the child labor. She wondered if he had ever observed it. One must take great care that the children were not abused.

She started when he addressed her firmly. "Miss Charlotte? I think your mind has wandered. You are, perhaps, not interested in mills and such?"

"On the contrary, sir, I am much interested. I mean to visit the mills as soon as may be," she told him, quite startling him.

He stared at her. "That will not be your duty, I assure you," he said with a frown.

"Oh, I assure you, sir, that I am a modern woman, and much more interests me—than you can imagine!"

He stared at her, and so did Pamela. It was like a gauntlet flung down. Well, if he must marry her, he need not expect her to stay quiet in her corner, and tend to her sewing and sweetly wait her lord! He would be in for a shock, Charlotte promised herself.

Aunt Lydia came in presently, and the tea tray arrived with her. Pamela helped hand about the cups and glowed when her father patted her head. Charlotte wondered how much attention he paid to her when they were not on public view. She would find that out soon enough—if she went through with the marriage!

Fergus Gordon came in from the street, and joined them. Presently Neville and Kenneth came also, Kenneth in a mood of suppressed excitement. Charlotte noted his wink at her and wondered at him.

Darcy and his daughter took their leave. Pamela dared to kiss Charlotte's cheek, and Charlotte gave her a little hug. Darcy kissed her hand as usual and bowed to the company before departing. Aunt Lydia remained to murmur about the next preparations and a dinner they must give the next night. But finally she departed, and Fergus went to his study.

Charlotte had poured herself another cup of tea she did not want, and now she stretched out her slippers to the fire, and looked up at Kenneth. Neville went to shut the door, cautiously peering around it first.

"Well—well, what news? You are like two cats on hot bricks," she said impatiently.

Kenneth came to sit beside her. His brown eyes were dancing with excitement, his thin face glowed with his gossip. "You knew? I find it hard to hide my expressions," he said ruefully. "Listen, we have great news for you, Charlotte!"

"Finally dared to go see the lovely Mrs. Holt," murmured Neville, sitting across from them, and nodding at Charlotte's amazement. "Yes, we went to call upon her. Lives in a luxurious flat, she does, all black and gold and silver, and thick fur rugs, and tons of gold china and that."

"Well—well, what did you say, what excuse—" She was stammering with eagerness. She sat up, pulled at Kenneth's hand. "Tell me, do! I am all eager to hear—"

Kenneth took her hand gently. How different his touch from that of the arrogant marquis, who held her so tightly she felt trapped. "The lady is furious over Arundell's marriage. She received us only out of curiosity, she admitted later. We had heard stories about her—" He hesitated, looked at Neville who nodded.

Neville said, "We heard she has the dressing of the child, garbs her the way she would a blond-haired little girl of her own, which she ain't! Seems that she was friends years ago of Arundell's first wife, name of Lucille. Got invited often to Arundell Castle; always sitting in each other's pockets in London. Anyway, she adored Darcy Saltash, to hear her tell it. And years ago she was even prettier than now. She cut out the wife—"

Charlotte felt the blood draining from her head. She gripped Kenneth's hand. "What do you mean—cut her out?"

"Well, it was a scandal of the time. Seems Darcy Saltash got involved with Iris Holt, and his wife was angry, and turned to someone else. Arundell was in and out of England, off to the Peninsula, and all. Fighting fierce, could get home only now and then. While he was gone, his wife finds she is going to have a second baby. London doesn't know if it was his—or maybe someone else's! Arundell returns, Iris Holt and he thick as thieves. Lucille has the baby, the baby dies, so does she. The story is he wasn't sure the baby was his, mad as fire at her, quarreled so it was all over England. If she had lived, he might have put her aside, the story is. So Mrs. Holt tells it, that he didn't love Lucille at all, he loved her, wanted any excuse to marry her."

"Then why didn't he?" cried Charlotte, feeling pale as death. This was worse than she had dreamed.

The men shrugged, embarrassed at all they had said. "Well, she was married to her old husband, thought he would die any time," said Kenneth finally. "She wasn't about to give up his money. Then she finally got a divorce, but her husband saw to it that the Prince Regent got his ear first. She is disgraced, not received where he is about. So Saltash won't marry her. He doesn't want to be set down, not when he's close to the throne. Anyway, Mrs. Holt was interested in what Neville said, that you were reluctant to marry."

"You told her—that?"

"Oh, just hinted," said her brother uneasily. "Told her we was scouting about for his reputation—"

"She assured us that Darcy Saltash was very close to her, that their association—" said Kenneth unhappily, squeezing her hand, "was continuing. She has the dressing of the child. She practically lives in his pocket! And she wants to meet you, talk to you herself."

"Oh!" Charlotte put her hand to her mouth, made it a fist. She felt rather sick. She had not wanted to marry Saltash, she detested him, but she had not thought him so bad as all this. She wondered at herself. Here was a chance to get out of the marriage—and yet—to meet that woman—"I don't know—"

"Day after tomorrow," said Neville, pale but resolute,

"papa is going to be from home. I'm going with him to the 'change, he wants me to learn about it. Kenneth thinks he can get his mama to go somewhere with him. We'll send a note to Mrs. Holt to call on you—maybe in the morning—as soon as it is safe—what do you say?"

Charlotte thought about it, twisting her hands together. It might be a terrible encounter—but truth was better than wondering, wasn't it? Finally she nodded.

"Yes, yes, I'll meet her," she said faintly. "Do arrange what you can, and send her the note. I'll see her—the day after tomorrow."

"You know," said Kenneth gently, "this will probably be for the best. You can tell your father, he won't insist. We have heard that Mrs. Holt deliberately ruined Darcy's marriage, that Lucille was heartbroken. We wouldn't want that to happen to you. Your father wouldn't want it—and if Darcy loves her—" His shrug was eloquent.

Chapter 6

Charlotte wanted, yet dreaded, the meeting. The next day flew past; she was pale, distraught. She was so quiet, that her father was concerned for her and urged her to stay in for a day or two.

"You are gadding about too much," said Fergus. "You'll be worn out for the wedding. Get some rest, call off some engagements."

She managed a smile. "I think I shall. I have just an engagement at the dressmaker's tomorrow—and tea. Perhaps Aunt Lydia would make my apologies, and I'll stay in by the fire. The rain makes the day so cold!"

Truly, she had felt chilled whenever she went out, the rains had come down almost without ceasing for four days. London in the rain seemed dreary to her. In the country, she had gone riding in the rain, loving the smell of the hedges and fields, putting her horse to the gallop over the wet hedges, returning covered with mist and glowing. But London—splashing about in dirty puddles, the horses tangled in their shafts as the traffic became snarled, coachmen cursing each other—she was becoming very weary of London.

So they left her alone the next day, Kenneth with a wink, and a word to her ear. "She'll be coming at eleven, on the quiet, you may be sure!"

She nodded, and thanked him in a whisper. She did not want to see the woman, it would be most unpleasant. But it might be just the thing to call off the wedding. Her father must be convinced. She shrank from meeting Darcy Saltash, and was grateful she had no engagements with him for two days.

The next morning, the others set off, leaving Charlotte to the house, and the fire in the drawing room. She had dressed carefully in a casual white muslin dress with green ribbons, and a comfortable mob cap trimmed in lace and green. She stretched out her slippers to the fire and mused, unable to read or think properly. Her father would be furious—but better his fury than a lifetime of regret, married to a man she despised.

The butler came to her just before eleven, his mouth turned down in a disapproving frown. "Miss Charlotte, there is a female here who would see you."

"Oh, yes, who is it?" Her heart was thumping hard, she could scarcely keep her tone casual.

"A Mrs. Iris Holt, ma'am." He presented the card on a silver tray, stiffly. She wondered if even the butler knew who Mrs. Holt was, and her association with Charlotte's fiancé. Probably. The servants missed little.

"Show her in, then."

She waited, then stood as the delicately beautiful woman swept into the room. They measured each other, like two beautiful cats, carefully, before Charlotte bowed slightly. "Mrs. Holt, how kind of you to call."

"Ah, Miss Gordon, it is delightful to meet you." Mrs. Holt waited until the butler had closed the door behind her, then she advanced to the chair Charlotte indicated. "What a charming room. Your doing? I hear you are quite the housewife. And so very young."

She sighed, as though in regret, gently. She wore a thin black lace gown, setting off her fragile beauty, the magnolia white skin, the soft blond puff of hair, the helpless fluttery hands. She carried a small black taffeta and jet bag, which she set beside her.

"May I offer you tea?" Charlotte hovered near the bell rope.

Mrs. Holt shook her head, and set the black plumes on her head waving. "No, no, Miss Gordon. I must not remain long. Your dear brother urged me to call, but I must not stay. So many engagements—" She let the words trail away, studying Charlotte's face under her long darkened lashes.

"Then let us to business," said Charlotte, and sat down opposite the woman. "You know I am engaged by my father to Lord Arundell. My brother and cousin indicated that—may I be blunt—you have a relationship with him."

The delicate brows raised. "But of course—the world knows," she said simply. "Darcy and I are always discreet, he is the greatest gentleman in the world. So generous, so loving—he gave me this only last evening," and she held out her wrist, drawing back the lace sleeve.

Glittering there was a wide diamond bracelet. Mrs. Holt fingered it, touched the stones, a faint smile on her lips. Charlotte felt vaguely ill.

"You have been—associated with him—long?"

Mrs. Holt nodded. "I tell you this only because, poor dear child, you are so young! And I understand you are being coerced into the marriage. I cannot approve. I understand that Darcy cannot marry me, he would not be received by His Highness again if he did. Since I am divorced, many doors are closed to me and would be slammed in his face. I cannot do this to him." Sadness tinged her lovely face, the wide blue eyes.

"A great pity," said Charlotte drily. If she had loved a man she would have wanted him with her, and the hell with the world, she thought, surprised at her own fierceness. She forced herself on. "And you have loved him long? Even when he was married before?"

Mrs. Holt nodded, lashes down. "I loved his wife too, that was the trouble. She was such a flighty but adorable creature! Her daughter resembles her not at all! But Lucille—all the world loved her! Too many, and Darcy discovered her indiscretions. He turned to me—I comforted him—"

"He seems a very jealous creature," said Charlotte slowly, wondering at herself. Sitting in her own drawing room, calmly discussing her fiancé's nature with his mistress—! How low had she sunk! But she must know. "I—find him very jealous, very possessive. He seems to expect absolute discretion from me, while continuing his relationship with you—perhaps others."

Mrs. Holt delicately shrugged. "That is a man for you, and he is every bit a man," she smiled. "Poor child, your illusions shattered! But he is generous, you will see. He has given me sets of sapphires and diamonds, he settles all my bills for me, and all he asks in return is that I dress his little daughter for him, and help him in little ways— And of course—if he has other women, they are only for the moment, you understand? He is very much a man."

Charlotte gazed at the fire. She felt such nausea rising in her she wondered how she would endure it. She knew other London rakes lived like this, but her father had not. The trouble was, she decided bitterly, that she had a middle-class upbringing, and could not settle to noble ways! Affairs and casual amours were not for her. How could she endure a husband such as Lord Arundell? He would not allow her to change him, she was sure of that. And he had no incentive to change. He had the whip hand, and could rule her absolutely. That was the law.

Mrs. Holt was fingering her diamond bracelet meditatively. After a short pause, she said, "You know, I was thinking of the family gems, the fire opals. They were brought from the Orient by the first Lord Arundell, more than two hundred years ago. They have brought misfortune on the unhappy wives of the Arundells time and again. I tried to warn Lucille, but she would not listen, she would wear them. And sure enough, she became entangled with a man, just as Darcy was returning from the Peninsula, wounded, and in no mood to be generous with her faults. And so she quarreled with him—bitterly. I often wondered if that brought on her death, that quarrel, with her so near her time." She sighed deeply.

"And she died in childbirth—" Charlotte's voice was low, she felt caught up in the bitter drama of long ago, five years ago.

"Yes, she was brought to bed with the child almost a month early. She and the child both died. Arundell was wild with misery, jealousy, rage. He turned to me for comfort—I was able to help him. Poor darling," murmured Mrs. Holt, with a sigh, her mouth curling in a slight smile. "Men can be so like boys when they are hurt. And his poor dear shoulders covered with scars, scarcely healed. I used to cover them with ointment and rub it in for him, he was so grateful."

Charlotte winced. Every word was damning. This woman had known him so intimately. She could not endure much more.

"If he gives you the fire opals, my dear, I think you should refuse to wear them," said Mrs. Holt seriously. "They are so very unlucky, you know."

"What could be more unlucky than marriage to a man already deeply in love with another woman?" Charlotte burst out angrily, then bit her tongue, as the blue eyes sparkled with eagerness.

"My very thought, Miss Gordon! If you could only persuade your father to allow you to cry off! It would be a scandal for only a short time, I assure you! His reputation is well known in London. Even I was amazed when he chose someone so young and innocent, and meeting and talking with you I am confirmed that you are just so! He should have chosen someone older, less sensitive, less—vulnerable," said Mrs. Holt, and her eyes glistened.

Charlotte stood up. "I must thank you for coming," she said, formally.

Mrs. Holt rose also, gracefully, picked up her handbag, and adjusted her slight black woolen wrap about her shoulders. "If I thought I had helped you in any way, my dear Miss Gordon—"

"You have been most kind," Charlotte told her, and rang for the butler.

He came so promptly he must have been just outside the door, thought Charlotte. "You rang, Miss Gordon?"

He was probably expecting her to order tea. "You will see the lady to her carriage. Thank you."

The ladies did not shake hands. Mrs. Holt, her head bowed as though in deep sorrow, left the room with her light small steps. Charlotte pressed her handkerchief to her mouth. Yes, she was going to be ill!

As soon as she heard the heavy front door close, and the voices cease, she left the room, and raced upstairs to her bedroom above. In her room, she shut and locked the door, and ran to the washroom. There she was violently sick.

She returned to the bed and lay down weakly. Her stomach was churning and churning, but not more so than her mind. She must get out of this abominable situation! She could not endure it! That woman in her heavy perfume, fondling the bracelet that Darcy Saltash had given her only last evening!

Noreen came to her presently, her Irish face concerned and ominous all at once. Charlotte knew the word of her visitor had sped like wildfire through the house.

Charlotte let her in. "I want no luncheon," she said at once, before the maid could speak. "Inform me when papa returns, if you will. I will speak with him at once."

"Miss Charlotte, you won't listen to what that woman said!" burst out Noreen. "It was wicked of you to receive her!"

Charlotte only shook her head and turned away, to sink into a soft chair near the window. She stared out at the rain, her fingers clenched about her silk handkerchief, her shoulders stiff. Noreen sighed and departed.

Charlotte waited. Near her on a stand was a cunning music box. Darcy recently had given her the gift as though from Pamela. One lifted the lid, and it played a gay tune, and there was room in it for a tiny pair of earrings. He had placed in it a pair of emerald earrings, small and adorable. She gazed at the box, she had been pleased with it—if only it had come from someone else!

On the dressing table stood a beautiful cut-glass bottle of her favorite lilac perfume, another gift from Arundell. Her jewelry boxes overflowed, he had bought her another velvet lined box made of Chinese lacquer, of black and gold, to hold more that he gave her, the pearls, more emeralds, some beautiful cameos from Italy. He had spoken of Italy—she would enjoy a visit there, he said.

She pressed her hand to her eyes. All mockery, all mockery. He cared nothing for her. Why would he marry her? She could not understand his motives. Except that he must have an acceptable wife, someone to look after Pamela, perhaps to breed more children for the estate. She shuddered.

Noreen brought a tray of tea. She ignored it, while her mind went on churning around and around. She must cry off, she must escape this silken net. Surely her father would know *now* that she could not go through with the wedding. He would not expect it.

Finally Noreen brought word about four o'clock that

her father had returned, and would see her in his study. "I'll but brush your hair, it is sadly in disarray," said Noreen, and brushed it out and combed and plaited it into a coronet about her head. "You're pale, a bit of color in your cheeks?"

Charlotte shook her head, uncaring. "I'll go down," she said, and picked up a fresh handkerchief. Noreen shook her head as she saw her mistress go out, so dazed, so shocked looking. What that woman must have said! The butler had not overheard words, but they had talked and talked, he said.

Charlotte avoided the drawing room. Aunt Lydia's voice was going on cheerfully about her day. She slipped past it to the study, tapped on the door, and went in.

Her father was pacing before the fireplace. He stopped, and studied her under his rusty-brown eyebrows, so bushy and expressive. He waited.

She came and stood before him after closing the door. She felt amazingly calm now.

"Father, Mrs. Iris Holt came to visit me today."

"So? And is that why you're so pale and sickly?" he shot at her.

She swallowed. Gently he pushed her into a big chair and stood over her.

"Don't torment yourself, Charlotte. Gossip ain't always to be believed," said Fergus Gordon.

So he knew also! "She told me the truth of her relationship with Lord Arundell." She was amazed at the calm precision of her words. She twisted the handkerchief in her fingers. "Father, I cannot go through with the marriage. She is his mistress, has been for years."

"Pooh, nonsense! He assured me he would take every care of you, that he has a fondness for you." Fergus scowled and stamped back and forth, more uneasy than he wished to show. His daughter was too quiet, it was unnatural. Usually she stormed and raved just as he did, letting loose her temper, then regaining it with a laugh.

"She told me—that their relationship has lasted for many years, even before—the death of his wife." She swallowed convulsively, gazed from his face to the fire. How complacent the woman had looked! How she had recited the details of that relationship!

"Pooh, you can't believe her. The woman is jealous, that's clear! She's warning you off, means to have him herself."

"She said she could not marry him, he would lose the friendship of His Royal Highness. She—she showed me a diamond bracelet he gave her—only last evening," she said in a low tone.

Fergus shot her a worried look. The girl looked really sick. She wasn't used to the high society, that was sure. She had been gently bred, and in nature was much more like his dead wife than himself. He had tried to shield her from the nasty facts about life and men. Now perhaps he had been wrong, she should have been told the rumors he had heard and made to laugh about it.

"Father, I cannot marry him," said Charlotte, more positively.

"Yes, you will," he said heavily. It hurt him to bully his girl, but she did not know what was best for her. And he had set his heart on having her marry into nobility. And sure, but Darcy Saltash was one of the highest of the ton, with pluck and grace, and manners and all. Decent to talk to, also, none of your settings down when he spoke with Fergus Gordon! Could talk with the best about politics and labor and all.

"Would you—not call for him to come here—speak to him?" she pleaded. "When he knows that I understand his relations with—that woman—he will not insist—"

"No, I will not," said Fergus, more firmly. Talk to the ton about his affairs, never! "You'll marry him, and he'll settle down, you'll see. Nothing like a good marriage to settle a man like him. He'll be a fine husband—"

"But I don't want him!" she wailed, losing her composure.

"But you'll have him," said Fergus crossly, fighting his impulse to pull her into his arms and pat her head as he had done when she was small. She was hurt, and no wonder, but this was best for her, and he would go through with it. She had run wild, and he could endure no more London seasons for her! "The marriage will go through, and you'll do nothing to make him cry off! He's a good match, the best I could get for you, and you'll marry him! I mean this, Charlotte, my girl! You'll not defy me!"

When Fergus talked like this, Charlotte knew there was not much she could do. Her shoulders sagged, her proud head bent. She made one more effort. "Papa, to please me? You'll talk to Lord Arundell and hear the truth for yourself? I would not marry a man whose heart is elsewhere!"

"No, I'll not speak of it to him, nor will you! Listen, my girl," he said, more gently, his hands behind him, scowling. "A gentleman ain't like me. I married your mother, and never wanted to look at another woman. She was—everything to me. But the ton ain't like that, Charlotte, and the sooner you learn that, the sooner you'll settle for what you got, and don't cry for the moon. Gentlemen like their little affairs. Darcy Saltash is a discreet gentleman, he won't shame you in public. You got that to be grateful for. He won't cause you humiliation. You'll live with it. Just think—the Marchioness of Arundell!" he added, encouragingly.

She stood up slowly, in silence, and made for the door. She turned her head as she reached it, and Fergus was never to forget the wounded incredulous look of her green eyes. "The marriage will be a disaster, papa," she said simply. "You will see—when it is too late."

She left and shut the door gently, and went up to her

room. She sent Noreen with the message that she was ill
and would not come down to dinner. Then she lay in
the semidarkness of her comfortable room, too hurt to
weep, too discouraged to plan, seeing no light in her
future.

Even her beloved papa would not listen to her or
help her. He did not care about her happiness, he wanted
only to marry her to nobility! Nobility! They could have
it, she thought bitterly. To her it meant only heartbreak.

Chapter 7

The wedding gown was of white lace over creamy white satin with trim of palest green velvet ribbon. The bodice was demure, with lace about the firm breasts, a tiny waist tied with green ribbon, then a bouffant skirt that billowed about Charlotte's long legs. Her veil was of precious lace from Brussels, and flowed about her curly red-gold hair, down to her waist. Her mitts were lacy, ending at the fingers.

Noreen kept saying how beautiful she looked. Charlotte scarcely heard the woman as she stood in the vestibule of the grand church, waiting. The days had passed in a dream. She had gone out with Lord Arundell, kept her feelings coldly to herself, but showed him such chill that he often looked at her with puzzlement.

Kenneth and Neville had begged to know about Mrs. Holt's visit. She had said only, "I learned enough. I shall not discuss it. Papa forbids me to say anything."

And the marriage plans had continued. So today she stood in the church, and waited for the music to begin. Fergus Gordon stood nearby, fiddling with his white gloves, his nervous eyes on his too composed daughter.

The music began. In a daze, Charlotte took her father's arm, and they went up the aisle where Darcy waited with his best man, someone from his former regiment. They were in morning dress, semiformal. It was one of the weddings of the season, but they had agreed—for once—that it was to be quiet. There were only about one hundred guests, mostly relatives and close friends. Someone had come to represent the Prince Regent. Charlotte had looked about for Mrs. Holt but did not see her.

She did see Pamela in one of the front rows. To her surprise, the brown-haired girl was decked out in a pale yellow muslin, of simple pattern, and a yellow chip bonnet with ribbons. She was on the aisle. As Charlotte came near, Pamela turned and smiled radiantly.

Pamela and Fergus Gordon must be the only happy persons here today, thought Charlotte ironically.

She met Darcy Saltash at the altar, not looking at him, keeping her eyes on the rector of the church as he stood in his vestments. She heard the sonorous words. And suddenly the realization swept over her that she was putting herself into the keeping of this hated man forever! There would be no divorce, it would be too much a scandal. Darcy reached for her hand, started a little as he felt the coldness of it. He pressed the golden ring on her finger, replaced the emerald over it.

She said the words mechanically, in a low choking voice. She wanted to cry out, "No, no, no!" but what good would it do? She was trapped. She was a woman, and women had no say in their own lives.

Darcy held firmly to her hand. His was warm, and some of the chill went from her own as they listened to the final prayer. Then he turned to her, drew back the lace veil, bent and kissed her mouth. She started at the touch and drew back, her own mouth trembling.

He looked down at her, strangely, then took her arm, and turned with her toward the registry. They signed their names. She wrote "Charlotte Mary Gordon" for the last time. He scrawled his in his firm black handwriting, a long name, a title. Then it was done, and the rector smiled and wished them both happiness. Fergus kissed her cheek.

Pamela was there, beaming tremulously. Charlotte bent to kiss her cheek. The girl whispered, "Papa chose my dress, is it not pretty!"

"Very pretty, my dear. You look lovely," said Charlotte gently.

The girl sighed with pleasure. "Are you my mama now?" she murmured, her eyes anxious.

Charlotte nodded, and took her hand. This was her one consolation. The child would be better off with her, and they would care for each other.

The reception was in Darcy's town house. She stood in the line, the pearls he had given her heavy about her neck, her slippers tight, and smiled and smiled mechanically. Neville's anxious face appeared, he squeezed her hand. "We'll be up to see you soon," he whispered.

"That will be nice," she said politely. Her brother stared at her. She was feeling so bitter, so full of rage and hate. Men! They could do nothing but harm one, she thought. A woman was a poor creature to be pushed and shoved into her place in life, forced to it whether she fit there or not. Even her beloved brother had not helped her to escape this marriage. She was tied tight, with the golden chain of the ring about her finger, invisible chains about her neck—the pearls a visible symbol of his domination of her.

Darcy led her to a chair, and forced her to sit down, gently. "You are weary. I will bring something to eat and drink," he said. "Pamela will sit with you."

She nodded wearily. Soon they would change their clothes, and set off in the carriage. He wanted to leave at once for his Cotswolds castle. Much of her luggage, four trunks, a dozen hatboxes and other items had gone ahead in carriages three days ago. A small procession of carriages would take them to his home in a two-day trip. Pamela would ride with Noreen and her own maid, and footmen and coachmen would take care of the trunks and cases. And she had come to London with her brother, with laughter and merriment, enjoying their nights of staying at inns, finding much to amuse and entertain them! How different this trip would be!

Fergus hovered near her anxiously, keeping a watchful eye on his unpredictable daughter. He would not be satisfied until she was off with her new husband. Then he could concentrate on his son's future. He would not be one-tenth the trouble, thought Fergus, trying not to worry about Charlotte. How her face looked! As though she had been sentenced to death. Her face had always been so revealing, so frank. Now she did not even look at him.

He suppressed his guilty feelings. Charlotte would be able to settle down now. Darcy was a good man. Fergus felt he had done his duty by his daughter and found her a fine respectable man, for all his little flaws. He would call on them in good time and be relieved that she had settled into her new home.

Charlotte sipped a little champagne, ate a bite of cake and managed to set the plate aside. Pamela drank of her fruit drink, and was quiet beside her new mother, as though she sensed that all was not well.

Once she touched Charlotte's skirt with a gentle hand. "It is so lovely," she murmured. "And you look like— like an angel."

Charlotte's mouth curled up involuntarily. She felt little like an angel today! "Thank you, darling. Are you— looking forward to going home?"

"Oh, yes! I will see my dog again, and my horse, and I like the gardens to play in." Then she subsided into silence again.

Kenneth came up to them, his face troubled, though he tried to smile. He picked up Charlotte's hand, kissed it quickly. "I must say farewell, I understand you are leaving within minutes," he said. "If there is anything—ever—"

"Thank you, Kenneth." She gave him a genuine smile, and Darcy watched with a look of envy in his eyes. "You must come and call upon us before long. Neville has promised to come."

"I should—like that, my dear." He gazed down at her for a long time, then turned abruptly away.

Darcy frowned, and said to Charlotte, "I think you will go and change your gown now. Be sure to take a cloak, the ride may be cool. Pamela, go with your maid."

"Yes, papa," said Pamela. Charlotte only rose and turned away, to look for Noreen. The red-haired woman came up to her.

"We have a room on the next floor, my lady," said Noreen, her cheeks poppy-red with excitement. She guided Charlotte up there and helped her change to a traveling costume of dark green trimmed with brown braid, and a matching green and brown bonnet. Then she took her down the back stairs, to where the carriages waited. Darcy was already there, in a black and gray traveling suit and matching cloak, holding his tall hat in his hand.

"You are very quick," he said, in approval, and helped her into the carriage. Pamela ran down the steps eagerly, and was put into the next carriage with Noreen and her own maid.

They were off, and Charlotte cried out suddenly, "Oh, I have not said goodbye to papa—and Neville!"

"I made your farewells to them both," said Darcy.

She sank back against the velvet squabs. So he made her farewells for her now! She was not expected to speak again for herself! She bit her lips and drew the green cloak closer about herself.

It was a silent ride until noon. They had little to say to each other. Darcy seemed preoccupied with his thoughts, Charlotte took off her bonnet and leaned her head back and closed her eyes. She had slept little lately, lying awake to brood and make futile plans.

They finally stopped to change the horses and have a light luncheon. Pamela seemed weary already, but brightened up when she sat next to Charlotte and confided more information about her pets and the life in the country.

They rode on. Darcy still had little to say, beyond asking if she were comfortable. "Quite," she said, without opening her eyes.

"We stop for the night at a comfortable inn. We shall dine there, and then start again early in the morning. It is yet a long journey," he said.

"I understand it is a distance," she said without interest.

"We are near the Cotswold hills," he said. "I have told you of the place. I think you will find the scenery improves tomorrow, as we journey through the countryside. You are fond of the country, I believe?"

What difference did it make?

"I have lived in a village and in town," she said indifferently.

He was silent then for a long time. They finally stopped in late afternoon, to change the horses and stretch, then went on for three more hours.

It was dark, and the twinkling lights of the inn were very welcome when they finally stopped for the night. The inn stood alone on the highway, and the innkeeper himself ran out to bid them welcome. The horses were taken away, their trunks carried inside to the best rooms. Charlotte was pleased and relieved to find she had a bedroom to herself, with Pamela on one side of her and Darcy on the other. Their maids were on another floor, and the footmen and coachmen were accommodated elsewhere, perhaps over the stables, she thought.

They were served dinner in a pretty sitting room, with rustic table and chairs, flowered curtains and a cheerful fire in the fireplace. The meal was excellent, however, with freshly caught fish, then a side of beef with many greens and fruits. Darcy drank a red wine with his meal. Charlotte refused all wine, she was weary already, and wine made her head swim. She and Pamela had hot tea. The girl was nodding, and Darcy sent for her maid to carry her off to bed as soon as she had finished.

· They sat then before the fireplace, saying little. She wondered if all their married life they would have little to say to each other. It was a dreary thought. She and Neville and Kenneth had always had much to say, of reading they enjoyed, of gossip about society, of their work in her father's mills.

Darcy finally stirred, set aside his cheroot. "You must be weary. Do you wish to retire early?"

She nodded. "Yes, I think so. You said the journey tomorrow would be long."

He hesitated. "I hope you are able to get more rest at home. You have run about London until you are exhausted, I believe."

She would have flared up at his tone of censure, but she did not care enough. "Probably," she said indifferently. What had kept her awake nights had been trying to think of ways to get out of marrying him! Much good it had done her.

She rose as Noreen came in, and bobbed to them. "I will say goodnight then, my lord," she said, and left the room. She went to her own room, questioned Noreen briefly. "You have been well cared for, Noreen? You enjoyed your dinner?"

"Oh, my, yes, Miss Char—my lady! It was fair grand," said Noreen enthusiastically. "My lady Pamela's maid is a fine one, and we get along perfectly. We have a room together next floor up, with curtains and all, and hot water to wash. My lord gave orders we was to be treated so."

"That's good." He could be kind to the servants then, that was a relief, thought Charlotte. For a moment she thought of the housekeeping tasks that would be hers soon, in a castle, no less! But she would manage somehow. She had been well-trained in that.

She slipped into the pale green negligee that Noreen held for her, washed, braided her hair as she always did, in a long braid over her shoulder, and slipped into bed. Noreen put out all the lights but one near the bed, then bade her "Good night," and left her.

"Silly girl—she forgot the last light," muttered Charlotte, and leaned over to blow it out. Then she lay back, half-asleep already, thinking about the next day, and the task of meeting all the servants in the new house.

She turned over, sighed, and stiffened. The door was opening. Darcy came in, in a dark wine-colored robe. She could just see him in the light of the candle he held. He set down the light on the table beside her and surveyed her. She sat up abruptly, tossing back the braid.

The door was closed behind him. "What are you doing here?" she cried out.

His dark eyebrows rose. "I came to see if you were all right. You seem overtired," he said.

She clutched the bedclothes about herself, glaring at him. "Leave me alone," she said, her jaw clenched in anger. Oh, how could she have forgotten that he might do this! No consideration! One would think he would at least leave her alone until she was rested.

"Is that an order?" he asked, almost gently. His dark eyes blazed in the light of the candle.

She drew a trembling breath. "If you think I shall endure anything more today—" she began. "I shall not! I

shall scream and then you will be the laughingstock—"
Her voice was rising.

"You sound hysterical," he said, his tone a dash of
cold water in her face. "Shall I send for your maid?"

"Just get out—leave me alone!" she cried.

He bowed sarcastically and picked up the candle. "My
intention exactly. I do not care for screaming females,"
he said. "May I wish you an untroubled sleep?"

He went out, taking the candle with him, leaving her
in the dark. She lay trembling for a while, for fear he
would return. Then she began to relax. She was so weary,
so bone weary—

She was just dropping off to sleep, when she heard the
weeping. She started up on an elbow, listening with a
frown. It sounded like a child. Pamela?

Though it was June, the room had turned cold as the
fire died in the fireplace. She rose, slipped into her green
velvet robe and her slippers, and then moved silently to
the door. She opened it, listened at the hallway. All was
quiet but the sighing of the wind downstairs in the hallway near the front door.

Then she heard it again, a soft sobbing. It came from
the adjoining room. She closed her own door quietly,
and tapping at the door next to hers, went in.

"Pamela?" she said, gently.

In the dimness, she saw the girl sit up. "Oh—is it—
mama?" she asked, on a sobbing breath.

"Yes, what is it, my dear?" Charlotte came over to the
bed, and sat down beside her on it. She patted the small
hands, felt with her free hand for the small face. It was
wet with tears.

"I had—a nightmare. A bad dream—I dreamed of my
mama, and she was screaming and crying out—" The
small voice shook.

Charlotte took her impulsively into her arms, and held
her close, patting her back. How thin the child was,

how she trembled with nerves! "Oh, I'm sorry, I hate bad dreams, don't you?" she soothed. "They seem so dreadfully real in the dark, I can hardly wait for morning. Then when the sun shines, I can't believe I felt so scared. Isn't that the way of it?"

"Oh, yes, yes," said Pamela gratefully, drawing a shuddering breath. "They seem so real—and I did hear her screaming—"

"Poor darling," Charlotte soothed her, and petted her for a time. But when she got up to leave, thinking the child was soothed, Pamela clung to her.

"Don't leave me—can't you stay?" Pamela whispered.

Charlotte hesitated. "Well—I don't see why not," she said practically. "But my bed is much bigger. You come over and stay with me, all right?"

She found the child's robe, and slipped it on her, and then half carried the drooping girl to her room. She tucked her in beside her, and whispered to her, and sang a little song to her, and presently the evenness of the child's breathing told her Pamela was asleep.

And finally Charlotte slept also, deeply, holding the child to her, unconsciously comforted by her as she comforted.

They both slept so long that the sun was bright in the sky when Darcy finally came into the room. He had wanted Charlotte to sleep, but the day was growing late, they would arrive late at home, and he frowned as he tapped lightly, then opened the door.

He came in, blinked. He stared at the two heads on the pillows, the bright golden-red of his new wife, and the dark brown one of his child, as they slept peacefully together. Tear stains on Pamela's cheeks told him the story. He looked at the protective arm of Charlotte as it lay across Pamela.

He gazed down at them thoughtfully. He rubbed his face with his hands, then shook his head.

"Charlotte, Pamela," he said firmly.

The larger body under the covers stirred first. Sleepy green eyes blinked open, gazed up at him. Then her lashes opened wide, she moved her head on the pillow.

"It's getting late," he said. "I'll send in Noreen with some tea. Do you think you can be ready to start in an hour?"

Charlotte moved, sat up. He saw the pearly glow of her skin under the sheer green nightdress. She tossed back the red braid across her shoulder, rubbed at her eyes like a child.

Her voice was husky with sleep. "Oh—yes—yes—I had forgotten where I was—"

Pamela stirred at the voices, slowly wakened.

"Wake up now, Pamela," Darcy said briskly. "I'll send in Noreen. We'll have breakfast before we depart." And he turned and walked out. In the sitting room he paced up and down before the fire, scowling in thought. The landlord peeped in, began to speak, then discreetly withdrew again. When his lordship looked like that, it wasn't safe to disturb him. He had a quick temper, and one didn't always know what he was up to.

But he scurried about, and snapped at the maids and cooks, and in half an hour the breakfast was on the table, piping hot. Nothing helped to cure tempers in the morning like a good hot meal of ham and eggs, hot breads, and good coffee, thought the landlord.

His lordship sat down at table, and soon my lady came in, looking brighter than yesterday, thought Darcy. He rose to greet her and apologize. "I began my meal, not knowing when you would come."

"Oh, yes, do please go on." She sat down, in some confusion as the landlord held her chair. She managed a smile at the innkeeper. "It smells and looks delicious," she said.

"There you are, ma'am, my lady," he said, beaming.

"Will you help yourself to the dishes?" And he moved them closer to her.

Pamela came in also and greeted Charlotte with a kiss, and then her father. She sat down, and made a better meal than usual, watching them both with bright eyes.

"I wondered if Pamela might ride with us today," said Charlotte, as she sipped at her hot coffee. She watched him warily under her lashes.

"I don't know why not, there is plenty of room," he said casually. Pamela beamed and wriggled on her chair.

"I'll show you the places as we near home," she told Charlotte, happily. "There are so many pretty castles on the hills, and my favorite woods where we sometimes see deer, and when we get further on, you'll see Arundell itself in the distance. It looks blue when we aren't close yet."

Charlotte smiled at her. "That sounds charming," she said. She had scarcely dared look at Darcy. Was he furious with her about last night? She could not tell from his cool expression.

The maids and footmen finished packing as they ate, and soon they were on their way again. But yesterday's uncomfortable silence was broken for Charlotte by Pamela's shy comments as she sat beside the window and pointed out places along the way.

Darcy sometimes added to them, explaining something of the local history of the various towns they passed through, or the manor houses which stood grandly on the hills, and a couple of crumbling castles near enough to the highway to be seen. He did not seem to notice when the closeness of the carriage and its rocking motion made her arm brush against his, or his thigh pressed momentarily against hers.

But Charlotte was aware of it and aware also that he had every right to be angry with her for refusing him.

Would he take it out on her later? Or didn't he care enough to make an issue of it? Only time would reveal his thoughts to her—if ever.

Chapter 8

It was a very long trip, and Pamela went to sleep against Charlotte's shoulder long before they arrived at the castle on the hill. The past two hours she had seen nothing in the darkness. They rattled and jolted along the road. Finally they entered a village, saw some lights at an inn, others in small cream-colored cottages, then they were in the country again.

After another half hour, the carriage was climbing, the tired horses straining uphill. "Almost home now," said Darcy, stirring in his place. "Are you very weary?"

"Yes, tired," she said, with a sigh. And there were ordeals to come, she knew, the introductions to the staff, finding her way about a strange place.

The carriage turned into a dark drive, around in the semicircle, and came to a halt before a wide doorway. Men ran up with flares, she saw beaming anxious faces, a door flung open, ranks of servants drawn up in the hallway inside.

Gently she moved her hand over Pamela's forehead, and the girl wakened. "Oh—we are home," cried Pamela. "How lovely! It was such a long way."

A footman let down the steps. Darcy stepped out, then turned to help Charlotte out. She was so stiff and tired, she stumbled on the step. She felt for a minute the iron hardness of his arms as he helped her down and held her until she regained her balance. Then he turned to help Pamela out, lifting her by the waist and putting her down on the ground.

They went inside, to be greeted by a long line of servants. Darcy introduced her formally, to the butler, the housekeeper, a Mrs. Nettleton of whom Pamela had spoken, and several of the footmen and the chief cook and some maids. Finally it was over, and Mrs. Nettleton stepped forward to show Charlotte to her rooms.

They stood in a wide tall hallway. The great gloomy central hall reached up three stories, and was hung with tattered red and gold battle flags with a dimly seen device of a golden leopard rampant on a red field. At the back, on the second floor, was a minstrels' gallery, and above that another balcony. On both sides were balconies over-looking the great hall, showing doors that evidently led to rooms. The castle was in the form of a great letter E without the central sign, and Mrs. Nettleton informed Charlotte that beyond the great hall was a long gallery of cloisters containing family portraits and a conservatory for plants. Above that was the ballroom, the length of the castle.

They climbed the great circular staircase of polished rosewood that wound around the minstrels' gallery, and past it to each floor. They passed a drawing room. Mrs. Nettleton indicated the doors. "These lead to the grand dining room and breakfast room. On the next floor, the first floor of the castle, my lady, are the libraries and music rooms. My lady Pamela's apartments are on the second floor. Yours are on the first floor beyond the library."

She turned off, went by the library, to the corridor

beyond, and into a suite of rooms. She led the way past the first rooms "for your maid, if you desire it, my lady," and to a grand bedroom.

There Charlotte found her trunks already open, and Noreen scurrying around to unpack the night valises. She was so dazed she could scarcely take in the contents of the great room. A huge four-poster bed with a green tapestry canopy embroidered in gold, with gold tassels. A charming mirrored dresser in rosewood, a matching wardrobe of full height to the ceiling, and set with double mirrors in the doors. A green and gold stuffed chair, and matching sofa. French doors showing a patch of sky beyond the balcony.

Mrs. Nettleton, a brisk, plump, graying woman, with keys rattling in her belt, threw open another door and indicated the room beyond. "Your sitting room, my lady. Beyond it is the great drawing room of the suite. You'll see it all later, I'm sure. Shall I send up supper at once, or will you have dinner?"

It was past ten o'clock. Charlotte managed to smile; the woman seemed anxious to please. "I should prefer a light supper, Mrs. Nettleton, and an early bed. I thank you for your kindness. We shall talk tomorrow."

Mrs. Nettleton bowed and retired. Charlotte went over to her sitting room. It was enormous, twice the size of the family room at home in Leeds, and four times that in the London town house. She blinked at the furnishings. They might have been chosen by herself, to suit her own coloring. A Persian rug of green, gold, off-blue, rose. Sofas of turquoise taffeta set off in gold, a lounge chair and footstool matching. Chairs of comfortable proportions, stuffed and straight, in gold and green and two in rose. An elegant desk with many pigeonholes, with pale green stationery, pens and ink. An empty bookcase of rosewood.

Noreen said proudly, "Mrs. Nettleton informed me, my

lady, that all was redecorated for you in just four weeks! Imagine his kindness! He is a fine lord, he is." She eyed Charlotte out of the corner of her eyes. Charlotte turned away abruptly and sat down wearily in a chair, passing her hand over her eyes.

Yes, he would do the proper thing. She wondered if these were the rooms his previous wife had had, and what color they had been. If she had been dark like Pamela, then— But no, she must not think like that. The past was past.

She retired after a light repast, the tray having been brought up with admirable promptness. Evidently Lord Arundell ran a tight household. She was able to sleep, but wakened early in the unfamiliar room. She lay staring at the drawn cream draperies for a time before Noreen tapped and brought in her tea.

"Ah, good, you are awake, my lady," said Noreen, and proceeded to set out her clothes. "You'll wear a muslin this morning? It's fair warm already."

Charlotte sat up slowly, stretching. At least today she would not have to ride out in a carriage. "Yes, the green muslin with the darker green ribbons, and the morning cap of lace."

Noreen set them out, then prepared the bath. "A tub bath, my lady, all proper and nice," she beamed. "The pumping is as up to date as London. I poured in your lilac salts."

Charlotte was refreshed by the warm bath, luxuriated in the tub and the pretty fittings. A bathroom of her own, and no need of having footmen bring up buckets of water to a tub before the fire. That was luxury indeed. She lay back in the bath, planning her day. An interview with Mrs. Nettleton, meeting the servants again and getting their positions straight in her mind, touring the castle, especially the kitchens and staff quarters. Perhaps there would be a time to view the gardens. Pamela seemed particularly fond of the gardens.

She breakfasted alone in a grand room, all blue and white, cheerful with the sun shining in the French windows. The room was just below her own, on the ground floor. One could step out from it into the gardens. She meditated on the delights of the garden from her seat at the table, two footmen hovering at her elbow. My lord had risen early and gone riding, one said, when she questioned him.

"And Pamela?"

"My lady sleeps late," said the footman, bowing. "Will you have aught else, my lady?"

The formality was strange to her, their stiffness and anxiety to please. At home it had been informal, she had known the servants all her life. She finished her tea, then inquired where she might find Mrs. Nettleton. They would have sent for her, but instead she insisted on being shown the way to her workroom.

The housekeeper arose at once, coming to her. "My lady, I would have come to you!" She was pleased and anxious all at once.

"Nonsense. I must find my way about," said Charlotte briskly. "I must beg your indulgence as I do that. Such a huge place is new to me, though I have managed my father's home in Leeds."

She found the woman most efficient, with all in hand about the house. Mrs. Nettleton gave her a brief tour of the kitchens, explained the arrangement of the staff rooms, asked what she liked on the menus.

Then the housekeeper proceeded to show her about the great castle. "I am sure my lord will wish to tell you himself the history of the place, if he has not done so already?" A fleeting look at Charlotte. She shook her head.

"No, we have not spoken much of it. He said only

that it was built on the site of a ruined abbey, and was a fortress for some years."

"Yes, my lady. Much has been added to it. The Great Hall was built first." And Mrs. Nettleton pointed out where additions had been made. They walked along the cloister walls, rebuilt where the Abbey cloisters had been, examined the many plants and flowers at one end. She indicated only the many family portraits at the other end of the cloisters. "My lord will explain these," was all she said of them.

Charlotte had a hasty impression of many dark-haired men with arrogant chins like Darcy's, and some sweet-faced ladies in many costumes of the past three hundred years, some in ruffs, some in great embroidered dresses with enormous sleeves. One man caught her attention—he looked like a pirate, with a fierce grin, and a short sharp-pointed beard, his hand on his sword. She would like to ask Darcy about that one, she thought.

It was soon time for luncheon, which she shared with a bright-faced Pamela. It seemed that Lord Arundell had gone to the mills to consult with his foreman.

"Oh, they are great huge buildings, mama," said Pamela. "We make wools for all over the country. Sometimes we have orders from France and Italy and Holland and Sweden. It is amazing. Papa talks to me about it sometimes."

"Do you know what work is done? Is it the spinning and the weaving, or do they process the raw wool as well?" Charlotte did not really expect the girl to know, but she nodded intelligently.

"No, not the processing of raw wool. Papa buys the best wool already processed, and it is dyed here in our vats. He is very particular about the colors. Then the spinning is done here, with very clever girls and boys. They train them here. Papa is able to get orphans from many places." The girl's face shadowed a little, she frowned slightly. "It is very sad to be an orphan, I think," she said in a low tone.

Charlotte's attention was caught by that. She resolved to visit the mills soon and examine the situation for herself. This efficient mill foreman might be a good man— or he might be a bully. She had met both kinds in her work for her own father.

During the afternoon, Pamela went with them to tour the remainder of the castle. It was truly immense, with a dozen guest rooms in several floors of the wings. Pamela's own rooms were large, and next to them were two nurseries. Charlotte went hastily through them. She did not want to think about that now.

Many of the draperies had been made in their own mills, Pamela told her eagerly as they walked about. Charlotte paused to admire the work, the satin velvets were beautifully done, and the colors exquisite, some mulberry, some wine, some emerald green, and one set in a marvelous pale golden color. There were two drawing rooms on either side of the Great Hall on the ground floor, where Mrs. Nettleton said formal receptions were held. These mammoth rooms held half a dozen sofas each, and numerous chairs, small tables of mahogany and rosewood polished to a fine gleam, some glass-fronted cupboards holding precious objects from the Orient and Europe. Charlotte promised a closer inspection, for they looked entrancing with their ivories and miniatures, jade and porcelain, and blown glass in many delightful shapes.

Pamela went to bed early that evening, and at dinner Charlotte talked about her tour of the castle. Darcy was frankly amazed at all she had seen.

"I had intended to show you about myself. I think you have done much in a short time," he said, helping himself to the cold dish of asparagus and dill which the footman held. He took a little of the trout with it and nodded his thanks. "I do not wish you to burden yourself overmuch with the housekeeping. Mrs. Nettleton has that well in hand—has worked here for many years."

Charlotte was puzzled at his remark. She had thought he had married her for the housekeeping she could do. Then she remembered—and flushed hotly. He would want an heir for the estates also. Only a wife could give him that.

She changed the subject, asked about the portraits. That seemed a safe subject. After dinner, they strolled in the long gallery, and he pointed out some of his ancestors and told stories of them. She was impressed in spite of herself. She had thought him a rake, and his family accustomed to wealth. Instead, they had fought in many wars, traveled in the Orient on business for the Crown, interested themselves in many businesses and enterprises. The fierce looking one had indeed been a pirate for Her Majesty Queen Elizabeth, fighting the Spanish in the Caribbean, and bringing home much booty in the form of emeralds, gold, silver, and flowers.

"Flowers?" questioned Charlotte, in surprise.

"Yes, indeed. You will see some of the specimens in the gardens out there." And he nodded toward the darkened grounds. "Also in the conservatory, there are some rare plants which bloom only in warmth. You will see some orchids from Brazil. If you are interested, we shall go now." And he motioned to the footman who followed them with a many-branched candlestick to light their way. They went into the warm humid conservatory, and she was amazed at the beauty of the pale mauve orchids, the bright yellow allamanda, a rare green orchid with silky brown fuzz on it, and other species she had never seen before.

It was a most enjoyable evening. She thought as she lay in bed that night that Darcy's chill had begun to thaw. But the next morning, he had disappeared for the entire day. After dinner, he excused himself to work in his study beside his room. He had much ledger inspection to do, he said.

Charlotte selected some books from the library and carried them off to her room to read. At least Arundell boasted a fine library, and she promised herself a search of its contents at length. Many fine old books in rare leather bindings contended with shelves of recent publications. She had spotted some of the works of Lord Byron, Mr. William Wordsworth, Mr. Coleridge, Walter Scott's novels. There would be enough to fill her idle hours for quite a time.

She made up some tentative menus and resolved to ask Mrs. Nettleton about Lord Arundell's special likes and dislikes; also to ask about wines—she had not yet inspected the wine cellar. She wrote herself several notes, then settled down to reading.

Another day passed. She found time to examine some of the gardens with Pamela, to meet the lively black-and-white cocker spaniel, Macduff, to meet the head gardener and walk with him about the formal pond, and through the trees to the lovely little silvery lake and the white gazebo beside it.

And one day she took a carriage to the mills. She had found herself more and more curious about them. Darcy said little of the mills, Pamela had been troubled about the children. So she took Pamela with her, a coachman to drive the carriage as the horses were strange to her, and set out without informing Darcy.

The several great gray buildings were set on the hillside, beside a watercourse, with a water mill churning slowly beside them. One could smell the mills from far off, the odor of sheep and grease and wool, and of the dyes. Charlotte was accustomed to them, and began searching keenly for signs of neglect.

She found none at first. The buildings were sprucely kept, the wood fences about them were freshly painted.

But inside—she caught her breath. A small child, clad in rags and barefoot, was lying on the ground a short distance from the weaving sheds.

She started over to the child. It looked about five. Her path was barred at once by a great man in shabby gray shirt and gray trousers.

"Where would you be going, ma'am?" he asked sharply.

The coachman left his horses. "This be the new Lady," he told the man hurriedly. "My lady, the Marchioness of Arundell."

The man backed off, pulled his forelock hastily. "I'll see to Mr. Botts," he said, looking about furtively. "You stay here, he'll come out to ye—"

And he was gone. Charlotte went over to the child, bent down, and the child cringed, and put up his arm to his head as though fearing a blow. "What is it, my dear?" asked Charlotte gently.

The child seemed unable to speak. A booming voice behind her made Charlotte start, and swing around.

The man behind her was of medium height, heavy set, red-faced, with a rolling gait. He was balding, his black hair set in strings pasted over his forehead. He had sly, small black eyes. His dirty hands had blackened cracked nails.

"My lady, you don't wanna come in here! I was fair 'mazed when Hank here says you was coming."

His bold eyes looked her over. She lifted her chin. "I am interested in the mills, Mr. Botts—you are Mr. Botts?"

"That I am, my lady. At your service." He smirked, gazing at her from chin to skirt hem. She longed to slap his face, but would not have touched him. Something about him was dirty, filthy.

"Why is the child lying here? Is he injured?"

The sly eyes went to the child who lay there on the earth seemingly without strength to move. "Hank!" he bellowed. "I tol' ye to move the child! Get him over to the medical place. He's sick!"

The huge man, Hank, seemed amazed at the order, but finally moved awkwardly to scoop up the small child and carry him off. Charlotte looked after them, frowning. "I should like to tour the mills, Mr. Botts," she said finally.

"Today, my lady?" He looked about, spat on the ground. "Ain't nothing to see today, no, ma'am."

"I know much about mills, my father owns several woolen mills," she said pointedly. "I should like to tour them today."

Pamela's hand slid into hers and clutched it tightly, but the girl said never a word. Botts huffed and protested, but Charlotte stood her ground, and finally the man reluctantly took her inside the first building.

They walked on the slippery greasy floor from one operation to another, observed the sorting of the wools, the vats in which the dyes were boiling, then on to the spinning and the weaving rooms. At some of the wooden machines were women, at some were men, mostly in poor rags and with bare feet. But many times the operators of the looms and wheels were children, very small children. Their tiny fingers moved rapidly among the tops and the twisting of the yarns, not giving a look to the visitors, intent on their tasks. All were barefoot. Of course, it was summer, thought Charlotte, but they seemed so poorly clad. And thin—they were thinner and smaller than Pamela. Pamela, slim as she was, seemed husky beside some of the frail tots. Some of the youngest could be only four or five.

Her mouth set grimly. Botts did not have them at the dyeing, they were nowhere near the hot liquids. But these children were definitely ill-fed, ill-clothed. What wages did they receive? Where did they eat and sleep? What food did they eat?

She asked casually, "Where do they eat luncheon?"

He indicated a bench at the side of the room. "They takes their turn and sit there." The bench was about ten feet long. It could not hold more than a few, and the stench of the dyes and wool would be in their nostrils as they ate.

"And where do they sleep, Mr. Botts?"

He seemed to lose his composure. "My lady, I ain't in charge of their eating and sleeping! There is those who care for that. If you want to tour their quarters—" He paused suggestively.

"Not today, thank you."

She had seen enough to make her feel sick and apprehensive. They took orphans from the poorhouses of Wales and Scotland and brought them here, far from home. It was the practice, her father did so also. But he saw to it that they had beds to sleep in, nurses to care for them when they were ailing, good food to eat, proper working quarters. And none were so young, so frail as these little ones.

She must speak to Darcy about it, and soon. She did not trust the mill foreman. She had rarely felt such dislike and disgust of a man in her life.

She knew little of Darcy. He probably knew and cared little about the working conditions of his factory hands. If so, she must persuade him that good work could not come from such bad conditions, that it was to his advantage to feed them well, sleep them well, clothe them. She sighed as they went back to the carriage, and was silent on the way home.

Pamela's plaintive voice interrupted her thoughts. "Mama, I smiled at some of the girls, but they did not even look at me. Why was that?"

Charlotte roused. "Well, I fear it would have interrupted their work, darling. They might have made a mistake with the threads."

"Oh, I thought maybe they didn't like us coming

there. Mr. Botts doesn't like it when Mrs. Nettleton comes and takes food there. She scolded him once about their clothes, and he said he would get papa to dismiss her if she interfered! Would papa do that?"

Charlotte squeezed the small hand in hers. "I don't think so, Pamela. Your father likes his good food and service," she said drily. She thought she must proceed slowly, or she would get in trouble herself. It might result badly for the children. She frowned, not seeing the bright June sky, the golden-gray of the stone fences, the small yellow cottages tucked into the folds of the hills, the white sheep grazing. In her mind was the picture of the gaunt children, their fingers working swiftly in the threads of wool. Not daring to turn and look at her. Not daring to speak or murmur a word.

Chapter 9

Black Satin arrived a few days later, in the care of Charlotte's own groom. She went out to meet the tired dusty horse and the small grinning jockey, to pet her horse, and murmured praises in his perked-up ears.

"Oh, I am so glad to see you both," she said impulsively. "You are all so tired."

Her groom had ridden his own horse and led Black Satin. He grimaced, shook his head. "Ain't so bad riding, but Black Satin, he attracts that much attention, wasn't sure we'd get through without him being stole, my lady." His eyes were red-rimmed from lack of sleep.

She gave him a gold coin for his trouble and bade the other grooms at the stables to find him a good room and care for the horses. She left them deep in conversation as to the merits of various horses and went back through the gardens.

She found Pamela wandering about, chasing her small black-and-white cocker, and enjoying the blooms. Pamela caught up with her and put her little hand in Charlotte's. "Oh, don't you love it here, at Arundell?" she asked, half proudly, half anxiously.

The castle was beautiful, so were the grounds, Pamela was sweet, the servants attentive. But Darcy Saltash—oh, he was spoiling it all, thought Charlotte. She shook off her feelings, and managed a smile at the girl.

"It is magnificent here, my dear," she said. "I can see why you are so proud of it. One day we must ride to the village and make my acquaintance there. I am sure you know the rector and all the main people there, the grocer and all?"

"Oh, yes, indeed." It changed the conversation successfully. They wandered about, and presently Darcy Saltash came out, smart in his gray morning suit.

"Ah, so here you are." His gaze flickered critically over Charlotte, in her pale green muslin gown, her hair in a neat chignon at the back of her neck, a scarf about her shoulders. "You have been seeing the gardens?"

"Yes, they are beautiful," she murmured. She turned to look about. Roses in their neat array, hedges trimmed to the inch, beds of pinks and peonies—all very organized. Beyond were the woods, near the stables, and the lake. She longed to ride out and find some of the wild forests to ride about, and over the distant hills. Soon she would do it, she vowed.

"I was telling mama," said Pamela, rather shyly, "that we might call upon the rector soon?" She ended in a question.

Darcy frowned slightly. "It is for them to call upon us first," he said, in his arrogant fashion. "And you will see the rector and his good wife at church this Sunday. We go to the service at ten," he told Charlotte.

He glanced about, curtly bade them enjoy themselves, and returned to the castle. He would probably work in his study for a time, she thought, as he usually did, then ride out and inspect the fields, or the mills, or whatever he pleased. He was a man, and could do as he wished.

She resented it deeply, that he so plainly confined her

to the duties she had here. She did not mind working, she enjoyed having work to organize, and plans to make. But during her own hours, her father had permitted her to ride, or to go to the village in a carriage and do the shopping. In their home in Leeds, she had often walked out with her maid to choose fabrics, shop for herbs, and call on her friends, all without asking permission.

When Black Satin was rested, she decided to ride out with her groom. And she did so. Early in the morning, she dressed in her dark green riding habit, with the full skirt, severe bodice, and velvet revers, the tall green bonnet with green plume. She went out the back way to the stables, past the gardens and the ancient round tower. It was a brisk, beautiful, blue morning, with the early breeze stirring the gardens and spreading the scent of the grasses and herbs lavishly about.

Hobbs was waiting for her, with Black Satin saddled and eager to go. She petted his black neck, stroked his nose affectionately, then let Hobbs put her into the saddle. Oh, it was glorious to feel the muscles straining to be off, the prancing gait as they set out.

Hobbs did not know the countryside any more than she did, but they set out with a will, past the stables, and the silvery lake, rippling with the early morning wind. She headed for the forest beyond, and they galloped along a dim path for a time, Black Satin finding his stride and lengthening it, head up and tossing.

"Oh, you beauty," she praised him, stroking his neck. He pricked his ears to listen. "You missed me as much as I missed you, I do believe! You shall like it here, the country is lovely, and we shall roam far and wide!"

Hobbs trotted along behind her, eyes alert and interested. They cleared the forest, and came out on a hill, overlooking the valley where lay the nearest village. Charlotte remarked on the creamy-golden walls of cottages, the brownish turf of the roofs, a single spire of the

church, the wandering brown lanes. Beyond her on the
other side sheep grazed on the green hills, and far beyond
them were the sharply blue chain of the Malverns, the
jagged edges against the blue of the sky. To the east
were the smooth Cotswold hills, rounded, beautiful. In
the distance, to the north of the valley, a river wandered
through, cutting the fields of gold and green with its
winding banks.

She pointed out some places to Hobbs, ranging up
beside her. "It is lovely here, isn't it?"

"Yes, Miss Charlotte," he said, eagerly. "I remarked
how purty it was as I come. Not like the big cities in
the north, with the smoke and all."

She sat on Black Satin, automatically stroking his
sleek neck, then they rode on, discovering small copses
of beech trees, the beauties of a June treasure of wild-
flowers beside a stream, an unexpected white waterfall
in the hills. Finally, reluctantly, they turned back, to
arrive at the stables past nine o'clock.

She went to her room, changed to a green muslin dress,
and went down to the breakfast room. Pamela was there,
lingering over her meal. Her face brightened.

"Oh, I wondered where you were!" she said, ques-
tioningly.

Charlotte only smiled, and sat down. She valued her
freedom too much to reveal everything, even to this eager
child, she thought. Most of her time must be given to
taking care of the household, to caring for Pamela, and
seeing that all was in strict order for her new lord, she
thought with a hidden grimace. She must have some time
to herself.

She ate, then conferred with the admirable housekeeper,
Mrs. Nettleton. Later she strolled in the gardens with
Pamela. Then luncheon, from which Darcy was absent.
He could come and go as he pleased, she thought with

resentment, but she must account for all she did! It was not fair.

On Sunday, she dressed demurely in a white muslin gown and a cloak of dark green, with bonnet to match. They set out for church in a carriage, a groom driving, with Darcy silent and abstracted. In the simple village church, they sat in the tall front pew, grandly carved with the heraldic symbol of the Arundells. The pastor was a kind-faced man of some fifty years, with white hair curling about his face. He read in the sweet accents of a man over whom life has passed gently. Charlotte thought of the fiery accents of the Leeds pastor, who was fighting for reforms in the slum areas, and better working conditions, and more doles for the poor.

After the service, they met several of the leading persons of the village, the pastor and his wife and two elder daughters, the squire and his lady and two sons, the innkeeper who seemed to have some status here and kept an inn which had been there for five hundred years, as he said. Several elderly ladies peered up at Charlotte from under their bonnets, and whispered sharply to each other, little black-mitted hands waving.

As Darcy seemed bored and stood with his hands behind his back, Charlotte was the more gracious. "You must call upon us soon," she said to the squire's lady and the pastor's wife. "Some afternoon—why not come for tea on Tuesday, if that suits?"

Darcy frowned. They faltered and finally agreed to come. Later in the carriage, he said, "I do not care to become familiar with the village people, Charlotte."

An imp of perversity overcame her. "You do not need to, my lord," she said, with mock innocence. "You may be away on business when they arrive. I am sure our gossip will not amuse you, anyway."

His mouth tightened. "I mean," he said deliberately, "I do not wish you to encourage them to become familiar with us! We have little in common."

"I beg to differ with you," said Charlotte, losing her temper. "It is the duty of the Marquis of Arundell to see to the welfare of the people of Arundell. That I do know! I mean to meddle quite a bit in their affairs, I give you fair warning!"

Pamela gasped. Darcy seemed startled, then he gave a little laugh. "Your passions do you justice, my lady," he said drily. "Well, then, go about doing good if you choose, but don't come crying if they take advantage of you!"

He mocked her! She compressed her lips, turned her head away, so that her face was hidden from him by the wide brim of her green bonnet.

A Sabbath calm settled on the household that afternoon. Charlotte read to Pamela in her favorite room, the large drawing room at the end of the private apartments. Just beyond her own sitting room, it was a huge room with circular windowseats, one in each of the towers of the East Wing. It could be a delightful place but for the formality of its arrangements. Charlotte, looking up from her reading, decided she would change it about. The furniture was pretty enough, of deep green sofas trimmed in gold, green velvet draperies, small golden chairs, larger plush chairs of green or gold. The colors suited her well, but she would push the furniture about, she thought.

With the sofa before the fireplace, and the chairs grouped about it, there would be a conversation place for herself and Pamela. She would order a small rug brought in for Macduff, just now confined to Pamela's own rooms or the gardens. Some cushions on the padded windowseats in the round towers would make them charming informal places to sit. The insipid picture over the mantel could be replaced by something else—she would find something in strong beautiful colors—

"What are you thinking, mama?"

The small voice recalled her.

"Oh, I was thinking about changing the furniture about," she said absently. "Making it more comfortable."

The brown eyes widened. "Change it? Oh, but papa arranged it especially, and ordered the colors when he knew he was going to marry you," she said naively. "Don't you like it? My—my other mama had it done in pink and silver, which papa said would never do for you."

Charlotte felt herself wincing inside. She had wondered often what Pamela's mother was like, but suppressed her curiosity. But Pamela's mother had sat here, perhaps on this very sofa, reading to her small daughter. She had looked from those windows, she had slept in the huge four-poster bed under that canopy—

She took a deep breath. She must not, must not hurt Pamela by showing any jealousy or lack of feeling.

"I like the room immensely," she said. "I imagine you came here often, with your—own mother."

"Oh, no," said Pamela. "She was rarely here. She liked London. I—I was here with my nurse. Papa was at war. These rooms were all closed, much of the time."

Charlotte repressed a gasp. She had said it so innocently. But surely this was not her only memory of her mother, a woman who left her here with her nurse? Then she remembered what Neville and Kenneth had said, about Darcy's first wife. The rumors must have been true, that she had had a gay time of it in London, and run about with—admirers.

After Pamela had left her to return to her own rooms, Charlotte began pushing and pulling the furniture about. Noreen came in and found her doing so and gasped her disapproval. "Now, Miss Charlotte, forever more! What would you be a-doing with all this?"

"I want it changed," said Charlotte. "Do push the sofa over this way!" She enlisted Noreen and a footman to help her, and soon had the sofa shoved to a comfortable position before the fire, plush chairs moved to group about it, a rug brought in for Macduff, and cushions piled in the windowseats. Finally she was satisfied except for the picture on the wall. That she would change when she found something more suitable.

She was curled up in the windowseat that night after dinner. Darcy had retired to his study next door, and with papers being rustled about, he spoke to his secretary brusquely from time to time. Charlotte read for a while, then let the book drop to the padded seat as she gazed out. She could see little but a slim sickle of the new moon rising in the east, against the deeper blue of the hills. Light flickered, reflected in the silvery lake beyond the stables. She looked up, at the calm brilliant specks of the stars, moving their majestic way across the purpling sky. She could love this place, set on a hill, with the beauties of the Cotswolds and the Malverns, the creamy gold of the cottages, the peace and happiness of the people here—if only—

If only— What do I want, thought Charlotte, restlessly. My freedom, completely. But no one was free, she had learned that. All had duties, responsibilities, no matter what his station and class. It was not that, she did not wish to shirk her work. But with the rings on her fingers, and under the frowns of Darcy, she felt rebellious and hedged about with restrictions. She wanted to throw them all off, and run free—

"What are you doing here in the darkness?" said a cool amused voice behind her. She started violently. She had not heard him come here; his boots made no sound on the thick Persian carpets of green and gold and rose. She turned about, to see him standing at the fireplace, gazing at her from under those dark heavy brows.

"Oh—just—looking out," she stammered.

"Do you like the countryside by now? I know you are riding about quite a bit."

She stared at him. Did he make it his business to know all about her activities?

"So long as you ride about with your groom, I have few objections," he continued, in his cool deep voice. "However, it might be wise at times to take another groom along with you also. Your own man is unfamiliar with these hills, and you could become lost!"

"We have a good sense of direction," she said, sliding down, and standing at the windowseat rigidly.

"And you enjoy the Cotswolds?"

She softened a little. A genuine interest seemed to show in his face.

"I think they are beautiful, so soft and green, with many trees. It must be beautiful in autumn, all the oaks and maples. The hills must seem on fire then."

"Yes, they are most beautiful. I have lived here all my life, for my relative had no immediate heirs, and my father was heir to him, then I to my father. I grew up riding these hills, fishing in the streams, hunting deer— oh, not with a rifle, for I was not old enough then. But a friend and I went out with bows and arrows and pretended to hunt as in the old days."

His voice was curiously soft as he spoke of the past. When he indicated a chair and held it for her, she sank down, and they talked for a time—of the castle and the hills and the pleasant prospects to be seen from the windows. He said nothing of how she had changed the room.

She was surprised when the clock chimed eleven, she had not thought the time had passed so quickly. She rose, said goodnight, and went to her room in a musing mood. He could be charming when he wished, he had smiled more frequently tonight than usual. He had seemed sincere when he asked if she was settling in, and was comfortable with her rooms.

Noreen came, and she made ready for bed, in the creamy lace nightdress she preferred on the warm nights.

Settled in the huge four-poster, she was on the edge of sleep when the door opened again. Thinking it was Noreen, she asked sleepily, "What is it?"

The door closed again. Her eyes popped open, to see Darcy coming in, wearing his dark robe.

There was no light in the room—only that from the opened windows. She sat up abruptly as he approached the bed.

"Don't come in here!" she said harshly, abruptly, so startled she did not guard her tongue.

"Why not? I am your husband," he said smoothly, a sort of laugh in his voice. "You have had time to adjust to that idea, have you not? And you cannot plead weariness. You seem quite lively."

He was at the bed, his robe was off. He was reaching for the sheet to lift it up. In a panic, she started to slide off the other side of the bed. He caught at her, pulled her back, his arms warm and close about her.

"Don't touch me—don't!" she cried, in a desperate way. She could not endure to be touched, and she was afraid, afraid, of what he would do.

"Nonsense," he said softly. "You are a grown woman, are you not? Old enough to marry, old enough to bed. Are you afraid of being hurt?"

He did not give her time to answer. He pressed her back against the pillows, and his head came down until his rather rough cheek pressed against hers, then his mouth came to cover her own. She fought him desperately, but he simply wound his arms about her and held her still. His body lay half on her, and his legs pinned her down. He was much stronger than she was, she was amazed to find. She had to fight to get her head moved, so that he could not kiss her mouth. Her head jerked back and forth on the thick pillows. He only kissed her cheek, then moved to kiss her throat.

She was trembling with fright and some emotion she

could not define. No other man had ever touched her like this. Nothing was like this, the closeness of a man's hard warm body to her softness, the strength of his arms pressing under her body, the feel of his bare legs against hers, the hardness of his mouth as he kissed her silky flesh.

She tried to protest, her words were muffled by first the pillow, then by his mouth again. He stroked his hand over her, from bare shoulder under the lace, down over her arm to her wrist, then over to her waist, up to her breast. He found the soft skin of her breast under the lace bodice, and pressed his fingers to it. His mouth covered hers, and his breathing was more rapid.

She struggled under him. He let her move, then shifted his weight, so he was more over her. She was terrified, and cried out, when he released her mouth.

He soothed her gently. "Easy, darling, easy. I shan't hurt you, don't be frightened. I know it is your first time, but I shall not hurt you. If you struggle so, you will only hurt yourself."

She knew what he was doing, but unconsciously the voice soothed her. It was as though he gentled a horse, coaxing it to him with voice and hand. She was shivering as she finally lay still, and his hands moved over her, learning the soft curves of her breasts, and her waist, and her rounded thighs. He drew the nightdress from her, and he was naked also, there in the darkness, with only the dim light of the moon making slivers of light in the bedroom.

His mouth moved over her body slowly, as though he delighted in her soft gentle flesh, her fragrance. His fingers cupped her breast, he kissed at her and played with her, until she was weak and unable to struggle against him. How sensuous was his hand on her, the stroke of his leg against hers. She tried to rouse resentment and fighting fury in herself by reminding herself that he was skilled from long practice with women.

He put her arms about his neck. She lay passively, but she became curious as he continued to caress her. What did his head feel like? She stroked her fingers tentatively over his hair, his neck, down to the scars on his shoulders.

Then she did remember. Mrs. Holt's words about his scarred shoulders. She stiffened, in shock, to recall. That other woman, how intimate she had been with him! And now he lay with her—

Her fingers traced over the scars. They were deep cruel scars. How they must have pained him. He lifted his head.

"Do they shock you—those scars?" said his deep quiet voice, a little uncertainly. "You would not like to see them, I know. They are ugly—"

"Oh—they must have—pained you—" she murmured. She felt the rigidity of his body under her fingers. All her mind was bent on consoling him, why, she did not know. "They were—from the wars?"

"Yes, on the peninsula. I was shot up—the wounds did not heal for more than a year," he said, lying back slightly. It seemed so very intimate, to talk to him, with their lips only inches apart, his arms wrapped about her, his naked body so close. "I was healed in time for Waterloo, however. Then I was shot in the hip. I still limp from that. You must think me quite old and wretched—" His voice mocked himself this time.

Without pausing to consider her words, she said vigorously, "Oh, pooh, nonsense. You waltz very well, and you ride splendidly. One would not think at all of the injuries if you did not speak of them."

He laughed softly, turned over, and began to kiss her more passionately. His hands roved more boldly over her, the sensuous feel of them was rousing in her some strange feeling she had never known before. She felt soft, weak, yet her blood was pounding in her head and in her chest. When he moved over her, and began bringing their bodies together, she did not even want to fight him.

He made her his wife then, in fact as well as words. And her body responded, timidly, unsure of itself, her hands gripped at his arms, until it was over, and he lay back.

"There, now, it wasn't so bad, was it, darling?" he whispered against her ear, and kissed the lobe, and nibbled at it.

She could not answer, she felt in a daze. Was this the man she had hated so violently? He seemed different in the darkness, younger, more eager, not so cynical—almost romantic, she thought, as she sought to recover her breath. His arm lay across her, possessively, and she did not resent it. She was weary, and soon slept, in his arms, against his body.

She wakened at first light. She thought she might go out riding, then she felt the arm across her, and remembered it all. The struggle, her surrender without much of a fight, she thought ruefully. She turned to see the dark face so near hers on the pillow, the eyes shut in sleep. He had such long lashes for a man! She noticed a small scar on his cheek she had not seen before, and examined it in wonder.

He wakened, his eyelids flickered, he opened his dark eyes and looked right into her green ones. He seemed almost shocked for a moment, then smiled, right at her.

"Good morning, darling. How are you?"

She flushed violently, all her body one big blush as his hand went down to her thighs. She pushed his hand away vigorously. "Don't do that!"

"Aren't you going to become accustomed to me?" he mocked her gently. "We are married, you know."

She sat up, forgetting her nakedness, then snatched a portion of the sheet up to her breast. He had done it, and she had let him, in spite of her fierce anger against him. She stared at him resentfully. He had made her give in easily, and he knew it.

He sat up, reaching for his robe. "Are you always cross in the morning?" he added. By the twitch of his mouth, she knew he laughed at her.

"What kind of women are you used to?" she blazed.

"What?" he barked, staring at her, as he put on the robe. He was standing, his naked body splendid, the muscular shoulders firm, the waist slim and taut as a very young man's. She was glad when he fastened the robe about himself—the sight of his firm hard body disturbed her. "What are you talking about?"

"Your other women," she said, pulling the sheet up about her shoulders. "You are—very experienced, aren't you? That's why you had such an easy time of it—with m-me!"

He flung back his head and laughed. "An easy time—with you? You're a firebrand, my dear! No other woman would have made me wait so long after our marriage!"

She was hotly angry, not counting her words. "Oh, and no other woman did make you wait, then? Too bad! Perhaps you had best find some other woman again! For I shan't be so easy again! I—I have to respect a man b-before I would—would—" She faltered before his fiery look.

"You have said quite enough, Charlotte," he said quietly. "Be still. You are my wife, and I shall take what I please when I please. What I do with other women is not your concern, either before or after marriage!" His voice was cold now, and cynical, his eyes a dark blaze. He turned and walked out, closing the door softly behind him. She would have not felt so uneasy if he had slammed it.

She dreaded his cold anger. It was much worse than when Fergus Gordon had flared up at his children. His anger was soon over, burning itself out. She had a feeling that Darcy Saltash was the kind that burned slowly and for a long, long time.

She washed and dressed without calling Noreen. She would have no sly comments from the red-haired Irish woman—the blood on her nightdress and the sheets would tell their own tale. Her mouth compressed in anger. She was a woman, a wife now, and she hated him for doing this to her. All he wanted was a male heir. He had no feeling for her. As for her, she hated him!

She went down to breakfast, to find Darcy there before her. He greeted her politely, rose until the footman had seated her. Then he resumed his breakfast, giving her only a cold look when she spoke.

She hated that cynical gleam in his eyes. When Pamela came in, beaming and shyly pleased to be with them, he kissed her affectionately and seated her beside him. Charlotte, at the other end of the table, felt far away from their warmth. Presently he went away. When Pamela asked where he went, he said absently, "I must ride out. I'll not be back until dinner this evening. Be a good girl!"

And he said not a farewell to his wife. Charlotte's compressed lips told of her fury. Yes, he would use her, but the rest of the time he had no use for her, not even giving her the courtesy of a nod. Then she thought how unreasonable she was, wanting it all ways. She wanted him to let her alone, that was what she wanted!

She left her breakfast unfinished and went to confer with Mrs. Nettleton. The details, the fussy matters of the servants, the menus, plans for the tea the next day, all filled her mind, and she tried to put away from her the sensuous feel she remembered, of Darcy's hands on her, his voice whispering in her ears, his kisses on her body.

Chapter 10

Monday passed quickly, then it was Tuesday. Charlotte fussed about the large formal drawing room on the first floor, had two footmen changing the furniture about until she was satisfied with a more informal arrangement.

The room was very grand, with gilt chairs and sofas, fine furniture from the Queen Anne period, several fine glass-fronted cases of ivories and porcelains. She had the footmen arrange the more comfortable sofas and stuffed chairs about the fireplace, then brought in a basket of flowers which one of the gardeners had cut, and arranged them herself in some blue porcelain vases and a low bowl on the shining rosewood table.

Promptly at four o'clock a carriage rolled up, bringing the Reverend Mr. Potter and his good wife, both white of hair and serene of manner. Behind them came another carriage, with three persons, Mr. Herbert Crotchett, Mrs. Crotchett and Miss Dorcas Crotchett. The squire and his wife and sister were all plump, in their late forties, with keen eyes which seemed to see everything. Miss Dorcas was particularly interesting to Charlotte, as she was a schoolteacher in the village and knowledgeable about all that went on.

To her amazement, Darcy arrived soon after his guests, properly attired in afternoon suit of gray silk, a fine white neckcloth fastened about his throat in the latest fashion, ruby stickpin in that, and a ruby ring. He looked much as he had when he had appeared in her London town house, to converse.

Pamela was attentive to the guests and sat beside Miss Dorcas on the good woman's invitation. Darcy stood before the fireplace, conversing gravely with the squire on matters of the village. Charlotte wondered if he had been teasing her about not wishing her to become much concerned with village matters. Or had he been testing her willingness to do so?

She kept a watchful eye on him as she spoke with Mrs. Potter. They found a common interest in the children of the village. Mrs. Potter spoke of the orphans employed by the mills and seemed to feel that something should be done about them.

"I think you should know, my lady," she said in a low sweet tone, "that we feel they are much abused. You have visited the mill yourself?" The faded blue eyes studied her face in concern.

"Yes, only once, however. I mean to go again. You know perhaps that my own father was a mill child, and I have worked in his offices, now that he owns mills." She said it a little defiantly, to see if the woman would go proud and contemptuous.

Instead the woman smiled and seemed relieved. "Oh, indeed? Then you will comprehend the problems. The poor dears seem not to have sufficient clothing or food. We sometimes take baskets of food to them."

Darcy was watching them, a slight frown on his face, and moved closer to hear the conversation. "I shall visit them soon, I promise you, Mrs. Potter," said Charlotte, and turned the conversation to Miss Dorcas and her school.

"You might recommend a governess for my daughter," said Darcy to Miss Dorcas. "She has been without one for some months, and will soon be sadly behind the other children of her age."

Pamela's face drew into a frown, amusingly like that of her father. "Oh, papa, I do not want a governess! May I not go to school to Miss Dorcas? It would be so much more interesting than having an old governess!"

"Hush, child, you are being rude," he said sharply. "You will do as you are told," and he gave her a fierce look.

Pamela pouted. Charlotte was somewhat amazed. She always seemed a meek child, now she was beginning to show the stubborn nature beneath. She did have something of her father in her after all! Miss Dorcas gave her a keen look and a smile, and a brisk nod of her gray head, as though to say she had dealt with many such and was not put out.

Again Charlotte changed the conversation, turning to the rector. "I understand you have lived in the vicinity much of your life, sir? How pleasant is the area! I have often admired the valley, with the river running through it, and the views from the hills."

The rector gave her a pleased smile, his gentle face beaming with gratitude. "Yes, my lady, all my life have I lived here. The Cotswolds are my family's home, for many generations, and my good wife's also. I would find it hard to live elsewhere, though we made up our minds and hearts that we would go where the good Lord sent us. Fortunately, my lord gave us the living here, and we are well content."

Charlotte glanced at her husband. She wondered if he had given the living to this gentle soul because he wished to do so, or out of laziness for not wishing to look elsewhere, or perhaps because he preached kind, gentle sermons. She knew so little about him. He had so many sides to his nature. She mused on that, coming back to her guests to find Mr. Crotchett and Mr. Potter discussing the history of the region and of the small village they had both lived near all their lives.

The town, with its narrow cobblestone streets, its market place, and central location, had known more than four centuries of strife, had seen the farmers' income decline, then the brighter picture when the woolens were in demand. The advent of the watermill had increased the good lives of them all. The shepherds were able to sell their wool to the cottagers, who processed it, some weaving it in their front parlors on their own looms. When an earlier Arundell had built his woolen mills there by the waterfalls, where the water power could turn the wheels, some of the cottagers had been upset, thinking all their livings would be gone. But the Arundell had employed them in the mills—all who wished it.

"And some continue to weave and spin in their homes, and the tops are taken to the mill to be made into cloth or finished," said Mrs. Potter with great satisfaction. "So the mills have made the village and the countryside about. We are most grateful to my lord here for continuing his policy. We had feared he might shut the mills, as he has many other interests." She gave my lord Arundell a shy smile.

He bowed to her, Charlotte thought a shade mockingly. "It is a good income, though I am being teased for being in trade. I was grateful enough in the wars to have a good woolen suit over my back, and another woolen blanket to keep me at night. No, the woolens have been good for me, and the money is not to be sneezed at. I find in London it is the fashion to sneer at trade, but a man's money and jewelry are not so despised! They are willing enough to take it from him, I assure you. Pastor, do you not find that a man's deeds speak louder than his words?"

All the company had a good laugh over that, and the atmosphere seemed to ease. Charlotte was surprised at the difference laughter made in the countenance of her husband, softening the hard cynical lines, and making the blue eyes warm and sparkle.

The guests rose promptly on the hour to leave. Charlotte accompanied them to the door and was pressed with invitations to call upon them. Also there were sometimes dances in the country hall, and would she come at times and honor them? She promised to consider it, and they parted with warm expressions of gratitude for her invitation.

She returned to the drawing room with Darcy, and he promptly began to scold Pamela. "I am ashamed of your behavior, pouting and quarreling with me over your governess," he said sternly. "You will not embarrass me in company again so soon, I promise you. If it should happen again, you shall feel the whip!"

Charlotte gasped, as Pamela turned to her tearfully. "Oh, Darcy, do not speak so to her! She did but speak her mind! Shall she be punished for that? She has had poor experience with her governesses, they understand that!"

He glared at her. "Do you defend her behavior before guests? It is bad enough to be defied in private! I will not endure such behavior in public."

Pamela's lips trembled, she hung her head. Charlotte hesitated, then spoke more calmly. It would not do for all of them to lose their tempers.

"My lord, permit me to send Pamela to her room. She is overtired and excited."

He nodded curtly, she turned Pamela gently to the door and bade her go and rest. After the child had left, she made sure the door was closed. Darcy was watching her with a sardonic twist of his lips. She sat down, and folded her hands in her lap.

"Now, sir—"

"We are alone. You may call me Darcy again," he sneered.

She held to her temper. His seemed about to slip the leash. "Of course, as you will," she said carefully. "About Pamela, it will be soon enough to obtain another governess or decide about her education when autumn comes. I hope to look about for someone for her. Or I might investigate the village school, for Miss Crotchett seems most wise and amiable."

"Pamela does not go to a village school," said Darcy, pacing about restlessly. "She is sensitive, quick of mind. I wish her to be tutored at home, as you were, I believe."

She hesitated. With her father, she would have argued the point heatedly, they would have quarreled, then come to some decision. Darcy was of a different nature. Pacifically, she said, "Let us think about this for some time before deciding, if you will, please? I wish to become better acquainted with Pamela's mind before my decision is reached. And," she added quickly, "if we decide to remove to London for the season, and take Pamela with us, it would be better to have a good governess hired and willing to travel with us."

"I do not intend to go often to London for the season, Charlotte," he said heavily. "I hope you do not count on frivoling about, now that you are married! It was the one thing your father did not wish! And I think you had best make up your mind to settle down and be a wife and mother! Your youthful flings are over!"

She stared at him, gulped down angry words. She wanted to ask him if he himself intended to settle down, if he intended to remain away from London.

She managed to remain calm in manner, though she was seething inside at his insults. "Then the matter may remain at rest for a time, I believe," she said, and rose to her feet. "May I be excused? I wish to change for dinner."

"Do as you wish," he said, and opened the French windows and went out into the gardens. She stared after his stiff back, heard the stamping of his boots, and guessed he was raging about something, but what she did not know. Probably that she dared to defy him, she thought, and sighed heavily, and went slowly up to her rooms.

For some reason, she wished to calm him down and please him. Perhaps he would be of a better nature then. For dinner, she had Noreen take out the cream dress with green trim, and in the bodice she set a small corsage of creamy white carnations from the garden. Her hair was dressed smoothly, with long curls on her neck, the red coloring taking fire from the candles in the chandelier above the dining table. She sat at one end of the long table, he at the other. She made whatever pleasant trivial conversation she could for the length, and they retired to the drawing room as soon as the meal was over.

There she poured coffee for him, watched him take brandy for himself, refused it for herself. "Thank you, I am not accustomed to it."

He nodded, curtly, flung himself down in a chair, and watched her broodingly over the bulbous glass of amber liquid. She wondered what went on in his mind.

She ventured some conversation. He had ridden far that day? How did the wheat? Had his stallion recovered from the lame hoof? He answered little at first, then gradually relaxed, and told her some incidents of the days past. Evidently his long absence from Arundell had caused some difficulties, and he was very busy making up for it. He had replaced one tenant, who was always drunken and abusive, and found another to take his place. He had decided to improve the herd of cows, and had acquired some excellent milk cows from the squire.

She retired for the night in some relief. The conversation had been heavy going, but he had seemed more amiable when she had left him. She went to bed.

Noreen had left her, and she had lain for a time, sleepily listening to the last soft calls of the birds, the whisper of a slight wind in the great oaks outside. The fragrance of the roses in the room gently scented the air.

Then the door opened, and Darcy entered abruptly, without knocking, coming to the bed. He removed his robe and slid into the bed, "without so much as a by your leave," she thought indignantly.

She began to sit up, shaking off sleep. "Lie down again," he commanded abruptly. He sounded so cross she decided to be meek and obey him. She lay down, and he put his arms about her and drew her to him.

In spite of his cross tone and his abruptness, she found him again sensuously skillful in rousing her sensations. He pressed his mouth to hers, then to her cheek, down to her throat, roaming greedily over the shoulder, to the breast where he lingered. She put her hands to his back, her fingers gentle on his many scars, then stroked softly to his back and spine. He seemed to shiver a little, then settled on her with a sigh of satisfaction.

He remained with her all the night, and in the morning she wakened when he left, pressing a kiss on her shoulder as she lay half-awake and blinking up at him. He seemed to be smiling. She went back to sleep.

She lay long abed, and when she finally wakened it was to find a tray of cold tea beside her on the table. Noreen must have crept in and left it when she found her mistress asleep.

She lay, yawned, stretched. It was late, she knew by the brightness from the windows. But she felt so lazy, so—so strange—so satisfied. She closed her eyes, thinking of the little caresses he had bestowed last night, the feel of his hands on her, the murmured words in her ears. He had meant them—or had he? Did he use words and caresses to get his will? Or did he truly think of her as an adorable woman, perfumed as silk—all the sweet words he had used on her?

She shook off her drowsiness and rose, bathed when Noreen drew the bath. The maid looked at the thoughtful face of her mistress, and forbore any jesting or serious comments. The girl was growing up, thought Noreen fondly. About time too. She only hoped the quarrels between her and the master would lessen as they learned each other's ways. The servants had been whispering nervously about their quarrel after the guests had left.

The days went on. Charlotte found them filled with her duties, some riding by herself or with Pamela, meals to plan, a slow exploration of the village in short shopping trips in the carriage. She called once upon the rector and his wife, met their elder children, and found pleasure in the sharp comments of Miss Dorcas when she met her outside the inn.

Her new lord and master came several times to her bed, not every night, but often enough to keep her stirred up and a little apprehensive. Always he was gentle enough in his love-making to quiet her fears, whatever he said to her in the daytime. Yes, he was a skillful lover, she thought, rather bitterly. He had the experience and the reputation to go with it. She was reluctant to admit she found pleasure in what he did, that she actually looked forward to the nights when he chose to come to her.

She had to remind herself that he wanted a male heir to his line, to inherit his estates. She might make the mistake of thinking that he wanted her for herself. His fond words were to soften her, she told herself, and refrained from becoming so moved that she would respond verbally to them. She wanted to some night, she wanted to whisper love words in his ears, and reply more passionately to his kisses. But something always held her back and made her cool to him.

One morning she found Mrs. Nettleton in the kitchen busily packing several baskets of food. She paused, looking rather guiltily at Charlotte as she entered.

"What is it, Mrs. Nettleton?" asked Charlotte, puzzled.

"I would be taking food to the children at the mills, my lady—if ye don't object." Her tone was uneasy, defensive. "They do look so starved sometimes."

"Of course," said Charlotte promptly. "I'll come with you this morning. I have been meaning to go again. We can converse on the way."

The woman looked much relieved. Charlotte wondered if she thought her new mistress would object to the giving away of food. They were rather silent on the way, sitting in the comfortable carriage with the baskets at their feet, the coachmen stiffly erect before them.

At the mills, Mrs. Nettleton stepped down with the coachman's help. "Ye might not wish to go inside, my lady," she began.

"Oh, yes, I shall come," said Charlotte, with decision. "I have been meaning—"

Her words were interrupted by a shrill yelp. As the ladies looked about, a young lad dashed around the corner of the nearest mill building, a long gray structure, and ran into the yard before them. His shirt was ripped and torn about, he was barefoot, and when he stared at them, Charlotte realized his face was bloody and his small sharp black eyes were glazed, as if in terror.

After him came Mr. Albert Botts, yelling, a whip in his hands. "Come back, you little thief! You bastard, you runt! Come here and take your medicine, or I'll make you sorrier—"

He lashed at the boy, and the boy screamed, falling to the ground before them. Charlotte screamed in her turn, in outrage.

"Stop that! How dare you! What has the boy done?" She stepped before the boy, as he groveled on the dusty ground, glaring at Mr. Botts in furious dislike.

"He's a bloody thief, he is! You step out of my way, woman, and I'll give him his just deserts, I will!" Botts waved the blood-stained whip in furious anger, threatening Charlotte with it in his rage.

Mrs. Nettleton cried out, "How can you speak to my lady like this? You forget yourself, Mr. Botts!"

The coachman was standing, watching in grave apprehension. He stepped forward, ready to take the whip, his eyes watchful for his mistress. The boy crawled under the carriage, mindless of the prancing horse, made restless by the screaming.

"What has he done?" demanded Charlotte again.

"Stole, he did! Come out of there, you imp of Satan! I'll teach you—by God, I will—"

"I did but take my morning bun, I did," cried the lad with some returning defiance. "He would not let me eat today. And I ate nothing yesterday, 'cause he says I was sassy! I be hungry, I be!"

Charlotte froze. The lad was so skinny, his bones poked from his torn shirt. His thin face was sharp as a pointed ax, the cheeks bruised and dark circles under the dark eyes. His arms were so skinny, and his long fingers seemed claws.

"Is that so, Botts?" she asked, in cold tones. "Mrs. Nettleton has brought food. Are you starving the children here?"

"None of your business," he sneered, and Mrs. Nettleton gasped. "You'll keep out of this, your man won't want you about! I run this here place, and I makes plenty of money for him, I do!"

His greedy piggish eyes were on the baskets in the carriage. She saw the way they lit up when he saw the loaves of bread sticking out, the cold hams, the pastries.

Why, he probably took much of the food for himself!

"You make money—by starving the children?" she inquired. "Mrs. Nettleton, do you and the coachman take the baskets to the children and see that they eat well. I'll wait here with the lad. Mr. Botts, I am sure you have more important work to do than to hang about whipping lads. Go on your way!"

Deliberately she was as crisp and curt with him, her chin up, her eyes fighting angry, as she would have been with an upstart worker in her own father's mills. He growled at her, cursed under his breath, then finally strode away. Mrs. Nettleton let out her breath and took the baskets from the carriage. She and the coachman hastened into the mills. Charlotte bent over and peered under the carriage, to meet the sharp black gaze of the lad there.

"What is your name, lad?"

"Me name is Edgar, miss."

He gave a distrustful glance about, then decided to crawl out. "How old are you, Edgar?"

"Fourteen, miss."

He looked ten, scrawny and thin, a hungry look to him. "Do you like the mill work, Edgar?"

He hesitated, then seemed to decide to trust her. "Oi wouldn't mind, miss, if 'e wasn't about—but Oi likes horses the very best." He gave the sturdy work horse attached to the carriage an affectionate look.

"Well, how would you like to work in the stables at Castle Arundell?" she asked briskly.

The black eyes lit up. "Ye wouldn't be fooling me?"

"I mean it."

"Oi'd like it fine. But what about his lordship? What'll 'e say?"

"I'm his wife. He'll—put up with it," she said, her mouth quirked.

He gave her a stare, then awkwardly pulled his forelock. "Ye'll be the new lady there? Ye mean it?"

"I mean it. Climb up there, in front. We'll take you back with us." And get him washed, she resolved, and the great welts cleansed with ointment, and food into him. By the time Mrs. Nettleton and the coachman had returned it was settled. Edgar was up on the seat, gazing about as though unable to believe his eyes.

"He works in the stables from now on," said Charlotte, at Mrs. Nettleton's eloquent stare.

"Ah, that's good." In a lower tone, she added, "I was afraid Mr. Botts would half kill the lad after we leave."

Charlotte nodded grimly, and took her seat in the carriage. As they drove away, she said, "You saw the children with the food, and they ate it?"

Mrs. Nettleton said, "Yes, my lady. And I fear you may be right to direct so—for Mr. Botts would take it from them, for very spite."

"Or for his own table," added Charlotte. She was lost in thought then, only rousing when they reached home. She directed the coachman to take Edgar in charge, getting him washed, and ointment for his back. "Then see to it that he is in the charge of my groom, to learn more of horses. I'll speak to Hobbs later."

Edgar beamed down at her. "I'll work hard for 'ee," he promised proudly, as they rode off.

"I don't know what his lordship will say," sighed Mrs. Nettleton.

"I'll speak to him," said Charlotte.

And she did so. She waited until Darcy had had his dinner with some wine—she had learned that much of men, she thought!—and then brought up the matter in the drawing room over coffee. She told him all that had happened that day. He stared thoughtfully at her, listened without interrupting as she told of the whipping, the boy's complaint about food.

"Truly, the foreman is not a good man, Darcy," she

said passionately, warming to her story. "I would hate to have him employed in my mill. I fear he is very cruel and abusive to the children. They looked ragged, and half-starved. Is no one in charge of them but Mr. Botts?"

"I employ several women to care for them, and make sure of their welfare," he said finally, crossing his long legs, and leaning back. "I must look into the situation. There may be some neglect there. But you wrong Botts, I think. He is a good sturdy fellow, always shows a profit."

She frowned. "At the expense of his workers, perhaps," she forced herself to say mildly. "I do wish you would inquire and see for yourself the situation in the mills. It is easy to get away with abuses, and it makes me ill to think of the children so treated."

"They do good work. They would not if they were so starved and abused," he said, still not angry. He seemed more amused at her seriousness. "You seem much concerned, my dear. Are you so fond of children?"

His dark blue eyes seemed to mock her, she thought again of his probable wish for an heir, and looked down at her coffee cup. "I do not like injustice," she said finally. "Father found it possible to turn a profit and still treat his workers with fairness. He gave them raises when their work warranted and saw to it that their homes were clean and well kept. And the children he uses are housed in dormitories, and good matrons are there for their welfare. You'll find no abused children, nor starving ones, in his care!"

"I'll see to the matter when I get time," he said, and turned the conversation to the farm he had visited that day. She was troubled but knew enough not to press the matter.

Chapter 11

It was but two days later that Darcy informed Charlotte curtly that he must be away for some time. "I have a property, a hunting and game preserve, which has been in some neglect. It is up on the border near Scotland. I shall be away perhaps a week or more."

"Oh—I see," she said blankly. He made no offer to take her with him. She found herself wondering if he would meet a lady there, perhaps Mrs. Holt. No, Mrs. Holt would not care for hunting—that is, not that kind of hunting.

"You will do well here, you have much to occupy your actions and mind," he said, rather drily. "I understand you go to tea to Mrs. Potter on Wednesday."

"Yes, sir. That is—you approve?"

He shrugged his great shoulders. "I have a feeling you do what you please, with or without my approval. Your father warned me of this. But so long as you do not make scandal, you shall go your own way," he said indifferently.

The words stung. He did not care at all, she thought. And wondered at the depression of her spirits. She wanted only to be left alone. Surely she should rejoice that she would be free of his attentions for more than a week!

He left early in the morning. He had lain with her that night, and he did not rouse her when he left the bed. He bent over, pressed his lips to her cheek as she half-wakened, and turned over. "Goodbye, my dear. You will take care of yourself, and of Pamela?"

"Yes, sir, of course," she said sleepily, and yawned.

"Go back to sleep. It is very early," and he left the room. She heard his carriage later, as it ground along the graveled path from the stables, and voices dimly raised in farewell.

The castle seemed strangely quiet. She went for a ride on Black Satin and questioned Hobbs about the lad, Edgar. "He'll do presently, he has much to learn," said Hobbs. He was not given to praise, so she realized the boy pleased him. "Half-starved, he be," added the groom. "And old and new welts on his back. I'd not be happy under that Botts, my lady."

"I must go again to the mills," she murmured, frowning at the glowing scene before her. She did not see the thatched cottages, the sharply cut hills, the mist that rose from the valley in the early morning. She saw the whip as it rose and fell on the bleeding back of a thin boy.

Would there be time to go today? She had not believed she would be so busy. There was always something, the staff, visitors, the stables, provisions, directions for the gardeners. They grew much of their own provision, and the kitchen staff was often kept busy with preserving the fruit and canning the vegetables.

But early in the afternoon, everything else was knocked from her head. A carriage with two dusty horses came up to the very door, and a man jumped down and came inside. The butler himself came hastening to her in the kitchens.

"My lady, there is one who says he is your cousin, my

lady!" He looked jolted from his usual calm assurance, and she hastened to follow him, to find Kenneth Mackay pacing in the hallway.

He turned to greet her, and clasp her hands warmly. Tired lines etched his fine face, his hazel eyes were dark in concern.

"Kenneth, how good to see you. You are well? What is it?"

He kissed her hand. "I would not be the one to bring you such news, but it is urgent, Charlotte," he said in a low tone.

He looked so stern, she led him at once to one of the smaller rooms, and closed the door on them. "What is it?" she asked again. "Neville?"

He nodded. His top hat, all dusty and browned by the dirt of the road, was being twisted in his long slim hands. He looked distressed beyond politeness. "There is no easy way to tell you," he said, finally. "Neville, well—he dueled with Rockingham, and of course, he was outmatched."

She put her hand to her heart. It was beating wildly, as though to thump itself out of her breast. "He—is—dead?" she whispered.

"No, no, forgive me for alarming you so!" He stepped forward, caught her arms in his hands, warmly, his concerned face just above her own. She thought he would have kissed her, but he restrained himself. "He is injured, feverish. I left him in an inn some twenty miles away, and hastened to you. He would not have his father hear of it, and London was too far to fetch him—"

"London? Father is there again?"

"Yes, on business. He had returned to Leeds, now is in London again, and all about. I have tried to keep my eye on Neville, but somehow Rockingham—"

"That bastard," she said bitterly. "He would torment Neville! Oh, God, I hate him—"

Kenneth looked very guilty. "Well, he is not so bad a fellow. You see, he was in his cups when he dared Neville—and the duel—it shook him up something bad. Rockingham is taking care of Neville at the inn, all remorse."

Charlotte stared at him, shook her head. She could not believe what she heard. "You left Neville—with *Fitz?*"

"There was nothing else to do. I said I would bring you to him, I promised. He would hear of naught else to be done." Kenneth sighed helplessly.

Charlotte rubbed her forehead. Darcy would be furious, she thought. But she must go to Neville. She could not leave him to Fitzhugh Rockingham. It might be another trick of his—in any event, Neville was ill and injured, she must go to him.

"What carriage have you?"

"The open one."

"We'll take my closed carriage, and two fresh horses. Twenty miles? We can be there in a few hours." She flung open the door, called to the butler, who hovered.

"You'll see to it that my cousin is fed. Advise Mrs. Nettleton to pack a large basket of food, and—oh, I'll tell her myself—" And she picked up her skirts and ran back to where the housekeeper was working.

The woman listened, her face grave. "You wish ointment and bandages? You'll go yourself, my lady? But allow me to accompany you—if you will—I know something of medicines—"

"No, no, there's no room in the carriage," said Charlotte impatiently. She softened at the woman's hurt look. "And we shall be going very rapidly." The woman was older, she could not stand such a fast journey as Charlotte meant to make. "Don't fuss, please, just pack the basket of food and one of medicines, and I'll be ready in an hour."

She dashed upstairs, ringing for Noreen as soon as she entered the room. She was changing her dress when the maid came in. "Pack two sensible dresses and under-garments," she said crisply. "My nightdress and a thick robe. My slippers—where are my boots? I'll wear riding garb, it will be easiest." She was flying about, the maid had her lips compressed and was shaking her head.

"Miss Charlotte, you won't do this? You shall not fly off on this errand. Let two of the footmen go—"

Charlotte turned on her, furious with her own anxieties. "Neville is shot, and gravely ill. And he is left in the care of Rockingham! I must go to him, don't you see?"

"Lord save us," murmured the maid, and went to see to the packing of a valise and hatbox. "I hope his lord-ship will understand when he returns," she added gravely, as she helped Charlotte change.

Charlotte frowned, but said nothing. She would face that later. "Noreen, you'll tell Lady Pamela where I have gone, but warn her and the household to say nothing to anyone in the village. Oh, and send word to Mrs. Potter that I will not come on Wednesday, I have been called away. I shall call on her as soon as may be."

She was ready in an hour. Kenneth, looking refreshed, came out, and the coachman handed her into the car-riage. Kenneth took the reins, and they were off.

Hobbs looked after them, shaking his head. Miss Char-lotte had ever been impulsive, but he had thought her married state would settle her. What his lordship would say, Hobbs dreaded to think. He had gossiped enough with the other grooms to know Arundell had a temper to match my lady's.

Once they were out of sight of the castle and the lands of Arundell, on the road to the east, toward London, Charlotte called to Kenneth to pull up. She climbed out of the closed carriage, and he helped her up on the seat beside him. She held onto her hat as they started out again. She wore the black habit, and smart black top hat with the veil and thought she might not be recognized.

"Now advise me of all that has happened, Kenneth," she asked her cousin anxiously.

He stared straight ahead, holding the horses to a steady clip along the dusty road. "Well—Neville did well for a time on his studies, but he became restless. His father finally said he might come to London with him. We both came down to London. Rockingham had lingered past the season, we heard he was drinking heavily. And—and he used your name, said he might have married you if your father hadn't wanted a better title. All that."

"The cad," she said, in contempt.

"I tried to keep Neville from him. But they met one time, then again, over cards. Rockingham was drinking, taunting him over the race you ran with him, you recall?"

She nodded. That race, it had brought on more disasters—her marriage, that dreadful frightening quarrel with Rockingham and Neville—

"I finally persuaded Neville to come with me to call upon you. He brightened up, we packed and left London. But Rockingham must have taken the same road, or followed us, I don't know which. We met at an inn, the Sign of the Black Hawk, some twenty miles from Arundell. Rockingham seemed jovial, but he started drinking. Then he taunted Neville again, called him a—well, I won't tell you," said Kenneth resolutely. "I tried to stop them. First thing I knew, they were outdoors in the innyard and starting to pace off. Stupid, all against the regulations, you know. They was counting for themselves, and the stable-hands cheering them on, gad, it was terrible."

Charlotte's hands twisted together in misery. "And Neville—was hurt?"

"Right off. First shot of Rockingham's got him in the hip. I think they was both aiming low," said Kenneth critically. "Rockingham flung down his weapon, swore, said he didn't mean to do it. Neville was laughing and cursing, and the innkeeper said he'd have to call the law, 'cause it was 'gainst the law—"

"Oh, he didn't, Kenneth, he didn't!"

"No, not for the payment of five pounds in gold, he didn't," said Kenneth gloomily. "But we couldn't call a doctor either. The bullet went through the hip, and I tried to bind it up. By morning, he was feverish, that was yesterday. Neville was out of his head, but he kept calling for you. Rockingham was sorry about it, seemed sincere. Said he'd stay with Neville while I got you, or he would come for you, either way. Figured you wouldn't want to be seen with Rockingham, might not come, either. And I couldn't move Neville, not the way he was."

He seemed glad to get it all off his mind and heaved a great sigh. Charlotte sat silently, thinking of poor Neville, furious at Rockingham.

The miles seemed to drag, but Kenneth cheered her up a bit with gossip about his mother, about her father and his work, about Neville's studies and his new tutor who was a cracking good one. He asked briefly how Charlotte got on in her new life. Charlotte replied in a courteous way, "I am doing well, thank you," and he shot her a keen look, and said no more of it. He knew her well, she thought. She did not look a radiantly happy bride, nor was she.

"There it is, the Sign of the Black Hawk," said Kenneth, pointing with his whip. It was a lonely inn on a side road, and he turned off the main highway to London to reach it. The inn when they drove in seemed neat enough, though small, she thought critically. Arundell had chosen better on their own journey from London. Then she wrenched her thoughts from him. She did not want to think of him.

She jumped down as the stablehands set steps for her,

and Kenneth gave the horses into their care. She went directly inside, to the bedroom where Neville lay. Rockingham started up from his bedside.

"Miss Charlotte, how can I look you in the face?" Rockingham began.

"Later, later," she said, curtly, and bent over Neville, who lay with his eyes closed. She pressed her hand to his forehead, it was flushed and hot. "Bring my bags in here, and bring some hot water."

She examined the wound, flinched at the great gaping hole of it. They must have shot each other from close range. She bathed it again and again in hot water, then applied some soothing ointment and set a loose bandage over it. Neville finally opened his eyes, seemed to recognize her, and tried to smile.

"Keep quiet, Neville, you are doing well," she said firmly, to soothe her own spirits. "Can you drink a bit of broth?"

He shook his head weakly, not trying to speak. But she herself prepared a broth of some beef and fed him with sops of bread, and a little spiced wine. He slept after that.

A flustered but competent chambermaid prepared the next bedroom for her, and she washed and changed to a light green dress. When she was comfortable, she joined the gentlemen in the parlor of the inn.

Rockingham was sitting moodily at the fire. He jumped up when she came in. "I must—must—make my apologies to you, Miss Charlotte!" he said earnestly. He was pale, and his usually immaculate self was mussed, his shirt open at the throat. "I cannot forgive myself for wounding your brother! It was—devilish—of me! I have never hated myself so much!"

He did seem sincere. Kenneth looked appealingly from one to the other of them, ever the peacemaker.

"Tell me how it happened, Fitz," she said in more

friendly tone and sank down gratefully into a chair.

He repeated his story, said humbly he had been drunken and quarrelsome. "I have been this way since your engagement, I do not deny it. I felt your father should have considered my proposal and given you to me."

"Father has little use for rakes," she said composedly. "My lord Arundell seemed the better match to him, because he works on his estate, and manages woolen mills, and all that. It was little of personal note, I assure you, Fitz."

He seemed a little relieved to hear it. Kenneth gave her another of his keen looks that went through her, and sent word to the landlord for some luncheon to be prepared.

She managed to be polite to him, but thought she could never like or trust him again for treating her brother so. His story was plausible, his regret seemed genuine. However, her love of her brother was too strong for her to feel kindness to the man who had injured him.

She ate a little, then soon returned to Neville, to sit at his side, change the bandages, soothe him. She was somewhat skilled at nursing, having seen her father through an attack two years before, and treating various injuries at the mills. She kept her head ever, her father had said proudly, and allowed her to learn something of medicines and herbs. The training served her in good stead those days.

Charlotte remained at the inn for three days, until Neville was able to sit up, and finally to move about. The wound began to heal.

They were taking all the good bedrooms in the inn, they occupied the parlor constantly, and the landlord of the inn was rather sullen, for all the gold they paid him. He was turning away all his local trade for them, he finally said, and Charlotte decided they must leave as soon as possible, or the man would go babbling all over about them and perhaps report the duel to the local sheriff.

Neville practiced walking about the innyard and seemed much brighter and more cheerful. On Sunday, Charlotte said finally she thought they might return to Arundell the next day. Kenneth could drive the closed carriage, the horses were well rested, and she herself would take care of Neville inside the carriage.

They packed up and were off early on Monday morning. The landlord beamed after them, pleased finally with his generous amount of payment, and Charlotte bestowed largesse on the stablehands, warning them bluntly not to speak of the duel. She thought they might keep their tongues long enough for the story to die or not follow them about.

Rockingham begged for her forgiveness one more time, and she said, "You must forget it, Fitz. I understand you were both drunken. However, if Neville had died, I should have killed you myself, you understand!"

He stared at her, at the flashing green eyes. "By God, you are a wonder, Charlotte!" he said, in a low tone. "If only you had married me! What spirit, what a woman!"

She frowned at him. "We should have clashed constantly, Fitz, you know it. Now, if you will only be silent about this matter, you will have my gratitude. And I do thank you for caring for Neville while Kenneth was coming for me."

He held out his hand. She reluctantly put hers into it, and was immediately sorry, for he raised it to his lips and lingeringly kissed the palm. She snatched her hand away, and he laughed a little.

"You will not begrudge me one little kiss, Charlotte?"

He was incorrigible. She shook her head at him, and allowed him to assist her into the carriage. Then her attention was all on Neville. She did not even see the attractive face of Rockingham as he watched the carriage rattle out of the innyard, with Kenneth at the reins.

If she had, she would have wondered, and perhaps worried a little. For the Greek-god face was set and determined, and an unusually resolute line was cast at his mouth.

Chapter 12

Kenneth drove slowly, and there were frequent stops to ease Neville's leg, to give him something to drink. Therefore, it was late afternoon when they approached Arundell Castle, and Kenneth pulled up before the front door.

The door was opened before they could stop, the butler, two footmen, and Darcy Saltash all came out to the carriage. Darcy himself helped Charlotte down. His face was too smooth, too polite, she felt by the grip on her arm that he was furiously angry.

But all attention was immediately on Neville. He was carried inside tenderly by the two footmen, and taken at once to a bedroom prepared for him.

"Mrs. Nettleton has been ready for him these five days," said Darcy, with a dangerous glint to his cold blue eyes.

"He was too ill to be moved," Charlotte said, hating it that she felt on the defensive. Without removing even her hat, she hastened after Neville, to see him comfortable in the guest room in the west wing, with a room for Kenneth next to him. A footman was assigned as their valet, a tray of tea was brought, she must change his bandages before returning to her own rooms.

Noreen came to her, her mouth compressed, her eyes anxious. As Charlotte removed her riding habit wearily, she asked, "When did *he* return?"

Noreen said, "Last Saturday, and fair furious that you had gone off with your cousin, and no word left where you had gone! Why didn't you leave word? He would have gone after you."

"I didn't even think of it," said Charlotte, in some surprise, pausing as she removed her boots. "Neville and I always deal quite well together."

"You're married now, my lady, and it's different," said Noreen, then closed her mouth firmly. It was up to my lord to do the scolding, and it might have some effect, thought the maid.

Charlotte had tea in her room, lay down for a short time, then slowly bathed and changed for dinner. She went up to see Pamela in her rooms. The girl clung to her tearfully.

"Oh, where did you go, mama? Papa was so furious, he stormed about! I had nightmares again—" She went on and on with her own troubles. Charlotte soothed her.

"There now, you knew I would return. My brother was ill and needed me. I could not remove him until he was better. Pooh, nonsense, of course I was coming back— home." She gulped a little over the word, patting Pamela's back soothingly.

Pamela was inclined to cling to her. Charlotte sighed deeply as she left the room, and went over to the west wing. The footman met her at Neville's door.

"He be sleeping now, my lady. I'll let you know, yes, ma'am, if any change in him. You may trust me, my lady."

"I'll come back later, then," she said. She smiled as Kenneth came from his room, the dust of the journey washed from him, clad in a fine pale blue silk suit, a white

silk shirt, and an immaculate neckcloth of white linen.
"You are looking much better, Kenneth! I must thank you
for all your care of me."

He tucked her hand in his arm, and together they went
down the stairs to the great hall, and the drawing room
beyond. Darcy looked up as they came in. He was pouring out a drink deliberately.

"Ah, there you are," he said, glancing at the clasped
hands. "Mr. Mackay, you'll have whiskey? Or sherry?"

Kenneth chose whiskey and water, Charlotte shook her
head. She was so weary, that any drink would have gone
right to her brain, she thought. And she must remain
through dinner before she could retire. Darcy looked
rather dangerous tonight. She would have an accounting
with him, she decided nervously, and hoped to put it off
for quite a time, until she felt able to fight back.

Dinner went off rather peacefully, under the circumstances. Darcy did not mention Neville or his illness,
which was ominous in itself. He would speak of it later,
she knew. Kenneth kept the gossip light, on the latest
on-dits from London, a splendid horse he had seen
racing, an amusing remark of the Prince Regent. He
could always be counted on for innocuous conversation.

After dinner, they retired to the smaller drawing room,
Charlotte's favorite. She relaxed before the small fire, for
the July night had turned cool. The butler placed the
coffee tray before her, but she waved to him to pour it
out. He gravely brought cups to each of them before
retiring.

She sipped at her coffee, leaned her head back, closed
her eyes. It was unexpectedly pleasant to be home, to
know Neville was in capable hands. Tomorrow she would
summon a doctor for him, Mrs. Nettleton would be con-
sulted, she must write a note to Mrs. Potter.

"What story do we give out about your brother?" asked
Darcy, suddenly, from his pose before the fireplace, one

foot on the grate. He sipped at the coffee in the white china cup with the blue rose on it, then set the cup aside, on the white marble mantel. "Is he ill, shot, or what? What do you say?".

Kenneth looked at Charlotte, who sat up. "Oh—I think it best that he be ill," she reflected. "He is, after all, feverish. That is illness. The doctor can be trusted to remain quiet, I presume? Not to report the matter?"

"And the gunshot wound?" asked Darcy, without expression. "His gun went off and he shot himself? That is the traditional story, I believe."

She nodded, not looking at him. From his quietly dangerous tone, she knew he was in a mood of suppressed fury. Kenneth sensed it also and looked worriedly from one to the other. Finally he made his excuses and retired, leaving them alone.

Darcy went to fling himself in an armchair near to Charlotte's pose on the sofa. "And now will you explain yourself?" he asked. Still his tone was soft. "You went off with your cousin, a young attractive man, were gone almost a week—unchaperoned. And I asked you to make no scandal! Is this how you obey me?"

"Good heavens!" she replied, sitting up straight. "Neville had been shot, he was alone at an inn in the company of—of Fitz Rockingham. I could not suppose he would be as well cared for as I—as I desired."

"You had best begin at the beginning, and tell me all. Who shot him? Kenneth?"

Charlotte looked at him. The blue eyes were not cold, but blazing with fury. "No," she said, just as quietly. "Rockingham had been drinking. He met Neville and Kenneth on their way to Arundell, there was some conversation, he—he challenged Neville to a duel. It was foolish, senseless—"

"Worse than that. Was your name bandied about?"

"And if it was? Fitz had offered for me before you,

father turned him down. He has been—furious about that, looking for an excuse—he said that to me."

"And you accepted Rockingham's attentions as well as your cousin's? Good God, your father has spoiled you completely, as he warned me! What am I to do with you? But pray continue your fascinating story, I would hear all!"

At his deadly sarcasm, she flared up. She told him the rest curtly, and explained Neville's condition when she arrived. "He was unconscious, feverish. I bathed his wound often, applied ointment, until the fever broke, and he began to heal. It was only then that we could return. You cannot blame me for waiting until it was safe to move Neville!"

"I blame you for not notifying Mrs. Nettleton where you had gone. I blame you for not taking at least your maid with you to give some semblance of respectability! I blame you for your heedless ways which give no thought to your responsibilities, my reputation, or your own!"

She jumped up. "Sir, I wonder that you married me!" she blazed hotly. He stood lazily, only for politeness' sake, and faced her. "My father warned you I was spoiled! I warned him that you are too fond of many women to settle for one! I told him outright the marriage would be a disaster! Well, it is, and I—I—I am ready to finish with it!"

"Not so easy, my lady," he said drily. "I do not give up at the first sign of cracks and strains. We shall mend and patch and do better together. Only you shall learn to listen to me, and obey me! I am not your father, and I shall not be easy with you!"

She glared at him, then afraid she would break down and weep for sheer rage, and disgrace herself, she whirled about and left the room. She fairly ran up the stairs, past the startled butler and two footmen who nodded at each other significantly. They had heard some of the words through the thick doors.

In her sitting room, Charlotte sat and fumed. She had been weary, now she was too angry to go to sleep. She sat in the candlelit room and stared at a book opened on her lap. When Noreen came, she snapped at her, the maid shrugged and left again. Finally, Charlotte went over to the west wing to see how her brother did. The footman whispered that he was asleep, and Charlotte peeped in to see that it was true. Neville slept deeply, in the comfortable canopied bed, and his forehead was cool.

Relieved, she returned to her own room, and without sending for Noreen she undressed, washed, and went to bed. She blew out the candles and climbed in, letting her feelings of indignation wash over her.

Oh, what a hypocrite Darcy Saltash was! To scold her for going on an errand of mercy, without a chaperon! When he might rouse about London, have his mistresses, all without a breath of scandal to it, because he was discreet! She did not invite the attentions of Rockingham, and as for Kenneth, he was her cousin, and dear as her brother to her.

She lay and fumed, more and more widely awake. She tossed and turned in the wide bed, unable to become comfortable. How hateful he was, how very sure of himself, and his mastery of her! He would be surprised to find how little she would give in to him! Just because he was stronger, and a man, was no reason that a woman should have to surrender her mind and her soul to him, and give in meekly to whatever he ordered! So long as she kept her character and her soul intact, he had no cause for grievance! She had done naught wrong, and he must see it, or be an idiot!

The door opened, a dark shape came, and closed the door after him. She sat up like a shot.

"Don't come in here! How dare you come after what

you said to me! Get away from me!"

"You sound like a fishwife," he said, in his smooth deep voice, a slightly amused tone to it. Deliberately he removed his robe, and drew back the sheet. She tried to slip out the other side, utterly furious and shocked that he should come to her after such a scene. He grabbed her wrist, and yanked her back cruelly to the center of the bed. "No, you don't! You are my wife, and you'll act the part whether it pleases you or no! You have caused enough stir, you'll not shut me from your bedroom!"

"All you care about are appearances!" she cried bitterly, writhing and twisting to escape from him.

"You show only that you do not understand me at all," he said oddly. He turned her so she lay on her back, pinned down her legs, and bent over her. She flung her head from side to side to evade his hated kisses. He caught her chin in his hand, and held her head still. His mouth closed over hers, and she felt the deep anger in him.

She struck out at him with her free hand. He caught it, and held it with the other above her head, holding her helpless. Then deliberately he kissed her again and again, on her lips, her cheeks, down to her throat, to her breast. When she writhed in protest under him, he ripped the nightdress from neck to hem, and pressed his face to her breast. She gasped, and gasped again at the fierceness of his caresses, the way he held and touched her. All previous nights were wiped from her mind, he had never been so wildly possessive.

But he made her respond. Against her will, her body softened, and curved to him. He released her hands and made her clasp him with her arms, and he caressed her until she felt her mind blurring with wild emotions. He was so skillful in his caresses, his hands were so knowing, he played her as a master played a violin, with the exact touch on her that made her moan and melt to him. Then he took her.

She slept in his arms, dreamlessly for a long time. She was vaguely aware in her sleep that he held her tightly to him, her back curved to his body, his chin on her head. Her hair had come unbound from its braids and curled down over her shoulders and breasts.

She wakened in the early morning, as dawn swept pink fingers across the windows. She heard the birds calling sleepily, a scent of roses crept in the windows from the vines outside. She stirred, and felt his arms tighten, and the memory of the night before made her ashamed.

She tried to pull from him, he wakened completely, and his voice murmured in her ear. "Come, now, you will not leave me, after such a night? You enjoyed it so much!"

He mocked her. She stiffened, and fought to win free, as futilely as the night before. He turned her round, and she gazed with wide green furious eyes into the cool blue ones above her.

"I hate you," she said clearly.

"You did not seem to last night," he mocked.

"Oh, you can take my body and make it respond!" she jeered, "you are so very clever with women! That comes from much experience, as I had heard in London! But the mind and the heart are different matters, as you may have learned also!"

His eyes shadowed. It may have been a trick of the early morning light, but his face seemed rather gray under his faint shadow of beard. She longed to strike out against him with her fingers, to scratch his face, to thrust him from her. Why were women born so much weaker than men? As he did not loose her, she tried again with words.

"But how if your body is all I want from you?" he mocked in reply, finally, and she closed her eyes tightly. He was more clever than she was, he could strike more deeply.

She knew her body was all he wanted, but her hungry

heart had always wanted more. She had longed for a marriage, with a man she could respect, whom she could come to love, who would love her. She had looked with interest at babies, wrapped snugly in shawls, and longed for a wee one of her own. She had smiled at children playing games in the parks, calling to each other, and wondered how it would be to have one such small boy, or an adorable little girl of her own.

But not like this! Not with a man whom she detested, whom she could not respect! Not with a man who went from her to a woman he truly loved and desired, a woman like Mrs. Holt! A hard woman who gave her scented favors for diamonds and made a mockery of the name of love.

She turned her face from him, he put his hand in her loosened hair and closed it over the curls, and forced her face back to him. His mouth covered hers, as she would have protested. She fought to free herself, in vain.

"When will you have done, sir?" she cried out, when her mouth was freed. "You have done enough for now— enough!"

"Oh, I think not," he drawled. "I still have a desire for you. Lie still for me!"

She struck at him, he only laughed, catching her hand easily, and forcing it behind himself. He held it there, caressing her, pressing his naked body to hers, until she knew he would have his way, that his desires had been roused by the contact, that he would go on and on until he was satisfied again.

She braced herself to endure it. But he would not have that. He caressed her, mocked her with words, but gentled her with his hands, until he had her moving in futile protest at this desire that had no sweetness for her.

And he went on and on. Her mind blurred. She could not endure it. He was making her respond, to hold to him with wet hands, and cling, and answer him kiss for kiss.

He drew up for a moment, looking down at her flushed face, the closed eyes. "You are very beautiful," he whispered. "Tell me you want me also, tell me."

"No, no," she whispered.

He moved, sharply, as though to her very vitals. Something seemed to break inside her, some wall of resentment, and she went weak. And she began to feel something she had never felt before, a quiver, slight at first, then stronger, something inside, forceful, like himself, at his every move.

"Tell me you want me," came his tormenting whisper in her ears. He nibbled at the lobe, she shivered. "Tell me—adorable—tell me—you want me—don't you—you want me—"

She would not reply in words. She felt as though there was something more, she quivered on the verge of a strange discovery. Only he could send her over the edge, into knowledge of herself, into some sweetness she had only dimly glimpsed before.

Slowly he drew back from her. She caught at him desperately, driven to pleading. "Don't—don't go—" she muttered. "Oh—Darcy—please—please—"

"Tell me you want me," he repeated inexorably.

Her eyes were tight shut, she would not see the mockery on his face. "I—I want—you—oh, please—" Something would come, something—

He gave a deep breath of satisfaction, then came down on her swiftly, and she went over the edge, into the falling singing wildness, the wilderness, where she had never gone before, the sweetness, the honeyness, the joy, the deepest pleasure— It shook her to the depths, and she could only lie there when it was over.

He lay there also, his arm about her. She could not look at him, he would be smiling in mockery, at her complete defeat. She had begged for him, she had begged.

She had fallen asleep then. When she wakened, it was late, and she was alone. Noreen crept about the room, opening the curtains, laying out her dress for the day. Charlotte opened her eyes, sighed without knowing she sighed, feeling the complete languor and satisfaction of her fulfilled body. Oh, what had happened to her? She wanted to roll over and think about it, and then sleep again.

"Now, don't ye be going back to sleep, my lady," said Noreen's sharp voice. "I know ye're tired from the trip, but there's much to do today. Neville has been a-asking for ye, and Miss Pamela too, poor child. Ye've neglected her enough!"

"Oh—what time is it?" She yawned, stretched, then saw the gilded clock near her bed. "One o'clock? Oh, it cannot be! Good heavens, how late I am."

"I told ye." Noreen gave her an anxious look. "And Mrs. Nettleton has been asking about ye, and his lordship will be back for tea, and Mr. Kenneth out riding these two hours. Now, come along, Miss Charlotte, I'll draw your bath."

Charlotte forced herself to rise, and bathed. She noted with wonder the marks on her body. He had been cruel last night, but she had not minded. She had enjoyed it! Oh, how could she! And he had left these bruises on her white body, on her breasts and thighs and legs and on her arms. She was flushed when she came from the bath. Nothing was enough to scrub away the memory of the night and his embraces.

She dressed in a white muslin with green ribbons, and fastened her hair back severely with a green ribbon. She tried to think of all she must do, consult with Mrs. Nettleton, soothe Pamela, see to Neville, catch up on her social engagements—

She went down late to luncheon, and excused herself

to Kenneth. Darcy was not there, thank goodness. She went up then to Neville, pleased to find him conscious and awake.

However, he was feverish again, and she was anxious over that. She sent for the doctor, urging him to come as soon as possible, and hovered over Neville with ointment, bandages, broth, spiced wine, until he slept again.

Pamela next had her attention. She must walk in the gardens with her and soothe her and listen to what had gone on in her absence. Then she must consult with Mrs. Nettleton, and then it was time for tea, and Darcy had returned.

Darcy seemed in a fine humor, laughing and chatting with Kenneth as though they were bosom friends—after all he had said about him yesterday, Charlotte thought with resentment. It was only on her that his displeasure fell. She hated it that she had given in to him so completely. She could not resist his skilled lovemaking. But he was experienced, oh, yes, he was experienced. She could not look him in the face. She looked everywhere but at him. Fortunately, she did not have to speak to him except for the polite queries about his day.

She went up to her own drawing room, to sit at the desk, and puzzle out menus for the invalid and the rest of the household for the next few days. She was busily scratching away, when Darcy entered from his study.

"Ah, there you are, Charlotte." He seated himself opposite the desk where he could watch her face. "I wished to consult with you about my message to your father."

Her face shadowed at once. "Oh, must you write, sir? I had planned to write—"

"And tell him a shaded version of the story? It would bring him packing down here at once, to demand what has happened to his son," said Darcy coolly. "No, I will tell him the truth. Only I mean to assure him we will have every care of Neville. Now, has the doctor been here?"

"Not yet, sir. He comes tomorrow morning, he sent word. He has a confinement today."

"Then I will await him tomorrow and have late word on the lad's condition. I shall have to tell your father, of course, that you went to Neville unchaperoned. I mean to inform him it shall never happen again."

The cool contempt of his words fired her up again. "And how do you mean to promise that, sir?" she flared. "I shall continue to do as I think best! Should such circumstances occur again, or something of such a nature—"

His blue eyes narrowed. "That is what I meant to talk to you about, Charlotte. I want your promise that you will never again do such a thing. Have I your word?"

"Of course not," she flared again, reckless of the consequences. "I shall continue to do as I think best, as I assured you! No man has such compulsion over me that I will keep from doing as I think I should do!"

He was rather gray under his tan, as he had been this morning. This time it was no trick of the lighting. The late afternoon sun shone clearly into the pretty green and gold room. "Do not force me to lose my temper with you, Charlotte," he said in a low tone. "You try me sorely."

Her fingers clenched over a paper, she crumpled it and flung it into the wastebasket beside the desk. "I warned you when I married you, sir, that you would regret it. I warned papa it would be a disaster. I wanted to marry a man I could respect!"

"And you do not respect me?"

Her green eyes met his blue ones. She was frightened a little, but she had ever had courage, a little too much, her father thought. "That is so, sir."

He rose, slowly. "Then I must teach you to do so," he said, and bowed to her mockingly. "I will write to your father tomorrow," he continued, as though they had not said anything else since he had first suggested this. "If you have messages to send to him, you might write them this evening. I will send a groom after the doctor has been here." He left the room and shut the door of his study behind him, very quietly.

She sat on, staring unseeingly at the white pages before her. He had said it so quietly, yet his words rang in her ears as though he had challenged her to a duel—and she had accepted the glove thrown down!

What could he do to her that he had not already done? It scared her more than a little. Surely he would not harm Neville, he was the one soul she cared about above all others. Or Kenneth, or Pamela? No, he would not hurt his daughter. He would hurt her some way, she felt sure. But how?

She must be on her guard. Oh, papa, she thought, how could you have forced me into this loveless marriage! I said you would regret it, but how much *I* already regret it!

Chapter 13

The doctor finally arrived and examined Neville. He pronounced him coming along well, prescribed a stronger medicine so he would sleep nights, and promised to come again in two days.

Darcy remained close about the house for a couple of days, but Charlotte saw little of him. She was anxiously nursing Neville, consoling Pamela, and sometimes she rested herself. She felt quite weary.

Kenneth came to her before tea one afternoon and urged her to walk in the gardens with him. "You are looking quite pale, Charlotte. Come, you must get some exercise. Have you been riding at all?"

"No, not recently." She did consent to stroll with him, and they walked up and down the garden paths for a time, and he even made her laugh a time or two. Darcy came out to them presently.

"You will come in to tea?" he asked, as the approach to their path brought him close. His tone was ironic, his eyes chilled. "You have guests, my dear, the Reverend Mr. Potter and his good wife, come to call on the invalid.

I showed them to Neville and asked them to remain for tea."

"How kind they are! I will come in at once." She turned back, her hand still on Kenneth's arm, and they walked together to the French doors into the drawing room. Darcy glanced at her hand once, and his mouth had a hard line about it.

But he said nothing to her nor to Kenneth. She was glad of that. She felt too tired to cope with his angers. He had not come to her rooms since that terrible, humiliating night.

The Potters were kind and offered some home remedies, and some little gossip of the village. After they had left, Darcy rose and paced about the room for a few minutes, pausing absently at the windows to stare out. Kenneth rose also, to excuse himself. After he had left, Darcy turned about. Charlotte felt his gaze on herself but could not read his face. She had never understood him, nor did he comprehend her nature, she thought, brushing her hair back from her forehead.

"I am going to London tomorrow," he said quietly. "I decided to invite some guests to return with me. I often have a houseparty in August. Your brother's illness has held up my plans, but I shall continue now, as he progresses."

She stared at him. A houseparty? At this time? "How—many guests?" she asked, carefully.

He shrugged. "About eight or ten, probably. I will speak to Mrs. Nettleton about their rooms. Oh, and you might plan some especially elegant meals, they are very particular. We shall have some hunting, and I shall open the ballroom."

Her heart seemed to sink down to her green kid slippers. "Who—comes?" she asked then. She was thinking of the effort of entertaining, how nervous she would be. She had never entertained on such a scale before. She had heard of houseparties in the country, but that kind of thing had been out of her orbit. Only high society did that.

"I have not yet chosen all the guests. We shall return in a week or so," he said, rather indifferent. "Excuse me, I shall prepare to depart." And he abruptly strode from the room.

She felt angry at his manner of speaking, as though she were a servant he commanded. She felt nervous of her own ability to cope with such a party. And she was weary from nursing Neville, she had been up several times at night. She rubbed her forehead. What could she do? Quietly leave with Neville and be away for a time? *That* would serve him out! He could entertain them himself!

But she could not move Neville again, nor would she desert him. She must remain and endure it and manage somehow.

Darcy left the next morning early, with no farewell to her. Pamela was quiet and gloomy. "I think he will invite some people I do not care for," she said, with a little sniff of ominous tears when Charlotte questioned her tenderly. But she would say no more of it.

Mrs. Nettleton flew about, preparing the guest rooms, ordering quantities of foods and wines. "For indeed, my lady, they can consume such amounts, you would not believe!" she sighed. "I must order more chickens—if only I knew when my lord would arrive!"

But my lord had not bothered to inform anyone of that. Charlotte set her mouth, ordered the ballroom opened and aired, polished and prepared, in case he kept his word to have a ball. While he was gone, she decided to do something she had planned for some time.

She prepared some baskets of foods and set out for the mills. Mrs. Nettleton was too distracted to accompany her; Kenneth refused to allow her to go with only the coachman. He sat in the back of the carriage with her, looking about curiously as they approached the bleak gray mill buildings set out along the pretty stream.

"And these are all Arundell's? Rum thing for him to handle," remarked Kenneth. "I thought he was a thorough rake. He has surprised me this week, all courtesy to me. I didn't think he liked me."

She managed a smile and a shrug. Darcy's manners were impeccable. He would be courteous to his deadliest enemy—while impaling him on a sword, thought his wife.

Several huge men were in the millyards, and gave Charlotte bold glances when she was helped down from the carriage. Kenneth gave them cold looks, but they only laughed and muttered to each other.

"Surely you will leave the baskets for the children, and depart?" he whispered to Charlotte. "This is no place for you."

She shook her head, picked up her skirts, and followed the coachman and Kenneth as they carried the baskets inside. She had not been inside the mills since that one brief visit, and she felt she must go and see for herself how matters stood. She had had enough of rumors.

Inside, she stood appalled. She was accustomed to the sound and rumble of the machinery, the heavy wooden looms thumping, the roar of the waters in the mills. But never would she get used to this sight. Thin women bent to the looms, threading the bobbins, tying thread. Thin men stooped beyond their years were moving here and there, rushing baskets of wool to the looms, carrying the huge tops of dyed thread. And the children—oh, the children—

Barefoot, with dull eyes set in small, wizened faces, they crept in and under the looms, catching the bobbins that fell, picking up threads, or carrying baskets of finished cloth too heavy for their frail sticks of arms. She saw one tot of about five, a curly-haired blond girl, sitting patiently before a loom ten times her size, thrusting up again and again to set the threads. None turned to look at her, though side glances told them she was there, walking slowly past them, pausing to watch the work, to see their faces, to study their condition.

She had not gone far, followed by the silent Kenneth and the coachman with baskets, when Albert Botts hurried down from his office overlooking the huge weaving mill. He rushed over to her, almost slipped on the greasy floor, where the hanks of processed wools had dropped again and again.

"What are you doing in here?" he bellowed, angrily. "No visitors allowed! Orders of his lordship, the Marquis of Arundell, and he will be—oh, it's you!"

Charlotte had pushed back her bonnet and veil and stared steadily at him. His face changed countenance, became more flushed.

"Ye cannot disrupt the work," he said more quietly, sullenly. "Ye cannot come in here. No women allowed."

"I wonder at you, Mr. Botts, daring to speak to me like this," she used her most frigid tone, her more imperious voice. "I intend to tour the entire site today, and see to the books also. I know much of milling operations, and never have I seen such disorder, such dirt and filth, such criminal conditions! There is no air in here, one can scarcely breathe!"

"But your ladyship is not accustomed to the air here," smirked Botts. "I suggest you go outside—"

"And I suggest you hold your tongue until I ask a question!" she flared in a rage, flinging back her head. "Now, show me about, I wish to see every building, every worker!"

She turned to Kenneth as the foreman gawped at her. "See to it that the children all receive some food, Kenneth. Much more must be done, but oh, God, how can he allow—"

Kenneth nodded, and he and the coachman efficiently

set the baskets on a bench, and beckoned the nearest children to them. They came timidly, casting anxiously their gazes at Botts before they went near the baskets. When food was given to them, they bolted it, pushing food into their small mouths as though starved, as indeed Charlotte believed they were.

"Now, Mr. Botts, the next mill, sir!" She said it crisply, and swept after him as he sullenly led the way. He showed her the spinning mill, then the sheds where the wool was sorted. They bought wools, some unfinished and some dyed and finished, and all was sorted here, then sent to the various vats to be dyed, or sent on to the spinning mill. All the way, she was conscious of the small children. The adults were pitiful, but it was the children that hurt her heart.

Small, anxious, weary faces, with great eyes in darkened circles. Thin sticks of arms, and legs like kindling wood, that might snap any moment. Ragged clothing, no shoes, some with a shirt, some bare chested with only a jerkin over the chest. Her mouth compressed in rage. So this was how her husband ran a mill!

In her thin muslin dress and light cloak, she thought she would faint in the hot airless rooms. Sweat streamed down the bodies of the men, women, and children. Their hair was thick with sweat, greasy, looking as though unwashed for years. Yet the finished products, the bolts of fine woolens, were beautiful, the threads perfect, the patterns finely created.

The tour took almost two hours, for she would pause to watch one work, to examine a machine that looked too fragile, worn with age. At the last, she said, "Now I will see the office. I wish to examine the books."

Albert Botts looked frightened, then blustered. "My lady, naught seems private to you! If his lordship wishes you to see the books, he will show them to you!"

"His lordship is vastly busy with his many enterprises,"

said Charlotte, with quiet sarcasm. He was even now with his mistress in London, probably. "So I shall look at the books, Mr. Botts. My father trained me well in their management. I shall not confuse the pages, I assure you."

He reluctantly showed her into the office, where nervous clerks sprang from their stools and bowed half way to the ground before her. He snapped at them to resume work, they were wasting time.

"Yes, indeed, do continue to work," Charlotte told them sweetly. "I shall not disturb you—much. I merely wish to examine the most recent accounts."

She took a huge ledgèr at random, set it on a shelf, and opened it. But Botts hung around, close behind her, and the stink of his unwashed body and his heavy, garlic-laden breath was too much for her. She could not concentrate on the amounts. She closed it, looked at two others, then decided it must wait another day. She would not be surprised if he cheated his master, but that was not so important as the workers.

"That is enough for today. Thank you, Mr. Botts. I shall return another time."

She swept out, collected Kenneth and the coachman, and they returned home. Kenneth did not speak, leaving her to her thoughts. She noted that the hem of her muslin dress was covered with wool shavings, and grease. The stink of the wool was in her nostrils, and worse, the memory of those children would haunt her until she did something about them.

She thought for a long time, but it was so vast a project that she was troubled. She could do little without Darcy's consent, and he was probably in no mood to listen to anything she said. She had complained before about the foreman, and he had evidently done nothing. She must conclude that he did not care.

Then everything else was wiped from her mind. Darcy and his guests came from London, in four carriages, grand guests, very demanding, sweeping in with laughter and drunken wavings of hands, demanding their rooms, places for their maids and valets, what entertainment had she provided, when might they go hunting, and so on.

There was Lord William Barkley—the sporting Billy, red-faced, hearty—and his wife, Lady Frances, blond, vivacious, catty, and smiling as she cut neatly through the reputations of half of England. There was Mrs. Eloise Connaughton, a widow, malicious, thirtyish, avidly fond of the hunt—both on horseback and off, thought Charlotte. Sir Blaise Percival was older than the others, but hunted devotedly. Lady Gwendolyn Guernsey, in her fifties, was a leader of society, witty, vivacious, seeing everything and telling all to her closest friends—who included most of London. Lady Horatia Settle was an echo of Lady Guernsey. Sir James Whitman seemed absentminded, dreamy, quieter—and Charlotte almost liked him until the maids began to complain to her of how he chased them about his room. And then there was Mrs. Iris Holt.

Yes, Mrs. Iris Holt had come. Charlotte thought she could not really have hoped she would not. In her favorite black—lace, or taffeta, or softest crepe—she drifted about from drawing room to dining room to Great Hall, out to the stables to cheer on the hunters. She hunted herself, in dramatic black habit and black plumed hat, and she craved Black Satin. Charlotte smilingly refused her own horse.

"He has been known to rear up and overturn anyone who tries to ride him, except myself," she said, explicitly, and gave orders to all the stable hands that the horse was her own, and no one was to ride him. She could not endure that!

It seemed the entire great castle was crammed full of guests and their servants. One could not stir, or walk through the gardens, without stumbling over them. Mrs. Nettleton grew flushed and perturbed, tearful when a dish was refused at table, fluttery when a servant was complained about. Charlotte had her hands full soothing them all, figuring out meals to serve which would be hearty enough for the men, with a dozen courses to please the ladies, and sweets for any occasion. More cooks were hired, and maids trained, Charlotte herself made some dessert dishes of odd flavors, such as she often prepared at home, almond cream, spice puddings, syllabub, seven-layer chocolate cakes.

One footman was assigned especially to the wines, served in quantities, with brandy often accompanying the coffee. Wagons rattled up to the kitchens daily, with loads of beef halves, whole lambs, baskets of chickens, huge hams and pork sides. More wagons of fresh vegetables, for their own gardens could not supply enough. Baskets of fresh peaches and strawberries, plums, oranges imported from London came up twice weekly.

Their demands for fresh excitements exceeded their interest in their stomachs. They would go hunting daily, crashing through the woods and fields, across the gardens. They wanted moonlight walks—preferably with their host to guide them. Charlotte asked the villagers for tea, and knew many were shocked at the heavy-drinking, maliciously gossiping Londoners.

She surprised Mrs. Iris Holt in her own private drawing room on the first floor, in the east wing, one day, returning for her bonnet before driving out. She stared at the black-clad woman, coming from her room.

"What the devil are you doing here?" demanded Charlotte, without thought. It enraged her that the woman made herself free of the entire castle. "These are our private apartments!"

The woman gave her a falsely sweet smile. "Oh, I often came here with Lucille, you know, my dear! I feel quite at home here."

"These are my rooms now, and you are not to come

here again without my invitation," she said shortly, not caring that the woman would probably complain to Darcy about her.

"I see he changed the decorations. I did not think he would so far forget the dear girl. He adored her, you know," and Mrs. Holt swept on with a sigh, leaving the dart where it had landed in Charlotte's tender flesh.

Charlotte went raging to Noreen. "That—that female! How dare she come into my private rooms! Did she come to the bedroom?"

"No, indeed, Miss Charlotte, don't fret yourself so! I kept her, indeed I did, right in the drawing room. She said she was looking for you."

Noreen looked at her mistress worriedly. "She has you upset, darling, don't let her! You're thin to the bone now. Can't ye rest for a wee bit before ye set out again!"

Charlotte jammed the green bonnet on her head and fastened it with shaking hands. The sight of that woman in her apartments had infuriated her. And she was already upset at the number of times she had seen Iris Holt strolling in the gardens, hand laid confidingly on the arm of Darcy Saltash. And he did not seem to mind at all!

He had not come to her bedroom once since he had returned from London. Some nights she had lain awake until past one, tossing in unusual frenzy, thinking over her plans for the next day, worrying over details, fretting over this and that. Sometimes she lit her candle and read a book until she was more calm. And he never came. He spoke only coolly to her, politely, of course, but with such chill.

"No, I can't stay, I must be off to the village. Mrs. Crotchett has promised me some cakes for tonight. And I must stay and call on her, she has been enormously kind."

The visit calmed her somewhat, the woman was so kind, and her sister-in-law, Miss Dorcas, was a fund of practical wisdom. Pamela enjoyed their visit also, and opened up brightly, and was a model of rectitude, which she had not been for the visitors. She had openly rebelled at coming to tea and sitting beside Mrs. Holt, her father had rebuked her, and she had fled crying from the room. Charlotte felt only a little more would be necessary to shatter the child completely, she was so on edge.

It was coming home with Pamela, hand clasped in hand, that a stunning truth was borne in on her. Pamela said, "I miss papa, he isn't very nice when those people are here, is he?"

"Um," said Charlotte, for she felt stricken by some sort of dizziness. She did miss Darcy herself! Why was that?

She examined the thought, turned it up and down, shook it inside and out, and could not evade it. She had come to love that sardonic curt creature, that abominable mocking man, and she missed his coming to her! She missed his polite conversations at table, for he kept his attention now on his guests. She missed his company at a quiet tea, when they had sat and talked to each other, and groped their way to a sort of wary friendship. And most of all, she missed him at night, when he had come to her bed, and caressed her, and she had felt alive and excited and more thrilled than ever in her life.

She loved him, even while she still hated him! That was the final crushing truth. She was fiercely jealous of his attentions to Mrs. Holt, even to the other women. She wondered how many of the women had known his caresses, his skillful love-making, how many he had gifted with jewels, dresses, exquisite expensive trifles.

She was wrestling with that thought late that night, as she tried to make out invitations to the ball to be given on Friday evening. The ballroom had been opened, polished, the chandeliers were shining clean, the candles set. It was short notice, but she hoped the villagers would come anyway. They would be curious—

She had made out a list, with the help of Mrs. Potter, Mrs. Crotchett, and Miss Dorcas, and now she was addressing and writing the invitations. Three dozen of the country folk would come, and mingle with the sophisticated London crowd. She rubbed her eyes, laid down the quill for a moment.

She started violently when the deep voice sounded behind her. "You are weary, why not leave that until morning?"

"Because they must be delivered tomorrow," she said shortly, not concealing to herself that his very voice and presence sent a shiver through her. The candles on her rosewood desk gave the only light in the room. The curtains were drawn against the night air, it was almost midnight. She had thought he was strolling in the gardens—again—with Mrs. Holt.

"I am sorry you have so much to do," he said curtly, not as though he meant it. "The company is much work."

She shrugged. "If it pleases you—" she began, with mockery.

"Well, I did not come to quarrel with you," he said after a pause. "I have just delivered to Noreen a gown I bought for you in London. I should like for you to wear it on Friday. It is of gray gauze in an overdress over an unusual shot silk. I thought these would go well with it—"

He set before her on the desk a worn leather case, and snapped it open. She stared, transfixed, at the gems revealed.

"These are the Arundell opals," he said, in a quiet tone, with something throbbing behind it. "I had them cleaned and some reset. Let me see if the ring fits."

He took her unresisting hand, and set the huge ring on it. The center was a fiery opal, almost orange in color, with colors of green, blue, cream, sparkling diamond-white flashing from it. About it were set small diamonds in a circle. It just fit her long slim finger.

The other gems were a lovely tiara, with a huge stone in the center, and smaller stones graduated to the sides; a silvery chain set with alternate opals and diamonds, ending in a huge irregular-shaped opal pendant; a bracelet of silver clasped with huge opals, another bracelet of opals set one after another on a crested band of silver.

"Do you like them?" he asked casually. "I think they will suit your coloring."

The fire opals, the unlucky fire opals of the Arundells, that Mrs. Holt had told her about. She felt a superstitious awe of them, but they were so stunningly beautiful, she could not but say, "I have never seen a set of stones so magnificent. They are truly lovely."

His voice warmed. "I am glad you like them. Please wear them on Friday, and the gown as well." He hesitated, then indicated the unfinished invitations. "May these not wait until morning?"

She said, awkwardly, "There are not many more to do, thank you. I should be better pleased if I could finish them, and send two grooms with them. It will take them all day to deliver them as it is."

"As you wish." He left the room, his study door closed. She finished the invitations more rapidly, conscious of the fiery ring on her finger, somehow warmed by his thought.

He had bought her a dress in London—he had given her the family jewels to wear. Surely that meant something, his tone had been more warm. Perhaps, one day, they might mean something in their relationship, a gathering warmth—

But no, he wanted Mrs. Holt, no matter whom he had married.

She sighed, finished, blew out the candles, closed up the jewel case, and went to bed.

At the end of the week, the ball was held. The candles shone on magnificent gowns, carriages rolled up to the door for an hour and a half, discharging the many guests. Long tables in the Great Hall were crowded and groaning with the massive hams, sides of beef, dishes of custards and creams, savories, cakes, pies, little pastries.

Charlotte and Darcy received their guests in the Great Hall and directed them to the long gallery, above the cloisters and picture gallery, on the first floor, around the corner from her own rooms. The entire length of the hall was used for the ballroom, and the musicians were already playing in the gallery which had been the musicians' place for four hundred years.

Mrs. Holt came down from her room, posing on the stairs, her hand on the railing, moving down further, all sweet smiles. Her misty black tulle gown was draped over black taffeta, and rustled as she walked. Diamonds covered her throat, her arms, her hand, and her tiara was of diamonds. Charlotte thought, a gift from Darcy, and felt an angry pang.

Mrs. Holt eyed the fire opals greedily, reached out to touch Charlotte's throat, and the pendant there. Charlotte shrank from her, she could not help it. She did not want the woman to touch her.

"Ah," said Mrs. Holt softly. "The Arundell fire opals. They have proved unlucky for so many Arundell brides, my dear!" And she smirked at Charlotte's frozen expression. She seemed full of a sort of subtle contempt, as though she knew something Charlotte did not.

Much of her pleasure in the misty gray gown and underskirt of fiery taffeta silk, the beautiful gems, vanished. Darcy had made a gesture toward his wife, a proper gesture. He was always proper. But this hard-as-diamonds woman had his heart. And Charlotte felt curiously forlorn as she turned to the next guests.

Finally, they were able to move to the ballroom. It did

look most beautiful. Charlotte had planned the decor, the masses of flowers from the gardens, the candles to match. Baskets of multi-colored gladioli were set near the ends of the room. The candles were of yellow, orange, flame red. The musicians' stand had been draped with red and gold silk. And banners with the Arundell device hung about the room at intervals, golden leopards rampant on red fields. Many of the villagers gasped in awed delight, and some dared to tell Charlotte how splendid it was, how much more beautiful than any previous ball they could remember.

She smiled at them, moved among them, greeted them all by name. She had become well-acquainted these weeks and months in her new home, and her natural warmth and friendliness and informality had endeared her to them. She thought her new friends, the Potters and the Crotchetts, had been spreading word in her behalf also.

Pamela stayed up for two hours, happy in a new gown of yellow silk her father had also brought from London, with a small becoming bangle of yellow sapphires on her small wrist, and a silver chain and pendant of yellow sapphire.

Charlotte was pleasantly surprised and relieved when Darcy came to her for the first waltz. He led her out, gravely, and they danced together for a minute, before he gestured for others to dance also. Neville was still too ill to come, but he watched from the musicians' gallery for an hour before retiring.

Kenneth claimed her for a quadrille, and complimented her on the arrangements. She smiled up at him naturally, and thanked him. Darcy was by now dancing with Mrs. Holt, and it pained her to see them together. He was stunningly attractive in pale gold coat and embroidered waistcoat, with rubies on his cravat and on his hands.

She danced with their guests in turn, one dance to each of the men, danced with the villagers, as they asked. When

Darcy came to her presently, he said, "You are most in demand. I must ask for the supper dance, must I not?"

"If you wish it, sir."

He bowed, and smiled, his face more relaxed than usual. The guests seemed to have softened him. "I should be most happy if you will allow me to take you in to supper, my lady."

She curtsied, with light mockery. "I accept your kind offer with deep gratitude, my lord."

He actually laughed aloud, and there was a funny, warm, hopeful feeling in her breast. Maybe—maybe—

But as they danced in a quadrille next, she was opposite the partner of Iris Holt, and she had the bitter sight of Darcy holding Iris Holt in his arms, swirling her about until the misty black skirts swung about the neat ankles. Yes, Darcy was happy—his mistress was here!

Chapter 14

The ball over, the guests continued in their mad race for pleasure. Some of the men hunted in the mornings, often the ladies slept until luncheon at noon, then demanded entertainment until late at night.

Charlotte began to avoid them. Seeing Mrs. Holt with Darcy stung her more and more. He seemed so devoted to her, his dark head bent to her blond one as they drank brandy, or walked the gardens, or rode together. The malicious gaze of the other women often went from Mrs. Holt's triumphant face to that of Charlotte, and she could not endure it.

She went more often to the mills. She examined the books to the rage of Albert Botts, and found some great discrepancies there. He was taking in much, and expending little, but where did the money go? Probably into his own pockets, she thought. She said nothing, letting him think she did not understand what he was doing. Time enough to inform Darcy when all her evidence was in hand. He paid the workers very little, the children nothing. They had their board and room, he said.

He was feeding them more regularly. She made a point

of coming sometimes in mid-morning, when they were supposed to receive their coffee and buns, or tea and cakes. Or she came suddenly in mid-afternoon, when they were supposed to receive dinner. If no food appeared, she waited until it was served. And the children did look brighter, though more ragged than ever.

She had discovered that the orphan children slept in a shed next to one of the mills, a former mill building. They had blankets on the hard floor, three children to a mat, in a hot airless room. Some of the older boys crept out to sleep in the near-by fields, on the coarse ground covered with mown hay, or in a field of stubble where cows or sheep had grazed, rather than be confined indoors.

She took some clothing to them, the women of the village contributed clothing their own children had outgrown. Shoes—she would get some by autumn, she vowed. But there were so many children, and they haunted her. She could not sleep nights for thinking of them in that shed, on hot nights stifling in that airless room, or huddling together for warmth in winter. When rains came, she lay and listened to the driving wind that blew against her windows, lying snug in her great bed. She thought of the children, so helpless and frail. And she thought of her husband, across the hall, uncaring either of her or the children.

August was drawing to a close, it would soon be September. The gardens bloomed with day lilies, brilliant gladioli, scarlet carnations. When she took one of her infrequent rides on Black Satin, she saw the hills turning to their autumn hues, scarlet, yellow, and brown, against the sharp blue line of the Malverns. The golden-hued cottages with their brown thatched roofs were covered with the last of the roses, and wild flowers of blue and rose and yellow dotted the grasses in the dim-lit forests as she rode along the paths with faithful Hobbs pounding behind her.

She felt more and more alone. Neville was recovering and grew fretful. He would return home soon, she thought, and Kenneth with him. Perhaps that was best, for Kenneth was earning some sharp looks from Darcy as he devotedly accompanied Charlotte to the mills, or on her outings to the village. And Kenneth was fond of her. He was enraged at her husband's flagrant attentions to the beautiful Mrs. Holt.

"How you endure it, I do not know," he said once to Charlotte. "He is not yet married three months to you! If your father knew—"

"He knows. I told him how Arundell felt about Mrs. Holt. He would not let me cry off the marriage," said Charlotte drearily. "Now, we will not speak of it again, Kenneth, if you love me," and she tried to smile over it.

"You know that I love you," he said, very quietly, almost under his breath. Charlotte, surprised, gazed into his gentle hazel eyes, and knew the truth. He did love her.

No, he must leave soon. She could not bear to hurt him, as he must be hurt. It would be best for him and Neville to leave as soon as Neville could ride. Then she would be truly alone.

She spent more and more time at the mills and in the village. And one day she went to the mills to find a surprise. Usually the children did not speak to her, other than to say "Yes, mum," to any question.

Charlotte had noticed this one boy before. He was blond, always with a muffler about his throat, and a hoarse mature-sounding voice odd in such a little boy. He looked about eight, so was probably eleven or twelve, she thought, with her new wisdom about the children. She had learned his name was Peter, and he had no other. He was from Scotland, near Glasgow.

That day, Kenneth had gone with the baskets of food to the bench with the coachman. As she walked slowly along the lines of weaving machines, watching the quick movements of the slim young fingers, a hoarse whisper stopped her.

"Mum? My lady? Do look at my machine, not at me." She halted, startled, and stared briefly at the blond head, then at the machine. The shaggy blond head turned briefly, then back to his work.

The oddly mature voice in the small body startled her.

"Yes, what is it, Peter?" She leaned closer to hear, pretending to gaze intently at the pattern he made deftly with the bobbins and the thrust of the wooden frame.

"It's Margaret. She be the girl at the end of the line, mum, with brown long hair and a purty face. Ye know Margaret?"

She glanced gravely down the line, focused on the girl he spoke of. She looked little older than the others, but was about fourteen or so, with a round sweet face and large dark eyes.

"Yes, I know her. What is it?"

"Mr. Botts, he be arter Margaret," said the hoarse voice, and Peter coughed harshly, bent to the machine. He recovered quickly. "Could ye use another maid up to the house, mum?"

She stiffened, studied the pattern without seeing the lovely brown and white stripe. "After her? How?"

"He be arter all the pretty uns when they gets older," said Peter bluntly. "She don't want no baby of his, she don't. She be a good girl, and quick and obedient. Could ye take her up to the big house?"

His voice was urgent now, he gave a furtive look about. Mr. Botts was pacing down the line toward them, his small black eyes suspicious.

"Right," she said swiftly. "Very nice work there, my lad," she said in a louder voice, nodded, and went on.

She was burning with fury at her new knowledge, but

she managed a curt nod to Mr. Botts. "Good morning, Mr. Botts. The children do quick neat work."

He gave a grimace for a smile, shot a suspicious look at Peter, bent to his task, and said, "What d'ya want today, my lady? I think you'd be tired of coming here so much. Don't ye like it up at your castle?"

His sneer almost broke her composure. She wanted to hit out at him. All the world knew how her husband acted, she thought.

"I am accustomed to working, Mr. Botts, as my father runs several mills. I enjoy the work, and it is a pleasure to see such fine fabrics coming from the looms. But do not let me disturb you. I am sure you have much to do. Pray return to your office."

She made her tone so firm that it was an order. He hesitated, about to snarl an impudent response, then swung about and went back to his office, where he watched from his window down at the workers.

Charlotte continued to walk along the line, back another line, then back to where the taller girl worked swiftly, her hands reaching up again and again to place the threads. She was thin to emaciation, but her round face was attractive under the mass of brown tangled hair. Her slim body was rounded at the breasts and thighs. Yes, Botts would be after her, thought Charlotte, in disgust at the ways of men.

"Pray continue your work," she said, at Margaret's side. "What is your name?"

"Margaret, mum," said the muffled voice, and there was a quick side glance, of fear and longing.

"You do quick neat work. Have you done much sewing?"

"Aye, mum." The soft voice was burred with Scottish accent. "At times I do."

"I could use a maid to help with the sewing. Will you

come up to the Castle Arundell and work with us there, Margaret?"

The girl gasped, swallowed convulsively. She cast a quick look at the small brown-haired girl just now crawling under a loom to pick up the bobbin there and hand it to her. A glance passed between her and the shy young child about five years of age.

Slowly she replied, "Oh, aye, mum, I'd like it—fine. I'd work hard."

Charlotte had no worry about that. The arms went on with their quick deft mechanical motion even though they spoke. "Good," she said. "You'll stop working now, collect your possessions, and come in the carriage with me."

Margaret leaned back, her arms dropped as though limp to her sides. "You—mean—it?"

"Yes, Margaret," she said gently. "You'll come in the carriage with me now."

Of course, Mr. Botts rushed down from the office as he saw Margaret leave her loom. "Get back to work, girl, at once," he snarled at her. She hesitated as though jolted back on her thin bare feet.

"Margaret comes with me, Mr. Botts," said Charlotte, calmly. "We have need of more maids at the castle, and she does quick good work. You know we have guests, and there is much to be done. Come, Margaret."

Gently she urged the girl to the entrance of the mill. Kenneth came up swiftly, followed by the coachman with the empty baskets strung on his massive arms.

"Ye'll not take her away! I won't have it! Ye can't come here and take my workers from me!" Mr. Botts was shaking with rage, his red face purpling, his black eyes almost disappearing in the folds of flesh.

She raised her eyebrows. "Of course I can. They all work for my husband," she said sweetly. "As you do, Mr. Botts. I hope you have not forgotten that?"

And she swept away, aware he was now a complete enemy of hers. Margaret came empty-handed to the carriage. "You have your possessions with you, child?" asked Charlotte.

"I left me blanket for—the others," said the girl, in a whisper of a voice. "I got nothing else."

The coachman lifted the child up into the carriage beside him. Kenneth helped Charlotte in, and whispered, "What are you doing, Charlotte? You cannot employ them all!"

"No, I know that," she said dully, thinking of the children left behind. Frail Peter with the heart of a lion, the dark-eyed girl under the loom, with her small, wasted features, small Jed only about five, fragile, and grimy, but with a cheeky grin for her when he knew he wouldn't get caught.

All the children, all the heart-breaking children. Their lives were often cut short there, Mrs. Potter had told her of a funeral last week for a ten-year-old. Breathing too much of the dyeing fumes into his lungs, they said. But Mrs. Potter said it was more than that—too little food, too little care, too much work. They haunted her. All the children. What could she do?

She was silent riding home. Margaret swayed with every jerk of the carriage, and could scarcely hang on. Charlotte watched the narrow thin shoulders, the drooping head.

At the back entrance of the castle, near the stables, the coachman helped Margaret down. She stood staring about, wide-eyed.

"You'll come with me, Margaret," said Charlotte, and led her to the kitchens. Mrs. Nettleton was there. She sprang to her feet from the desk where she sat, her eyes wide with amazement at seeing my lady come in the back way with the grimy child.

"Forever more," Mrs. Nettleton muttered. The cooks

glanced at her, eyebrows raised, the maids were silent in surprise.

Margaret's little hands twisted together.

"Mrs. Nettleton, this is Margaret, who has come to help us with the sewing for a time. We shall see presently if she shall be a housemaid as well. I think she learns quickly. But for now, a bath, and some fresh clothes. You have room for her with two of the other maids?"

Charlotte made it a pleasant question-order, and Mrs. Nettleton nodded, and took the child in her charge efficiently.

Mrs. Nettleton came to her in her drawing room presently, as Charlotte was trying to write a letter to her father. She wrote every two weeks, but her heart was not in it. How could she write happily, when she was not happy? How could she reassure him about her marriage, when she thought it would crack to pieces at any time?

"Sit down, Mrs. Nettleton." Charlotte turned in relief from the blank pages. "You deserve an explanation. You usually hire the maids. But this case—"

"There now, my lady, you don't need to explain yourself to me," said Mrs. Nettleton, quite gratified, her stern mouth gentling. She had told her confidantes in the village that she had never worked for such a lady, kind and considerate as she was, and so intelligent too, and such a housewife with an eye to everything.

Charlotte repeated what had happened, told her it was in confidence. "For I am sure small Peter will suffer if anything becomes known. Oh, Mrs. Nettleton, all those children—all those children—" Her voice faltered, she leaned her head on her hands.

"There now, my lady, don't take on so." Mrs. Nettleton was surprised to find herself soothing the lady of the castle. "You canna do much for them all. Botts is in control there, and sure as long as he turns out good fabrics there'll be nothing done."

"But when the winter comes——"

"We'll see to more clothes for them all. And mayhap more blankets, without causing a stir," said Mrs. Nettleton. "The food is improved, I heard from Mrs. Potter last week. He dare not withhold the food from them now, nor beat them so much, when all know you come often."

Her words echoed after she had departed. "Not beat them so much——" Oh, God, thought Charlotte, her mouth tight, her heart filled with fury against the coarse foreman with the bold hard eyes. And he was "arter Margaret" as he did all the pretty ones. He should not be allowed to remain. She must, must talk to Darcy about this. Would he not listen to her?

But she scarcely ever saw him to speak to, and never in confidence. His days were filled with entertaining their guests, especially Mrs. Holt. He seemed to think of nothing else.

She had heard grim stories of the children laboring in the mills of Manchester, of Leeds, of Glasgow. Even worse ones of the boys who worked on the docks, of the ones who worked as chimney-sweeps, forced up the chimneys if they did not go willingly, with torches at their backs. Small ones, dying of burns, of starvation, or disease, coughing their lungs out with none to care. Too many orphans, some said, just as well to use them up.

As though they were fragile flowers, to be plucked and thrown out, or weeds to be cut and thrown away. She remained with her head on her arms for a time, unable to finish the letter to her father.

Finally, wearily, she went to her room to change for the afternoon. She had missed luncheon, she could not eat, her throat felt full of unshed tears.

Noreen gave her a worried look. "The master said where was you this luncheon," she greeted her. "He was fair angry that you did not come. Miss Charlotte, you should not make me tell him stories, about how you ain't feeling well—"

Charlotte shrugged. "Then tell him the truth, that I do not like his fine guests," she said bitterly. "Oh, any dress will do! The gray one there."

Noreen compressed her lips, laid out the gray muslin with the black trim. Charlotte dressed rapidly, put on only her emerald engagement ring with the gold wedding ring, and went down to tea.

She managed to be in the drawing room, looking cool and composed, when the guests began to straggle in. The huge formal drawing room just off the Great Hall was her least favorite of the rooms now, where she had endured such agonies of spirit, jests at her expense, jeering looks from the guests of her husband.

She ordered tea, with brandy nearby for whomsoever wished it. The men usually preferred it, though they did not refuse the fine pastries on the tea tray. Charlotte managed to greet them courteously, asked how they had enjoyed the day. Lady Gwendolyn Guernsey drifted over to her, sharp eyes curious.

"You have been ill, Lady Charlotte?"

"No, merely quite busy about the house," she smiled. "May I offer you tea, my lady, or would you prefer brandy?"

"Tea, of course, I do not drink so heavily as the gentlemen," said Lady Gwendolyn sharply. "You look quite weary. Surely you're not in the family way already?"

Charlotte's delicate eyebrows raised. "Of course not," she managed to say, conscious of the entrance of Darcy with Mrs. Iris Holt on his arm.

"Of course not," repeated Lady Gwendolyn with a coarse laugh, also looking at Mrs. Holt. "I must say, I have not enjoyed a houseparty so much in years! I shall have tales for the whole winter at my dinners!"

Later Mrs. Iris Holt came over to seat herself beside

Charlotte. She was delicately beautiful this afternoon in a dress of sheer black chiffon with an underdress of gray shot silk. Her hair was piled up in wanton curls, delicately drifting to her fine neck. She put her hand to her throat, fingering the magnificent diamond pendant that swung there.

"Ah, you have been ill, Lady Charlotte? We missed you at luncheon," she murmured, accepting a cup. "What a pity your health is not good! I am sure Darcy was assured your health was the best! But you look quite gray in that gown!'

"I am quite well, only very busy," said Charlotte, wishing she dared dump a pot of tea into the woman's lap. With an effort she changed the conversation. "May I say how lovely you look? The country air seems to agree with you. And your gown is exquisite."

"Ah, do you like it? Thank you. Darcy insisted on giving it to me, on the latest trip to London," Mrs. Holt smirked. "And this diamond. Ah, he is too good to me." Her blue eyes watched Charlotte's reactions from under the long lashes. "And he has such exquisite taste! I told you before, how good his taste is, did I not?"

She was reminding Charlotte of her warning, before the girl's marriage. The hard blue eyes were unblinking, watching.

"I clearly recall everything that you said, Mrs. Holt," said Charlotte, and presently she stood up from the tea-tray, and walking over to Lady Frances, began a light conversation with her. Her hands were trembling, and she thought Mrs. Holt knew it.

Darcy watched them all, sardonically, from his stand at the mantel. It was his favorite position, as though he looked down on them all, with his foot on the fire-guard, his arm on the mantel, a glass of brandy at his elbow in the gleaming bulbous glass.

How could she go to him and talk about the children

of the mills? He would care nothing about it, she thought bitterly. He cared little enough about his own child, who remained in the nursery rather than come to see his guests. Pamela had shut herself in day after day, refusing to come, weeping when Charlotte pleaded with her. "I do not like them," she said stubbornly. "I cannot like them. Do not make me come!"

Charlotte left her then, conscious that she herself did not want to come. She detested them all, especially one of them. But she must appear—and be gracious. Kenneth often had his tea with Neville, and Neville did not choose to come down, after his initial acquaintance with the house guests. She thought bitterly how different it was from her own home, where guests were so much more congenial and intelligent, where the talk was not malicious gossip, where she felt warmed and loved and comfortable.

She was mistress of this house, but not mistress of my lord, she thought. And that made all the difference. It was not a home, it was a place of residence, a castle, with little warmth and no love in it. The very marriage she had dreaded.

Chapter 15

August turned abruptly to September, and the nights were cool. Winds blew across the valley, hemmed in on both sides by the steep hills, and the rains gusted day and night. The guests grew impatient as they were confined to the house for many hours.

Darcy seemed to make up his mind. He came to Charlotte one afternoon, a dark, gray day, as she sat in her own private drawing room making up menus, writing letters, her desk cluttered with papers.

"I shall take them back to London," he said abruptly, with scarcely a greeting. "I have business in Paris, they shall accompany me back to London. I think you will be glad to be peaceful for a time."

"You—go to Paris?" she said, slowly, blankly, laying down the quill.

"Yes, on business," he said. But she thought, he will mix business and pleasure, and take Mrs. Holt with him. The thought stung bitterly. Her father had promised her a visit to Paris one day, but had not taken her. Now Darcy went—without her. Ah, well, she did not wish to be dragged along with him, he would be reluctant to be in her company, she would be conscious of his coldness under the politeness. She swallowed angry words, avoiding his bright blue gaze.

His long slim brown fingers picked up a jade figurine which stood on her desk, he caressed it briefly. She looked at his fingers, at the slow sensuous way he held it. He had touched her like that—

"My guests grow impatient as the rainy days hem them in. It will be as well for them to be in London for a time," he said, and set down the figurine.

She thought of the long days without him. But at least she would not see him with Mrs. Holt, she would only know they were together. Then she thought of something else.

"There is something I would discuss with you before you go," she said quickly.

He turned as he was about to leave. "Yes?" he asked sharply. "What is it?"

His face seemed brighter, more warm, as he waited for her question.

"It is—about the mills," she said. "I have been there several times, and I wish to consult you about—"

He stared at her. "The *mills*? Good God, as though I cared!" and he slammed the door of his study after him.

Her knees felt weak. She put both hands to her face. He did not care about them—or her—or Pamela. He had said nothing more about the child, nor about a governess for her. Nothing personal. They were strangers to each other.

Darcy and the guests departed two days later, with much laughter and chaffing among them. Charlotte went down politely at noon to see them off, they were late as always. Mrs. Holt wished to shake her hand, Charlotte managed to turn to another woman and was able to act as though she did not see the hand. Mrs. Holt laughed, an amused tinkle of sarcasm, and swept out to the carriage.

The castle seemed empty without them. Neville came down to dinner, Kenneth frankly spoke of his relief. "What a crowd! I am surprised at Lord Arundell for caring for that sort," he said, in disgust. "I am sure your father did not know of it."

"I am sure that he did," said Charlotte, and turned the conversation. Darcy had not even said when he might return. Evidently he did not care to be questioned about his movements.

To occupy herself, and because it had been much on her mind, Charlotte went daily to the mills. Mr. Botts forgot himself so much as to snarl at her. One day, returning with Mrs. Nettleton, Charlotte said, "I must do something against the winter. The children will freeze there in that shed. What can I do?"

"Lord knows, my lady," murmured Mrs. Nettleton, looking anxiously at her. Charlotte had grown thin and pale since coming here, and all was not well between her and Lord Arundell, everyone knew that.

"If I could close the mills, I would," said Charlotte savagely. "The way he persecutes them—not just the children, but the adults as well! I wonder that anyone works for him!"

"Ah, well, they must make their living," said Mrs. Nettleton. "There be little enough work about. All the valley depends on the wool and the weaving. Whatever would they do when that is taken away?"

Charlotte bit her knuckles. "If there was somewhere to place the children, somewhere comfortable— There is not even an orphanage about—a large house—"

They sat in silence, riding along. She was blind to the gold of the birches, the brazen colors of the maples, the soft brown of the oaks. She passed the flowers without a glance at their flamboyant crimsons and golds and yellows.

"Lord Arundell has a town house," said Mrs. Nettleton suddenly. "He lived in it once, while the early Lord Arundell occupied this. My lord's mother did not care for him—they all lived in the town house. Then my lord's mother died, and his relative brought him to the castle. But the town house is empty. It sits idle in the park— rather near the church, you must have passed it Sundays."

Charlotte turned about in the carriage to stare at her good helper. "A town house? Oh, where—" But even as she spoke she thought of a vast empty house she had noted, on the edge of town, where weeds and grasses grew thick and tall on what had once been a pretty park land. The house was a gray and red brick building, of some three stories, with the empty look of blank windows.

"Sure, ye've seen it, my lady. Three stories and vast cellars to it, and a park about it. Would it not do for an orphanage for a time?"

Charlotte caught the woman's hands and squeezed them impulsively. "The very thing!" She called up to the coachman— "Turn about, turn about, back to town! I would see my lord's town house."

"Aye, my lady." The coachman was growing accustomed to her quick commands and whims now, and indeed it amused and entertained him vastly. Always about some good works, he told his fellows, proud that she trusted him to drive her about.

The town house was locked, but Mrs. Nettleton knew where the keys could be found. They walked about the house, peering into the huge windows, and planning excitedly. It was indeed large, and could be made into a very pleasant orphanage, with rooms for the children on the second and third floors, and a dining room, a lounge for them, and kitchens on the ground floor. "And they would be warm this winter," sighed Charlotte. "How far is it to the mills?"

"About the best part of a mile," said the coachman.

"They could walk it, my lady, if they had but shoes to their feet."

"They shall have, and shorter hours also," she vowed.

The next day she went to the mills, her plans made. Mrs. Nettleton had been dispatched with a small army of cleaners to the house. Charlotte would come later. She and Kenneth and the coachman proceeded to the mills, to inform Mr. Botts of her plans.

She entered the mill, and at once Mr. Botts came down.

"Here again, my lady? I heard his lordship had gone to London," he sneered, with a mocking grin. "Gone with his light o' love, he has, and you got nothing better to do than come and bother me, huh?"

"Mr. Botts, you forget yourself," she said frigidly. "I came to inform you that I mean to set up an orphanage for the children. They shall be placed there as soon as the house is made ready."

He gaped at her, showing tobacco-stained teeth. "Huh— you never—listen, that shed is good enough for them! His lordship will be right furious—"

"I am responsible for this!" she snapped. "There is no medical center here, no good women looking after the children. Since you will not pay out enough for that, they shall have an orphanage, a home to live in. And you shall not stop me, Mr. Botts!"

"Oh, no?" he raved. "Oh, no, my fine lady? Oh, no? Botts will stop ye, all right. He'll report to my lord, about how you eats into the profits, and makes trouble, and takes away my good workers, and ye'll be the one being stopped, my fine lady!"

Kenneth stepped forward to rebuke him. Charlotte held him back with a gesture.

"No, this is my doing. Mr. Botts, I discharge you. You are not working for these mills again, nor for anything I know about. You shall not remain here past this hour! Go at once, and do not return!" Her face was white as a lily, her hair flamed red under her green bonnet.

He glared at her. "You'll be sorry! My lord will hire me right back, see if he don't! You'll be sorry! He trusts me, he do, and I turn a right good profit for him!"

"Do you, Mr. Botts?" She managed to mock him coldly, though she burned with fury. "Or do you turn a profit, right into your own pockets? I have looked at the books, you see, and I am more intelligent about such matters than you seem to realize! When my lord hears how you have cheated him for years, and kept the money, he will not even give you a character! You will leave at once!"

He snarled in fury, but his eyes were frightened. He muttered something, some impudence, and the coachman growled at him. Then he turned and stalked away.

Charlotte told the coachman to follow him, and make sure he left without taking any gold with him. She went up to the office and took charge of the books of the past two years, and she and Kenneth carried them to the carriage and home again.

Once in her drawing room, with the dusty ledgers strewn over her neat tables, Kenneth said quietly, "Are you sure you are doing the right thing, Charlotte? Lord Arundell could be furious with you, if the man does turn a profit, as he says."

"If he cares so much for money, he should examine the books," retorted Charlotte with fire. "I can prove the man has cheated him for two years, and more. And he pays the children nothing, nothing! Darcy believes there are good women overseeing the children, that they sleep in cots in rooms. He will see for himself what has happened!"

"Will he care?" asked Kenneth, and left her on the question.

Charlotte went to wash her hands, and then to consult with Mrs. Nettleton. The good woman was keen to see her, and report happily on the opening of the town house.

Charlotte went with her the next day, and found the rooms large and imposing, empty of furniture, but in good condition, with little rot or mold, though much dust.

The army of workers cleaned up swiftly, and they roused much interest in the village. Mrs. Potter, Mrs. Crotchett, and Miss Dorcas were eager to come and approve and advise. They knew several females of good character who would come and work there, to do the cooking and supervising and laundry. They knew where Charlotte could purchase a number of small beds for the children, long wooden tables for the dining room, kitchen equipment, some chairs and tables and sofas for the lounge.

No sooner were the beds delivered than she had the children moved into the house. Sheets could wait, they had blankets over them, and comfortable warm rooms. The children wandered about, dazed, unable to believe they were in a house.

"I ain't been inside a house since I were a baby," said Peter hoarsely, and began to cough.

Small Susie looked in wonder at the little bed. "Mine? To sleep on?" she whispered. She was the brown-haired child who had crept under Margaret's loom. Charlotte was beginning to learn their names.

"Yes, darling, it is for you," she reassured the girl. Jed did not speak, he gave her his cheeky grin, bemused with wonder, and patted the end of his bed.

The women came, were brisk and quick and adaptable. They took the children under their wings at once. But they needed direction, confused by their new duties.

Mrs. Nettleton could come sometimes, but not all the time. And her work at the castle was suffering. "I must get someone to direct the orphanage," mused Charlotte to her brother Neville.

"You should get someone like your Miss Morris," he suggested. They all took an interest in the work, Neville had painfully climbed into a carriage to visit the project already. "She was a corker. Quiet voice, but one jumped when she spoke."

"Miss Morris? But she is working in a school for females—yet she might come—"

Charlotte thought of her good governess, the dear soul who still guided and directed her through letters. She sat down that night to write to her.

"Oh, my dear Miss Morris, if you could but see the children, how your good heart would ache! They need guidance and love, direction and help. I shall see to it that their hours are shorter, and they shall have lessons in the evening from you, if you will but come— Do let me know, I enclose a direction of money for you to use— pray do help me—"

In return post, she received an eager response. Miss Morris was too discreet to say so in so many words, but her post was ill-paid, and she had too many students to give guidance as she would have wished. Her employer was sharp, she worked long hours, had no room to herself. She would be delighted to come, and would hasten to pack and reserve a place on the next stage—

While they waited for her, Charlotte happily continued the work in the orphanage. At the mills, the clerks seemed able to continue their work. She went often enough to answer questions about which woolens should be made up first, whether to buy such and such wools, what to order ahead. But she was too busy, she could not go on like this. She must hire a new foreman, soon, but whom? Should she wait for Darcy to return? She had no word from him, none at all.

Sometimes at night she was too weary to sleep. Her bones ached, and she would toss and turn. She would think, inevitably, of her husband in Paris, the city of light and beauty, walking on the broad avenues with his mistress. Mrs. Holt on his arm, visiting the bright theaters, the gay restaurants, the night places— And staying with him, perhaps, in some discreet and luxurious hotel—together with him—

She pressed her hand to her dry eyes. She could not cry, she held it back, bottling it all up, ashamed of her emotions. He did not deserve to be loved. But she did love him—and hate him also—for what he had done to her. She wanted him to come to her, to be tender and gentle, to say he had some fondness for her. For why else had he married her? She had thought at first that he might have some liking for her as well as desire.

Probably she had soured all that by her defiance of him. He must like the easy conquest, the feminine woman with her flattering ways. She pressed her hand to her mouth, to keep back a cry.

"Oh, Darcy, Darcy, how could you? Bringing her to our home!" Only, it was not a home. It was a vast castle, which must be taken care of. He had needed a housekeeper, and someone to make a presence—and perhaps to have an heir— And she had fit into the picture, so he had married her. But he still longed for the lovely, frivolous, diamond-hard Mrs. Holt.

She continued to go to the town house, where the lawns had been mowed and made lovely again; the children sometimes sat on the grass, in wonder pressing their fingers to the ground, or touching the flowers timidly, in amazement at such color and fragrance. They made one's heart ache, sitting on the edges of chairs as though afraid they might harm them.

They were neat now, and dressed nicely in cottons and woolens. Some had had shoes fitted, and all would have shoes by late autumn, the shoemaker had promised. Curtains hung at the once bare windows, and the eyes of the children were brighter, as though they too had been empty inside, and now were beginning to be filled with hope.

Charlotte had shortened their working time. The adults still worked from seven until seven in the evening. But the children went in at nine, after a good breakfast, and remained only until six. They worked better, she thought, and their cheeks were filling out already. It would be a long time, though, before they were sturdy again, and Peter's cough would disappear. He still bossed the others about, importantly, a lion among them, urging them to do as he said. Charlotte smiled at him, he would make a foreman one day, she thought.

She was returning to her carriage that September day, the children following her shyly, into the autumn evening, when the smart carriage drew up. She looked up at the high-perch phaeton vaguely, at the smart black horses—into the face of the man in the gorgeous crimson suit with the smart black hat.

"Fitz— Good heavens—Rockingham!" she gasped.

He tied the horses, jumped down, took her hands, smiled into her eyes. "My dearest Charlotte, whatever in the world are you doing?" He nodded at the children following her. "Even you could not have produced so many in such a short time!" At his look of mock horror she had to giggle, gaily flinging back her red head, then laughing out loud as she had not for so long.

"Oh, dear—whatever are you doing here?" she managed to ask and draw her hands from his. Mrs. Nettleton was looking on disapprovingly, warily.

"I came to see you, my dearest," he said gaily. "I hope you will invite me to remain for a long time! I have been so dull without you! And I must inquire about your dear brother."

For the anxiety in his eyes, she forgave him. "Neville does quite well, you shall see him this evening for yourself."

"Good. And I may stay—"

She hesitated. She wanted to be gracious, but she did not yet fully trust Rockingham. She remembered that terrible race. And if Darcy should return and find Rockingham installed there—oh, no, she could not have that.

"I am sorry. Darcy is from home, I cannot invite you," she said frankly. "You may come for dinner this evening, indeed, do follow us along the road. But I cannot have you stay at Arundell. Darcy would be furious."

"Indeed? I have heard much about his houseparty, and some people your father would not have allowed house room," said Rockingham. Mrs. Nettleton drew in a quick breath.

Charlotte stiffened. "That is not your concern, my lord," she said coldly. "You may come to dinner, but you will not stay. Take that, or nothing."

"I shall take it, it is better than nothing." Rockingham laughed a little, but his handsome blue eyes flashed in the evening light. "I shall put up at the town inn and suffer it, gladly, my dear, for the chance to see you again."

And so he did, putting up at the inn, telling gaily and pointedly in her company of the many inconveniences he suffered—and coming over daily. Mrs. Nettleton sniffed at this, and Kenneth warned Charlotte that Rockingham's presence in the village would have Darcy Saltash furious.

But Charlotte turned stubborn. Rockingham amused her, he made her laugh and forget her troubles. And she had not suffered through Darcy's houseparty without wishing for a little revenge of her own. It suited her for him to remain, she said.

Neville sighed, and wrote to his father. Charlotte was a hand at the best of times, and he thought only his father could manage her. Darcy certainly could not, thought her brother, and told his father his wound still troubled him, and he could not return home—especially since Fitz

Rockingham was here now, and coming around Charlotte like a bee after honey.

He franked the letter with Darcy's frank, thinking with a smile that his brother-in-law should thank him for it!

Chapter 16

Charlotte took Rockingham with her on tours to the mills and the orphanage. If he was bored, he concealed it with his good manners, and managed to suggest improvements both to the factories and to the home. She took some of his ideas gratefully.

Kenneth accompanied them every day, sometimes silently, but determined to be with them, that there might be no scandal. Neville went sometimes, but though he improved steadily, he was not yet strong. Rockingham had gracefully apologized to him and to Charlotte, yet again, for the "asinine thing he had done to hurt them both," as he said.

He did seem truly sorry, and in the evenings he did not drink so much, and made them all gay with his wit and amused comments on society, bringing them up to date with his gossip. He was thirty, older than any of them, had been about for longer, and spoiled all his days, for his wealth and handsome looks. Truly, thought Charlotte, he did amazingly well for someone who had since childhood been nurtured with the idea that he was a favorite of the gods.

He had a fortune in his own right, and on the death of his "much-esteemed father," as he put it wryly, he would inherit more titles and estates. Though accustomed to flattery, he seemed to enjoy Charlotte's teasing, and Kenneth's grave conversations. Neville seemed more reserved with him, watching him warily.

He did make a remark about Darcy's absence, as one week stretched into another. "If I were married to such as you, my dearest, fairest lady," he said one morning in the garden, as she directed the gardener to the flowers she wished picked, "I should not leave you one day out of the year. You are not only beautiful, you have wit and intelligence and humor, all gifts not to be despised."

"I thank you," she smiled, over her hurt. "But he has much business here and about."

"What business in Paris?" asked Fitz. She frowned at him. "Very well, I am indiscreet. But I dread seeing you fall into the way of your—predecessor, the lovely Lucille."

She could not resist. "You knew—the first Lady Arundell?"

"Quite well. I squired her about London, as Mrs. Holt hung onto Darcy Saltash," he shrugged. "Mrs. Holt ever pretended to be a friend of Lucille, but such friends are worse than enemies."

He seemed unusually grave for him, frowning over the late roses. But the next instant he was teasing her to place a red rose in his hand, with her own fair hand, and she was laughing at him.

She did not forget his words, however. They caused her many a pang at night, as she tossed without sleeping. If only she could have persuaded her father to listen to her! Or listen to Fitz Rockingham, who had known the truth of the matter! He would not have insisted on her marrying Darcy Saltash, no matter how good the man's appearance. And she would not be turning about now, her fist to her mouth, longing unwillingly for a man she could only detest even while she desired him.

She loved—and hated herself for doing so. It was only desire, she told herself. But how she longed for the sight of his face, a quick flash of his vivid blue eyes, the rare laughter in him—a relationship which could mean nothing but humiliation for her.

Miss Gertrude Morris arrived on the stage within two weeks. Charlotte met her at the village inn, carriage ready, and impulsively clasped the slim tall woman in her arms and kissed both her cheeks.

Under the old-fashioned black bonnet, the gentle face glowed with pleasure at her welcome. Within the frame of light brown hair, her brown eyes were wistful as she peered in her near-sighted way at Charlotte's face.

"Oh, my dear Miss Charlotte! My Lady Charlotte, Lady Arundell," she corrected herself hastily. "How delightful to see your beautiful face again. What a charming village! I am all eagerness to hear everything!"

"And my dear Miss Morris shall hear everything!" laughed Charlotte, blinking back tears of delight. She had thought never to see her beloved governess again. She escorted her to the carriage. "This first week you shall be at the castle and rest before you take up your duties. Oh, I have so much to tell you!"

And she chatted eagerly, holding the slim hand in the worn black mitt all the way back to Arundell, telling her eagerly about the children, about the mills, the abominable conditions and the foreman, about the town house turned into an orphanage.

Miss Morris gazed at her thoughtfully, noting the thinness of the cheeks, the sadness of the green eyes. Something had happened to her charge, and she had a new reserve and dignity.

But, tactfully, she said nothing, only watched as Char-

lotte introduced her to Fitzhugh Rockingham, to Mrs.
Nettleton, to the others of the staff, talked to her of plans.
She contributed ideas intelligently, suggested books to be
bought, and visited the new orphanage the very next
day.

My lord Arundell was from home, and had been there
only with a houseparty that summer, she learned, and
the governess shook her head in the privacy of her pretty
guest room. Her beloved former charge was unhappy. It
did not take much to put two and two together.

Miss Morris had hoped so much that her charge's marriage would be a happy one, with respect and loving affec-
tion on both sides. It seemed it was not to be.

She flung herself with her whole heart into the work
of the orphanage, which she could see was Charlotte's
main concern. Charlotte arranged for regular delivery
of food from the village and from the castle. More cooks
and maids were hired, the children were fitted for more
clothing.

Now the children seemed much brighter, and they
chattered like little birds when they were free from work,
their high voices rising on the autumn air as they ran
about the park.

Miss Morris comprehended the situation readily, and
began to take charge in her gentle but efficient manner,
and soon they all came willingly to her for orders, reliev-
ing Charlotte of the day-to-day chores of the orphanage.

So she turned her attention to the mills. This troubled
her. She had dismissed the foreman, and they must have
one soon. She had inquired about, but none was suitable
to be hired there. No one had been trained to take his
place. The clerks could handle some of the work, but
the over-all direction must be by one who knew what he
did, who could see the markets abroad as well as at home,
decide on what tweeds should be made, how many bolts
of cloth produced, and in what patterns.

There was but one man to whom she could turn for advice, Fergus Gordon. So finally in one of her letters, she put it to him frankly.

"Dearest papa, I am deeply troubled by the mill situation. I wrote to you that I had dismissed the foreman, Mr. Botts, for insolence, for cheating on the books, and most of all for his cruel and callous treatment of the children.

"I have endeavored to correct the situation as much as I can. However, this requires more direction than I can contemplate. It also requires much time. I realize you are extremely busy with your own work. However, if you should know of a good man in the wool trade who might be available, I would be most grateful to you for sending him to me, for possible employment. I am at my wit's end as to how to deal with this, dearest papa.

"Neville is improving, but slowly. Rockingham has remained with us, and continues to divert us. You would be amused to hear the arguments he and Kenneth will make on a topic! And we play cards until eleven at times, for he will challenge us and you know how expert Neville is in this. Sometimes Mrs. Crotchett and her good husband come to us at dinner, and Miss Dorcas Crotchett is a match for any man at wit and repartee.

"Father, if you should be willing to come here and discuss the situation at the mills with me, I would be so very grateful. Arundell remains from home, having much business abroad."

She paused, bit the end of the quill pen absently. She would say no more of it. She signed it, "Your affectionate daughter, Charlotte."

Fergus Gordon received the letter in good time, sat down and read it ponderingly through a second and a third time. He was a shrewd man, he had not risen up from mill boy to mill owner by luck. And he knew his daughter well. He read between the lines, and he did not like what he read.

His affairs were in order, his foremen were too afraid of him to go behind his back and countermand his decisions. He packed his luggage and two trunks, ordered his coachman and valet about in a great hurry, and was on the road the next morning, bound for Arundell. He arrived, with no word before him, to find Charlotte in the garden with the gardeners—and Rockingham.

He paced out to the gardens, waving the butler away pleasantly enough. "No, no, I shall surprise my daughter," he said.

He came upon the scene and surveyed it under dark reddish eyebrows. His snapping green eyes gazed steadily as Charlotte laughingly gave a rose to the tall, handsome, foppishly dressed man beside her, the blond head devotedly bent to her hand, the kiss pressed on her fingers.

"Charlotte, what's this? No welcome for your poor papa, come these many miles?" he roared.

Charlotte whirled about, her green skirts flying, and raced to him, dropping the basket of flowers before her. "Papa!" she cried, and flung herself impetuously at him, as though a schoolgirl again. He received the attack tolerantly, beaming as she pressed a kiss on his tanned cheek.

He held her off then and studied her, shocked at what he saw. His girl had always been slim, vibrant with life. Now he saw a pale cheek, thin taut jawline, her waist so tiny it might break in two, a pink mouth that trembled as she tried to smile at him. God, what had that Arundell done to her? All in a few months, thought Fergus in a hidden rage.

"Well, me dear, glad to see me?" he asked, inadequately, inwardly wondering what he could do. He resolved instantly to remain until Arundell came home from his wanderings and then give him a sharp tongue-lashing he would not soon forget. No man could treat his daughter like this!

Fitzhugh Rockingham came up warily. Fergus looked at him with some dislike. This was the man who had done dirt to his daughter in that race in London, making her name a scandal for three days. He bowed to the man, who bowed back gracefully. Too handsome by half—he distrusted a man that handsome.

Charlotte left the gardener to attend to the flowers, and accompanied her father indoors. A suite was ordered for him, his valet dispatched to attend to the boxes and trunks and cases he had brought with him, Mrs. Nettleton brought in and introduced. Fergus Gordon liked her on sight, a nice sensible woman, who knew when a man was hungry, for she had already ordered a good luncheon to be served at once.

Neville hobbled down the steps, helped by Kenneth. Fergus held out his arms, made speechless for once by the sight of his only son limping. Neville permitted himself to be clasped, beamed at his father, wrung his hand again and again.

"Well, father, you came to see your poor injured son," he said chokingly.

Fergus clapped him on the back gently. "Had to, had to, what have you been about? Always into mischief, the two of you, had to come to see for myself," he boomed. He looked about the Great Hall, three stories high, hung with worn battle flags. "Good God, do you stand here long? My voice echoes as it does in Westminster Abbey!"

Charlotte hurried them into the formal drawing room, exchanging news with them, laughing aloud, but not getting much pink into her thin cheeks, thought her father, resolving to get his son alone before long and pry out the whole story.

But when he did get Neville alone, the boy was surprisingly reserved. He talked frankly of the duel, blaming himself as much as Rockingham. "Indeed, he has been a good friend to us these days, making Lotta laugh for the first in a long time."

Fergus gazed at him from under his thick red brows. "And why does Charlotte not laugh these days?" he barked.

"Marriage does not especially suit her, I suppose," said Neville at last. "I don't think it suits many females. And Lotta was always independent. It galls me when Darcy orders her about. She has taken on well here, though, I must say. The meals are always the best, and she entertains well—" He paused, frowned heavily.

"That houseparty?" asked Fergus casually, putting his feet up on a stool with a sigh of gratitude. Riding long was hard on his legs now he had gotten more stout.

"Yes, and—well—that Mrs. Holt came, you know. She's a hard piece. Don't see what Darcy sees in her, with Lotta about. Can't figure the man. Decent in many things, then inviting that—well, I am his guest, shouldn't say much." Neville concluded his piece unhappily.

"Um, yes," but he had said enough to set his smart father thinking. "I think I'll stay around a while. Charlotte wants my advice on the mills," he changed the subject abruptly. "You been there?"

"Yes, and they are a disgrace. Can't think why Darcy don't do something, except he is always busy about something else." Neville proceeded to enlighten his father on how the mills had appeared before Charlotte had begun to change them. "Still they look terrible, all the grease left to lie about, and dirt on the floors. Your mills were never like that, father. You kept a clean place, and happy workers. Been an eye-opener for me, for Kenneth also."

Fergus listened, keenly, hearing more than his son said. His heart swelled with pride. He hadn't done so badly, bringing up his son and daughter. Neville showed more than an interest in the mills, he showed more shrewd judgment and canny ability than his father had thought he possessed. Might make a business man yet, if he didn't become a marquis. Fergus had thought to buy him some title, through a skillful marriage and some maneuvering. But perhaps the lad was meant more for business. Might be a fine thing, that, to have his mills to leave to the lad, if he showed signs of being able to manage them.

Early the next morning, he and Neville and Charlotte went to the mills. Fergus paced back and forth, thoughtfully, observed the operations, then went up to the offices, and began going over the books. He made some remarks, thought about the matter, and scratched away at some papers in the evening, absently, not joining in the conversation. Charlotte observed him gratefully, happy to leave some decisions to him.

He went back again and again with her, and advised her to stop making one tweed which had proved unpopular, told her of another pattern to try, using a new attractive dye of a sienna color with a pale orange and a white stripe. She put them to work on it at once. He started going over the books.

"Truly, papa, I did not mean for you to do the work," she protested, openly relieved that he was. "I thought you might recommend a foreman."

"Oh, aye, we'll look about for a foreman, and recommend him to Arundell. Meantime, the work must go on," said Fergus. He enjoyed nothing so much as pulling up a slack operation sharply and getting it to show a good profit again. Secretly, he would have been happy to buy the whole works and take it over. He would show them a thing or three, he thought.

But it did show a profit, and Arundell would probably not sell out, especially since these were his people in the villages and the houses on the hills thereabouts. So Fergus happily pulled at the slack, went daily to the mills with his daughter, rode with her in the mornings.

She was getting a better color in her cheeks, he was thankful to see. They rode together daily, and talked operations at the mills, and he commended her on the way the orphanage worked out. And he easily nudged Rockingham from her side by the simple expedient of being there constantly himself.

Rockingham looked sullen at times, but he lived at the inn, he could not complain that his hostess deserted him, for she was not his hostess. He did come daily, and if Charlotte was not there, which she seldom was in the daytime, he applied himself to the amusement of Neville in cards, gossip, even reading some of the fine books in Darcy's library.

Mrs. Nettleton was relieved that Mr. Gordon had come. He seemed a sensible man, smarter than one gave him credit for at first. Sure, as the butler said, such a man had pulled himself up by his bootstraps, he was the true father of his daughter, and he was bound to be clever. Now if only my lord Arundell would come home and in a better mood than when he left, it should all be well again.

So the household ran along, waiting and watching, and the village also. They all admired Charlotte for her courage and her gentle ways with them. Mayhap if my lord should come to admire her also, their ways might be easier and their paths smoother than in the difficult past. And if she should give Lord Arundell a son, they would all be most happy.

Pamela was happier also. Her beloved new mama seemed brighter and her smile came more often. She had time for Pamela now, and Mr. Gordon was not so fierce as he looked at first. She had become accustomed to sitting at his feet on a little stool while he talked to her, even patting her on the head.

Chapter 17

It was early October, a heavy gusty rain blew across the hills and a driving wind banged at the windows when Darcy Saltash returned. Their first knowledge of his arrival came as he stamped into the hall, and the butler and footmen fluttered about him.

Charlotte came from the blue drawing room and stared. He looked at her across the Great Hall, dark and wet in his greatcoat, slapping his top hat against his legs, his boots muddy, the rain dripping from him onto the great stone slabs. She gasped, her hand to her throat. "Darcy— my lord—" she managed to say.

Then behind him she saw the two ladies coming in, complaining about the wetness. She looked beyond Darcy, saw Mrs. Iris Holt looking more delicate than usual in her black velvet cloak and soft new black bonnet with the narrow brim. She was accompanied by Lady Frances Barkley, and behind them came red-faced Lord William Barkley, grumbling about the weather and the slowness of the horses.

Her heart went down to her green slippers. She had to contrive a smile, and moved forward reluctantly to

greet them. It was to be the summer over again, and how
could she endure it?

Darcy was scowling at her, Mrs. Holt had her usual
mocking look. Charlotte did not bother to hold out her
hand. She curtsied, formally, to them all, then turned to
the butler.

"Pray, send word to Mrs. Nettleton to have the front
green room aired at once for the Barkleys, and the rose
room for Mrs. Holt. Send Molly up to attend Mrs. Holt,
and Frederick and Joan to attend the Barkleys."

She turned back to Darcy. "You have dined, my lord?"
she asked politely.

"Not since four o'clock, my lady," he drawled, in his
cynical way. "Can you spare a light collation for poor
travelers?"

"Indeed, my lord." She hesitated. "Pray go into the
drawing room, I shall attend at once to your wants. You
will know the company, I think." She smiled, as mockingly
as he, as he raised his eyebrows and went past her to
the drawing room.

She left to speak to Mrs. Nettleton. The good woman
went into a flutter, then composed herself to arrange for
a hot meal to be ready within half an hour. The others
had dined at eight, it was now past ten o'clock.

Then she returned to the drawing room, to find Darcy
in his accustomed stance at the mantel, leaning his elbow
on it, speaking to Fergus Gordon. Neville and Kenneth
had deserted their game of cards and were leaning back
to observe the new guests. Lady Frances was complaining of her weariness, Lord Barkley complained of the
miserable roads from London. "And Lord Arundell
would insist on returning tonight, we could have spent
another night in an inn, there are most comfortable ones
on the way."

Rockingham had left earlier in the afternoon, as the
weather had turned foul. She was grateful for that. Darcy

looked weary and exasperated enough. When he learned that Fitz Rockingham was here—

The guests were all weary. She attended them to their dinner in half an hour, saw to wine for them, went up to their rooms to make sure fires had been lighted and the beds aired. They were glad enough to retire for the night.

She was aware that night of the movements in the room across from her own. Noreen had commented on it. "Now my lord is home again, and you need not work so, my lady!"

"Do not count on it, he brought his guests," said Charlotte, her mouth wry. She felt shockingly disappointed. She had thought he might have enough of Mrs. Holt on their Paris journey, which must have lasted a month. Now he had returned with her.

She did not sleep much that night either, and wakened with the instant knowledge that their peaceful days of companionship, her father and brother and cousin, were over for a time. Mrs. Holt and the Barkleys brought the cynicism and wicked wit of London with them, and their critical gaze would follow her everywhere.

She could not sleep; she rose early, putting on her green riding habit. She would ride, even though it rained. She needed to get out, to gallop for miles.

Fortunately, Fergus Gordon was of the same mind. They met at the stables, and Hobbs saddled Black Satin at once for her. They were off in good time, with Hobbs following on his nag. They galloped in silence, then Fergus motioned for them to pull up so they could speak. A watery sun was beginning to come through the dark clouds, and the rain had ceased. Drops clustered on the dying leaves and dripped down on their heads along the paths, and the scarlet and yellow of the leaves crumpled under the hooves of the horses.

"Nice view from here," said Fergus, and they paused and gazed out over the Cotswold valley. Late roses still clambered over the walls of golden cottages, the thatched roofs looked wet and darker brown. A peaceful view after the wind and rain of the night.

If only her heart could find such peace.

"I'll be talking to Arundell today about the mills," said Fergus abruptly with a side glance at his daughter.

"If he has time to listen, papa," she said, with more than a touch of bitterness.

"Um-humph," said Fergus, and motioned for them to ride on. He misliked the deeper shadows under Charlotte's eyes. She did not have the cosseted look of a woman who had been the recipient of a night of caresses. She looked brittle, as though she might snap at a touch. Drat the man, anyway. He had thought Darcy knew how to handle a woman. Bringing that—that flibberty Mrs. Holt back with him! Infamous!

It was too late to cry off the wedding. The question was, could there be aught to mend, or was the fabric of the marriage torn beyond repair?

They returned in silence, but both felt better for the hard ride, and the quiet communion between them. Charlotte was glad of her father's company. He would see the situation now, the hopelessness of it. She longed to say, "I told you so, this is how it would be," but it would only have hurt him. She did love her father dearly, and she knew he was hurt already.

She was conscious that day of her father watching, keenly, every move she made, and Darcy, and Mrs. Holt. It was Fergus who brought up the topic at luncheon, breaking deliberately into the frivolous conversation of the Barkleys.

"You should see what Charlotte has been doing at the mills, Arundell," he said, attacking a slice of roast beef as though he longed for his knife to be elsewhere. He shot his son-in-law a fierce look. "Working like a dozen foremen, she has. Have ye seen the orphanage yet?

Fine piece, that. Miss Morris has come to tend the orphans, and get them some learning too."

Darcy gazed at Charlotte, at the other end of the long table. "You have been about some good works, my dear?" he said, as though he mocked. Mrs. Holt tittered.

"The children were in rags, with no shoes," she said, suppressing some rage. "They slept in an open shed. Winter was coming, and I thought something must be done about it. I learned of your town house and had it opened for them. I hope to show it to you before long."

He frowned slightly. "I am sure a word to the foreman, Albert Botts, would have tended to all this," he said, rather impatiently. "There was no need for you—"

"There was every need." Her voice rose, and Neville glanced worriedly from Charlotte to Darcy and back again. "The children were being abused and mistreated. There was no center for medical attention, no women to look after them, no place sheltered from storms for them to rest. Indeed, it depended on Mr. Botts's whims, as to whether they ate at all. The situation could not wait upon your return, my lord."

There was silence at the long table. The others seemed fascinated, or too wise to interrupt them.

"Indeed," he said, and laid down his fork with deliberation. "What has Botts to say for himself?"

"I will tell you of this later, my lord," she said, with more composure and turned the conversation. After luncheon, he drew her into his study.

"Now, I will hear of the whole matter," he said, more gravely, and seated her beside his desk. He took the chair opposite her. "What of the children? What have you done?"

"I—I have dismissed Mr. Botts," she told him quietly, her fingers twisting together nervously. "He was insolent, refused to listen to my instructions for the children. Indeed, I examined two years of the ledgers, and found he has pocketed much of the profits from the mills."

She continued her story, her cheeks flushing with her passion over the ill treatment of the children. She told of opening the town house for them, how the women of the village had helped. She told of dismissing Botts, of his threats to the children, how he lingered about the village, and she had heard he was threatening her. She spoke of her letter to her father.

"I did not know how to continue the direction of the mills, and had had no word from you as to your return," she went on, rather nervous under his silent intent regard. "I begged him for advice, as I knew he had much knowledge of mill operations. He came at once and takes great interest. I will show you, or my father will, what he has instructed to be done. He has not yet found a foreman to present to you for hiring. It may be you know of some good man who knows the work."

She finally halted, twisting her ring around and around her finger, that great emerald she wore day and night beside her wedding ring.

"You have done—amazingly, Charlotte," he said, finally, gravely. "I did not know you would be so concerned for the mills, for the children. I must speak to your father, and find his conclusions. Is there aught else I should know about, before I speak to Botts?"

She hesitated, then decided on frankness. "I have hired two workers away from him. You should know of this, for he will accuse me of it. I found him beating young Edgar, and took him away, and hired him for our stables. He is fond of the horses, and works eagerly, my man Hobbs tells me. And then there is Margaret—"

"Yes?"

"She was—is—an attractive girl of about fourteen. One of the boys at the mills told me that Botts was 'arter her' and she did not want Botts's child. I was stunned at this, and managed to take her away with me that day. She is employed here as a maid—you might have seen her. She is grateful for the work, and will do aught that Mrs. Nettleton or one of the others directs."

His great dark brows had drawn down to a frown of displeasure. "You—you dared defy Botts for this? He might have struck you down! What were the men thinking of, that they allowed you to confront that man alone?"

"Oh, I was not alone. Kenneth and the coachman went with me daily, or Mrs. Nettleton and the coachman."

"This does not please, not at all." He sprang up, and paced about his huge study, back and forth, back and forth. "You have too much courage and daring, Charlotte," he said sharply. "I think you had best leave the mills to me. I will speak to your father, and we shall see what is to be done. As to the orphanage, now that it is started, I wish you to leave it to the direction of Miss Morris. You might catch some infection—"

"Oh, pooh, nonsense!" she said, in her forthright way. "My visits to the children insure that they will continue to be cared for, and the interest of the villagers is high. If I deliberately stay away from them, so will the good females who make it their duty now to assist. No, my lord, it is best—"

He turned about abruptly, his nostrils taut with rage. "So, you continue to defy me," he said softly, then broke off. His hand rubbed his forehead. "No matter, no matter, I will speak to your father," he said wearily. "Do you go now, and for God's sake, get some rest, you are all bones. Your maid Noreen has already said to me that you ought to go away on a holiday, for you work from day's break to night."

"How dare she!" exclaimed Charlotte indignantly. "It was not her concern—nor yours." The "all bones" remark had stung. She had seen her wan, weary face in the mirror and disliked it.

"If not mine, then whose?" he said, and waved her away. "Go, go, get some rest. I must think."

She left the room, to go to her own sitting room, fuming. How like a man! She had managed alone for months, now he must pretend he was concerned for her and her health. Oh, yes, she thought, he might be concerned that she would carry a healthy child for him. He cared not a stone for her.

She went down early to the blue drawing room to see about a more formal tea. The additional London guests were accustomed to much more elaborate fare than the simple kind she preferred. After her instructions to the maids, she went to the drawing room, and found Mrs. Holt, languid in misty black gauze, draped over a blue sofa, her blond hair *à la grecque* with languid curls to her white throat.

Charlotte felt at once that her green velvet dress with the golden bands, which had looked so smart, was of a prosaic quality, too practical to be beautiful, though it felt good that cold autumn day. She told the footman to stir up the fire, and after he had left the room, she seated herself near enough to Mrs. Holt, far enough that she did not have to smell her perfume, a particularly clinging ultrasweet fragrance.

"Ah, my lady, you are so busy about your good works," said Mrs. Holt, smiling delicately over her lace handkerchief. "My dear Charlotte, you should not do so. Don't you know the men do not care for this?"

"I have not given you leave to use my own name," said Charlotte, bristling. She drew a deep breath to calm herself. It did no good to fight Mrs. Holt. The woman used subtle weapons, and who knew what tales she carried to Darcy?

The slim eyebrows raised. "No? But indeed, I feel quite friendly to you," she murmured. "I was ever a friend of Lucille. If she had followed my advice, she would not have chased after Rockingham, and made Darcy so jealous. For men like Darcy, that is fatal," and she sighed.

Charlotte stared into the fire, longing for someone to come, even the detestable Lady Frances Barkley, catty as she was. Mrs. Holt would not dare such an intimate conversation in the presence of another person.

"This scheme of yours, the orphanage," sighed Mrs. Holt, wafting her handkerchief before her to draw a luxurious smell of the scent. "You know, Darcy adores me because I am so feminine—so helpless, you know? He has always abhorred bluestockings. And do-gooders make him laugh. You go about winning him the wrong way, my dear!"

Charlotte moved abruptly in her chair. She was moved to snap she did not try to win him, but she would hand Mrs. Holt no such weapon. "Indeed?" she said very politely. "You know, I cannot imagine you doing any good at all, nor being anything but helpless. No wonder you charm him." And she managed a smile as demure as the other woman's.

The blue eyes narrowed. She waved the handkerchief at Charlotte. "Is this scent not divine? Darcy brought me bottles of it from Paris. I adore it. And this bracelet—" She waved it before her triumphantly. A carved gold bracelet set with diamonds of especially large and fine glitter. "Darcy knew I had missed him dreadfully, I told him so again and again. That is what a man likes, not long shrewish tales of what has gone wrong in his absence! You might learn much of me, my dear—"

Charlotte scarcely heard her, staring at the bracelet. Mrs. Holt had handed her rival something more precious than a diamond bracelet. Darcy had not taken Mrs. Holt to Paris with him! He had not taken her with him! All those weeks of anguish—and Darcy had not taken her—

"I wonder that he had time to shop for them," said

Charlotte casually. "His business seemed so all-consuming."

Mrs. Holt pouted, lusciously, with her red lips opened. "That nasty business, four weeks of it! I was enraged! And he was so tired, poor dear! But he managed to sign some important contract for his woolens, so he was satisfied. Business," she waved her handkerchief, as though to waft the hated word away. "I detest business!"

The door opened, and Fergus Gordon came in, giving them a startled look as he saw them alone and conversing. Charlotte managed a smile for him and saw him to a chair, with his leg up on a stool. "Tea will come shortly, papa, you look very tired," she said, patting his shoulder comfortingly.

"Aye. Your husband and I have talked long," he grunted, with a glance at Mrs. Holt from the corners of his eyes. "I think he knows the whole of that dratted business now. The mills need a good foreman, and we shall locate one directly."

"Good, that is good news," she said, and smiled as Neville came in. He was followed by Kenneth—and Fitzhugh Rockingham.

Mrs. Holt sat upright, in surprise, Rockingham seemed equally taken aback. "Good heavens, Rockingham," said Mrs. Holt, recovering. "What brings you to Arundell?"

Darcy followed him into the room, his mouth compressed tightly. "Yes, I am about to ask the same question," he said. "I cannot suppose it is the hunting, which is poor just now."

Rockingham smiled, came over to Charlotte, bent over her hand and kissed the fingers lingeringly. He smiled into her eyes. "No, not the hunting," he said gently.

Mrs. Holt rippled out a laugh. Darcy scowled, and took up his stance at the mantel, glaring at Rockingham. Neville looked uneasily about, Kenneth frowned down at the fire. Fergus leaned back in his chair and watched the little scene like a play.

The tea tray came in, and a tall footman handed about the cups. The Barkleys arrived, late as usual, and wished for brandy. As the footman served them, Rockingham came to Charlotte's side, and helped her hand the cups about, and the plates of cream cakes, little sandwiches of roast beef, and cheeses, macaroons, and apple tarts.

Mrs. Holt must comment on it, but Rockingham was not easy prey to her. "How devoted you are to my lady," she commented lightly. "I hear you have been in town for a month, driving my lady about on her—errands of mercy. How unusual for you, dear Fitz!"

"And how unusual for you to chase down to the country, when London is ablaze with lights of a new season, my dear Iris," Fitz countered smoothly. "And speaking of lights, do I detect a new and even more beautiful bracelet upon your fair arm? I do not recall ever seeing such diamonds before!"

Mrs. Holt smiled, glanced under her lashes at Darcy, then at Charlotte. "My lord Arundell brought it to me from Paris," she said gently. "A sentimental gesture, he knows I adore Paris."

Neville looked repelled and worried. Fergus snorted aloud. Darcy had turned rather red—strange for him. Charlotte continued to pour tea with a steady hand.

"And how you adore diamonds," said Fitz, with a laugh. "Here is your brandy, dear Iris. You adore diamonds more than anything in the world, as I recall."

Lady Frances Barkley was practically licking her lips over the delicious morsels of gossip being served up with her brandy and cakes. Fergus Gordon looked cross, Kenneth was grave. Let them think what they would, thought Charlotte. At least he had not been all that time in Paris with *her*.

"Of course, they are the most precious of gems," and

Iris complacently caressed the bracelet.

"Not always," said Fitz. "There are other gems, rubies, sapphires—and emeralds. Now, Charlotte here is best suited with emeralds. I am having a set designed for her and hope to persuade her to accept it. It will set off the fire of her glorious hair," and he caressed her hair lightly with the tips of his fingers.

It was outrageous. Darcy went pale under his tan, Iris stared. Fergus gave a great "har-rumph!" of outrage. Charlotte felt herself in a cold shock. How terrible of Fitz, though he was only playing off Iris. But to imply, to seem to imply understanding between them.

Darcy moved. "Emeralds suit my *wife*, of course, however, the most suitable gem for her is the fire opals. You would have been proud of her, sir," and he turned to Fergus Gordon deliberately. "The night of a ball here, she wore the Arundell fire opals and on her they were magnificent."

Fergus was inspired to turn the conversation to the ball, who had attended, the villagers, the squire whom he had met, and all seemed safe again. Charlotte began to breathe, but there was a pain somewhere in her breast. Fitz seemed content to let the conversation move on without him, he leaned back in a chair, looking mocking and watchful. Mrs. Holt caressed her bracelet absently with her slim fingers, her blue eyes narrowed on Darcy.

Rockingham remained for dinner, his lively wit amusing them all, except for Darcy who seemed abstracted, and Fergus Gordon who was unusually silent for him. Rockingham finally took his departure about eleven o'clock, to return to the inn. Under cover of final farewells, he murmured to Charlotte.

"May I not covet a room here in your so-ample castle, dearest? With other guests here, I do not see why I must be banished to the inn! It is most uncomfortable," he said plaintively. "And the food is outrageous."

"Since you eat most of your meals here, you have little room to complain," she said, coolly. "And if you are uncomfortable, I think your own estates probably could use some of your attention, my lord!"

"You are cold of heart, dearest, outwardly. But not inwardly, I think," he said, with a laugh, kissed her fingers, and departed.

Charlotte found Darcy behind her when she turned from seeing Fitz off in his carriage. The blue eyes flamed with fury, but he turned and went back to the drawing room.

She was weary, and there was a pain in her that would not be stilled. She made her excuses presently and went up to bed. She undressed and lay under the silk coverlet, in the pale green nightdress she preferred on the cooler nights. The wind hummed against the windows; she was conscious of every sound in the castle and outside.

But he had not taken Iris Holt to Paris with him! That much was granted to her, she thought, turning over restlessly in the great four-poster bed.

The door opened, a dark figure entered and the door shut after him. Arundell approached the bed, flinging off his robe and casting it to a chair.

Instead of climbing into the bed, he sat on the edge, and from his tone he was furious. "I have come to speak with you, Charlotte," he said, with controlled savagery. "I have thought sometimes you might learn discretion. But to have a lover here, the entire time I was gone, hardly argues you have changed."

She sat up in bed, holding the sheets against her. "How dare you! He is not my lover—"

"He implied such."

"He is always implying something," she said bitterly. "I would think you were so accustomed to society that you took words such as his with much salt, my lord!"

"You call him Fitz," he said, with seeming irrelevance. "I return home, tired and ready for some quiet and peace, and you are entertaining on a grand scale! Even Rockingham, who injured your own brother! You forgive easily, it must be—when you wish! Perhaps he gave you jewels after all!"

She flinched. "You know how little I care for gems," she said in a low hurt tone.

"Then it must be for love of him," he jeered, and flung back the sheets of the bed. He pressed her down against the pillows, and in the hardness of his hands, she felt the anger in him. She had longed for him—but not like this—not like this.

He pressed his mouth to hers, hurting her lips, pressing them against her teeth. "Did he kiss you like this?" he whispered, and ran his hand roughly down her side. "And caress you like this? Did he lie in your bed, or did you go to him at the inn?"

"I did not—I did not allow him liberties—" she protested weakly. She tried to turn her head from him, he put his fingers through her thick red hair and kept her face to him. He ran his fingers through the hair, pressed his mouth to her soft cheeks, down to her throat and to her shoulder, moving the nightdress from it to bare the soft flesh.

"You rode with him mornings? You went with him in his carriage?" he questioned again savagely, lifting his head.

"No—no—you have only to ask Kenneth—Neville—"

"Kenneth and Neville would lie for you!"

What good did it do to argue with him? He did not believe her. She lay back wearily, and let him do as he pleased. Her very passiveness seemed to infuriate him, and he made love to her cruelly, with little tenderness for a time. His kisses made her flesh sting, his mouth hurt her lips again and again. His hands bruised her arms, crushed her breasts.

"Well, are you not going to plead with me to leave

you?" he mocked, as she was silent under his attack. "Will you not beg me to leave, will you not order me from your bedroom?"

She was silent, only moving her head from side to side in weak protest. Her body was quickening under his skilled caresses, as his hands used her more gently. He took the nightdress from her, and his naked hard body lay against hers, and she wanted him, no matter how he treated her. It had been so long—

He came to her then, and they joined together in the bittersweet struggle of man and wife. But he did not linger afterwards to lie with her, or sleep with her. He got up instead, as soon as he had his breath back again, and left her, thrusting himself into his robe, slamming the door after him.

She lay awake for a time, salty tears trickling down her cheeks to her bruised mouth. She was bitter with the hopelessness of loving a man like that. He was tough, hard, cruel. He could do as he pleased, flaunting his mistress in her face, keeping her in her very home, giving her rare and expensive gifts. Why then did she persist in thinking that one day he might come to her in understanding, friendship at least, if not in love?

Charlotte pressed her arm across her eyes. She heard a clock striking in the little sitting room next to her bedroom, one, two o'clock, three, and still she could not sleep.

Chapter 18

Albert Botts came to Arundell the next day, and was closeted with him in the ground floor study for some time. The butler and footmen heard voices raised in anger, then a mumble, then more fury. They tiptoed about, scarcely daring to make a sound.

Botts slammed from the room, shouting after him, "Ye'll be sorry for this, ye will! No 'un will work for ye, not in them mills! I'll spread the words about—how ye're under the spell of that brazen female—"

"Enough! Go, or you shall be thrown out!" Darcy Saltash was pale with fury, as he followed him to the door. He curtly nodded for the butler to open the great doors and show the man out. Botts flung himself on his great horse, and galloped off. "Good riddance," said Darcy, with relief, and returned to his ledgers.

That afternoon, Charlotte was in the gardens, bending over the late roses, to see if aught was left to pluck for her vases. She spoke with the head gardener about the pruning that winter, about removing some plants to the conservatory in the cloister hall, about fresh blooms for the following spring.

The gardener straightened up, his old back giving him some difficulty, and put his hand to his hip painfully. He peered off into the distance, sniffed.

"My lady, do ye smell smoke?" He gazed with dimmed eyes.

She turned about, looked toward the horizon where he did. Then she put her hand to her throat. "Oh, God, smoke—yes! From where does it come? The village?"

He peered. "Looks to be the mills' direction, it be from the river."

She ran, picking up her skirts, dashing to the stables. Fire was one of the most dreaded of disasters. She cried out to the stable hands, "My carriage, quickly! And many hands to come with me! Hobbs, notify my lord and my brother and father—I think the mills are a-flame!"

Small Edgar went pale and ran to the nearest horses, and helped bring them out. "Let me go with ye, mum!" he begged, and she nodded. He was up beside the coachman in a trice, and a stablehand helped Charlotte into the coach. By that time Kenneth was running out, followed by Neville, limping.

Then Darcy came from one of the French windows, shouting at her. "What is it, Charlotte? The mills? Stay here, do not go!"

"I must go—tell Mrs. Nettleton, if you will—" She was gone, and Darcy cursed aloud, deliberately. He ran to the stables after Kenneth.

On their horses, they overtook the carriage, and passed her. Darcy shouted once more for Charlotte to turn back, but she shook her head, pressing back her flying hair with trembling hand. The children—oh, the children—were they inside? Had they been able to escape?

Her first thought was of Mr. Botts. Could he have done this? She had heard of the interview from Noreen and had felt relieved and triumphant that Darcy had not reinstated the man. But—oh—could Botts have been so cruel as to take this sort of revenge?

The mills were blazing with thick black smoke, greasy from the wools that burned inside. The gray stone walls were stained dark by the time they arrived. Children and adults stood back, forming lines of water buckets from the river, pausing to stare at the chaos before them.

Charlotte got down from the carriage, and ran forward to the source of the main fire, the weaving mill. "Is everyone out?' she cried to Kenneth, who was nearest.

"Not all," he said gravely. "Two men went in for a couple more children. The fire had started before any were aware."

She clasped her hands tightly. Darcy and Neville were in the water bucket line, Darcy directed them to fling more toward the roof, which burned like a torch. Inside the mill, the fire crackled through the looms, and now and then one went down with a great crash.

More carriages rattled up, villagers arrived with the Reverend Mr. Potter in the van. He had brought ladders with him, and more buckets, and they turned to soaking the other mills so that the fires would not spread. Mrs. Nettleton came in a carriage driven by Lord Barkley. The red-faced man helped her down, and also a slim girl, the maid Margaret, who gazed anxiously about the place.

"Well, well, quite a fire," said Lord Barkley, and to Charlotte's surprise, turned to helping Darcy direct the work quite efficiently.

"Are all the children out? Are all the children out?" asked Charlotte again and again of Mrs. Nettleton.

"Surely, dear, they must be," the woman reassured her. Miss Morris had come with Mr. Herbert Crotchett, and she went about counting, and drawing the younger ones aside out of the way of the men who were dashing about with buckets of water from the river nearby.

Margaret was also dashing about, and finally she returned to Charlotte, her face pallid. "I must go in," she panted. "Susie—she is missing—she must be inside—one said she was under a loom."

Charlotte caught her arm. "You will not go inside," she said firmly. "Susie—she is one of the youngest—where was she?"

"She allus works the loom at the far end," said Margaret trembling. "She be my sister. We was burned out of house and home, me parents died in it. She be skeered of fire, she be. I think she be hiding under the loom—oh, miss, I should ha' kept her with me—" And she was crying and wringing her hands.

With a great crash the roof fell in at the side. Soon it would be too late. Charlotte looked about frantically. Margaret made a move as though she would dash inside. Darcy was away on the other side of the building, trying to save the mill next to the burning one. The other men had followed him.

She caught up a full bucket of water, and dashed it over her head and shoulders. "Margaret—go tell my lord— I'll be in and out in a moment, I know the mill—"

Margaret gave her a frightened look and was off like a rabbit. Charlotte drew a deep breath, soaked her scarf in another bucket, wrapped it about her face, and without another thought ran into the flaming building.

The heat of it was like a blow to her whole body. She staggered, then forced herself onward. Ahead of her a loom burning brightly crashed to the floor. She edged past it gingerly, and down to the far end, not yet wrecked.

"Susie!" she called, her voice muffled by the scarf. "Susie, where are you? Susie, answer me at once!"

She groped her way through the blackened building, the fiery looms menacing her on each hand. The heat was appalling, the odor of the burning wool nauseous and overpowering. She pressed her hand to the wet scarf, and tried hard to catch her breath.

She forced her way to the farthest loom. She was feeling faint, she must go on—she must— She reached beneath the loom, found the small girl crouching there, her great eyes terrified, tears running down her grimy little face.

Outside, Darcy was working frantically, directing the bucket brigade. His jacket was torn and blackened, his face had streaks of soot. Someone laughed, and Darcy turned.

He saw Albert Botts standing there, feet apart, laughing at them all. "Ha, not so smart, are ye, my lord? Cannot do without me, eh?" he jeered. "If ye'd kept me as foreman, ye'd not have such a fire, eh?"

Something snapped in Darcy. He strode over to the man, faced him. Fergus Gordon hastened over anxiously, and Kenneth and Neville followed.

"You set the fire, didn't you?" demanded Darcy. Lord William Barkley ranged up to them. This was much more interesting than a London season, by gad! Never had he been so entertained as this summer and autumn, he vowed.

"Ye cannot prove nothing," sneered Botts. "Who would set fire? Your mills are heavy with grease and dirty, any fire would start. Ye care not how they are managed, ye leave that to yere brazen-faced wife—that doxy of the fine lord at the inn—"

Something raged in Darcy he had never felt in his life. He reached out for the whip with which Lord Barkley idly snapped his boots. "You cur," he said, in a whisper, and any who had fought with him would have known that tone.

The whip snapped out, caught Botts on the face. He cried out, pressed his hands to his head. Darcy whipped him mercilessly, the whip snapping about his shoulders, about the head and neck, until the man fell to his knees wailing. He whipped him until his arm was weary, and the man was on the ground, groveling, in a frenzy of pain.

Blood stained the whip as Darcy finally flung it to the ground. "Get out of here, get out of Arundell, away from this county! By God, if I ever see you again, I shall do more than whip you!" he ground out.

"Oh, please, sir!"

Darcy flung about, still fuming with fury, he glared down at the slim girl. Her face was wet with tears, she tugged boldly at his torn jacket.

"Oh, please, sir, please—"

"What is it?"

"My lady—she went in—after Susie—she said to tell you—oh, please, sir, she ain't come out again—oh, please—"

Darcy stared down at the girl incredulously. "Where— where did you say?"

"In there." The girl pointed, trembling, with her thin fingers. "My sister—Susie—under the loom—it's on this side now—she went right through the flames like she never felt it, my lady did—" she added proudly. "But— but she ain't come out—"

Charlotte had crawled under the loom finally and dragged the terrified child out. She was silent with horror, her great eyes dazed, the short dark hair wet with sweat. Charlotte took the wet scarf from her own head, and wrapped it about the child from mouth to knees.

She forced her to walk with her to the nearest door, but the effort of getting her out had taken the last fragments of strength from her. "Go—go—" she muttered, and gave her a great push that sent the small girl tottering toward the open door and freedom.

Behind her a crash—Charlotte tried to make herself go on. Unwittingly she held out her hand for something to hold to, just to get her breath for a moment.

She touched the scalding hot loom—and it tumbled

over on her. The burning wood seared her, knocked her to the dirt floor, and she knew no more.

Outside, Darcy was impatiently allowing Fergus to dash a bucket of water over him. "I'll go in—let me go—" breathed Kenneth anxiously beside them, staring at the door as though fascinated.

Margaret gave a scream, and darted forward. She clutched the small, crying child to her. "It's Susie—oh, me dearest—"

Kenneth caught the shoulder of the small Susie. "Where is she, where is my lady?" he cried sharply.

The girl could not speak, she raised her hand and pointed weakly into the now-flaming inferno. Darcy gave a curse, and ran. He dashed into the door, looked about wildly. "Charlotte!" he yelled, powerfully, and then gasped as the fetid burning hot air struck his lungs and grappled with his throat.

She was lying under some flaming timbers. He saw the green of her muslin gown burning, the flame of her hair about her on the dirty floor. In an instant he was beside her, he tossed the timbers off her, gathered her up. Ahead of them, another loom crashed to the floor with an immense scattering of sparks.

He picked her up, and carried her, staggering from lack of breath. The timbers had been heavy and hot, he did not feel the pain then. Charlotte was so still—so limp—

He carried her out, and into the open air, away from the burning building. Kenneth hastened to help him, Fergus was trembling too much. "My God, my God, my God," someone was saying. It was Lord Barkley, and he was clear-headed enough to snatch a water bucket and dash it over Darcy and his burning jacket.

Charlotte was laid on the ground, on someone's cloak. She did not stir. The children had clustered about, staring in awe.

"She be dead—" whispered Margaret, and Edgar echoed it.

"She be dead, my lady is dead," and they began to sob, clutching each other's hands.

Darcy knelt on the ground beside his wife, scarcely daring to touch her. Her face was covered with dirt, streaked with grime. Her hands were red, the sleeves of her dress burned away, and leaving red angry streaks up her arms. And she lay so quietly.

The doctor pressed his way through the crowd. "Stand back, stand back," he ordered, and they gave way to him. He knelt down on her other side, touched her wrist, then her throat. "Unconscious, not dead," was his verdict. "I'll treat her at Arundell," he added. "Come now, my lord, you'll get her up and into a carriage. She must be taken out of this cold air." He bullied the dazed man, and others until a carriage was brought about, and Charlotte wrapped into a blanket and put into it.

Fergus Gordon wanted to go with them, but the mill still burned, and his son-in-law was in a fine state of shock. "You go with them," he urged Neville. "See to it that he gets treatment too, and find how your sister is. See to them all, lad."

Neville nodded, pallid with the shock of it all. He rode with Charlotte, holding her tenderly against him. It was the first time he had seen his sister in such a way, and Darcy was not much better, staring down at his wife as though he expected her to expire at any moment.

At the castle, Mrs. Nettleton was close to fainting. She had gone ahead, warned Noreen to be ready with ointment and bandages, scurried about to have all prepared. When Charlotte was carried in, though, limp in the arms of two sturdy footmen, Mrs. Nettleton broke down and wept.

The footmen carried Charlotte up to her room, and assisted Darcy to his. He ordered curtly that his wife was to be seen to first, and the doctor attended her. He and Noreen cut away the green gauze dress carefully, what remained of it, from the burned limbs.

She was dressed with ointment, and it was found that her body was not badly burned. But her hands were the worst, with deep burns on them. And there were deep gashes across her arms where the timbers had fallen on her, and another great gash across one leg.

She roused slightly, and was given laudanum to help against the pain. She relapsed again into unconsciousness, more like sleep, and the doctor turned to Darcy.

His own valet had assisted him in removing his garments. He paced back and forth, demanding bulletins from his wife's bedroom, growling at efforts to help him. A deep scowl covered his face, but the footmen whispered to each other later that no wonder, he was in pain, his wife unconscious, the mills burnt. No wonder he was cross.

The doctor managed to ease his pain, covered him with ointment. He was persuaded gently by Neville to take some laudanum. "For father will see to the mills, and the doctor to Charlotte," said Neville practically. "You must recover quickly, and this will help you. The pain can be the very devil."

Darcy frowned at him, but finally took the medicine, and sank back on his bed with a sigh. "You must hate me," he said, presently, drowsily, as Neville waited beside his bed, patiently.

"Hate you, sir? Why, why should I?" asked the young man, cautiously.

"Letting your—beloved sister—get in such danger— terrible danger—" He turned his head, and was asleep against the pillow.

Neville gazed down at the black curly hair, the closed eyes, and shook his head. What a coil they were in, to be sure. He wondered if his sister and this man would ever reconcile their differences. Not while that Mrs. Holt was in the place, he thought. Who would have thought Lord Arundell would bring his light o' love to his own home? Charlotte was right to be cold to her husband. Married but a few months, and all this.

It would be a long time before Neville undertook matrimony, he thought seriously. What a chance one took, to be sure! He would devote himself to his studies more seriously from now on. Women could be the very devil—and men also. It was a profound reflection.

Chapter 19

The next days and nights were blurred into grayness for Charlotte. She was dimly aware of Noreen stroking ointment gently on her arms, her hands, her legs. She knew when the doctor came, and examined her hands; it was painful when he drew off the bandages, and tears streamed down her cheeks. She knew when her father tiptoed in, and clumsily stroked her forehead, and inquired of Noreen how she was.

But surely she was dreaming that Darcy came also, and touched her forehead gently with his lips, and even sat beside her for a time. He did not care enough for that, she must have dreamed it completely, she thought wearily.

She heard Darcy and the doctor speaking one morning when she was coming out of a deep sleep.

"But why is she so slow in recovering?" Darcy was asking, and his deep tones sounded anxious.

"She seems exhausted," said the doctor slowly. "She is not her usual self, the maid says, and tells me that she has not eaten properly for a time. She needs to be built up, I believe. And there is smoke in her lungs, that is why she coughs so much. She must lie quiet, have only liquids and sops for a time."

Charlotte opened her eyes with an effort, the doctor bent to examine her eyes and face. "There now, my lady, feeling better?"

She tried to say she was, but she could only manage a croaking sound. Her throat hurt, and she lifted a hand to touch it, only could not. The hand was covered in bandages.

"Do not move, Charlotte." It was Darcy's voice, and gently he placed his hand on her arm and held down the hand. "Would you like something cool to drink?"

She managed to nod. Noreen's head came into view, that bright red hair flaming in the sunlight, her freckled face anxious. She brought a glass of liquid. Darcy slid his arm under her top pillow, and raised her cautiously, putting the glass to her lips. She had a vague remembrance of something like that happening before—had it really, or was it something she had dreamed? She could catch the scent of his masculine lotions, feel his warmth against her shoulder, and somehow it seemed it had happened before—perhaps in her dreams.

The liquid was cool and she was grateful for it against her sore dry throat. She drank several swallows, then indicated she had enough. She could not speak, and as Darcy laid her down, she began to cough again, a racking sound she tried to suppress. Darcy stroked her hair back from her forehead, his dark face frowning. Was he angry again?

She drifted off to sleep after the doctor had changed the bandages once more. This time it did not hurt quite so much.

She wakened again in the night, the curtains were drawn back to show the night sky. She gazed out for a time, conscious of Noreen's deep breathing as she lay on the couch nearby. Dear Noreen, so faithful and good.

Slowly as she gazed at the stars, at the bare limbs of a tree outside her window, she began to remember—the fire, the greasy smoke choking her, and the child under the burning loom. Then the crash of the loom on her— What else had happened? She began to be anxious. Was Susie safe? Had all the children been rescued? What had happened to the weaving shed? Were the walls still standing?

She turned over restlessly, painfully. From here she could see the door to the hallway. It stood open. That was strange, it was never left open at night. Beyond was Darcy's door, and that also was open. She could see dimly the large bed beyond, and his form as he lay there quietly.

She frowned, puzzled. Why were the doors opened?

Stirring had made her choke, she felt stifled there with the covers piled on her. She stirred again, began to cough. She tried to hold it back but could not. She sat up, coughing hard. Noreen stirred, sat up, pulled on a robe, came to her.

"I'm—sorry—Noreen—couldn't help—"

"There, now, my dear Miss Charlotte, there, now—" Noreen hastily poured a glass of liquid and held it to her lips. "Try this, it will help your poor throat."

Beyond Noreen a dark form came into the room. "Is she coughing?" asked a worried voice. Darcy was pulling on his robe hastily, walking to the bed.

"I'm—sorry—woke you both up—" she managed to say between coughs. They wracked her body, they were so deep and painful. Her chest hurt when she drew a deep breath.

Darcy took Noreen's place beside the bed, sat down carefully on the side, gave her the glass again. She managed another sip, and it soothed her throat. The coughing finally ceased, and she lay back in relief.

Darcy stroked her hair softly. "Better now, Charlotte?"

he asked, his tone unbelievably gentle.

"Yes. What happened—to Susie? All—right?" she whispered against the soreness of her throat.

"Susie? The little girl you risked your life for?" His tone had turned grim. "She is all right."

Noreen said quickly, "Her sister is a-looking after her. They are both at the orphanage. Little Margaret is quick with her needlework, and a fair cook. And she's happier with her sister. Mrs. Nettleton thought she might as well work at the orphanage as here."

"Glad," whispered Charlotte. "Didn't know—her sister—"

"Don't try to talk more now," Darcy urged. "You'll strain your throat. Go back to bed, Noreen, I'll stay up with her until she sleeps again."

"No—need—" Charlotte managed to croak out.

"Stubborn child," said Darcy gently, and pressed his hand to her cheek. Noreen went off to her couch, and Darcy continued to sit beside the bed, his hand stroking her cheek, her hair, until she drifted off again.

She was a little improved the next day. At Noreen's urging, she was able to eat some sops dipped in warm broth, some eggs beaten in wine. Afterwards, she felt stronger. Fergus Gordon came to see for himself, nodded his head fiercely, and grumbled that she was ever foolish to dash into danger, and he would be hanged if he let her go near the mills again.

She laughed at him weakly, and he was satisfied she improved. "But you're to be a good girl, and be quiet," he said. "The doctor says you'll stay in for a week or more."

She was glad enough to do so. She felt tired through her whole body, as though she could not stir of her own strength. Noreen took devoted care of her. Neville came to see her twice daily.

It was Neville who told her that the Barkleys were

leaving. "They say they must attend to their town house, and be ready for the Christmas season," he said.

"Really?" she asked, longing to know if Mrs. Holt would accompany them. She plucked nervously at the coverlet with her just-freed fingertips.

Neville glanced at her, then away. "Mrs. Holt stays on," he said carefully. "She has taken an interest in the orphanage, and goes sometimes to take some clothing to the children."

Charlotte felt fiercely jealous of her and turned her head away. "I see."

"Father has an idea for building better weaving looms," added Neville, changing the subject skillfully. He was learning tact, she thought ruefully. "Darcy said he might go ahead and order some of his own design. It should be quite the thing."

"Fine."

"Father is having a great time straightening it all out," added Neville, after another pause. "He pointed out errors in the ledgers, changed the accounting system, appointed a chief clerk there. Now he's prowling about the weaving shed, getting the burnt looms all cleared out. They'll have it clean before long. By that time he'll have the first of the new looms ready to set up."

"That's—good."

"The children are having school while the shed is closed," he offered hopefully. "Miss Morris is teaching them reading and spelling, I go over sometimes and try my hand at teaching sums, and Kenneth has been involved in the scheme by teaching a couple of the older boys how to handle horses. Hobbs goes over with some of the horses. They might make good grooms, if they don't stay with the mills."

"I'm—glad."

She was glad, but she could not help thinking about Darcy and Mrs. Holt. If only the woman would leave, there might be some hope that Darcy would turn to Charlotte. She wondered bitterly why she even bothered to hope anymore. But if she did not hope, what was left for her?

No one had spoken much about the fire to her. She did know from what Noreen had let slip that Darcy himself had rescued her from the flaming inferno at much risk to himself.

"Neville—tell me about the day of the fire," she said abruptly. "Everyone avoids the topic, as though it could hurt me. Was it—Albert Botts who set it?"

"Right," said Neville. "He set it and was rash enough to stay around and taunt Arundell about it. Arundell took Lord Barkley's whip and gave him a whale of a thrashing! Good to see it," he said with great satisfaction. "Botts left town, sporting two black eyes and a face that will never look the same. He wouldn't dare come back now."

He proceeded to give her a vivid hero-worshipping account of what Darcy had done at the fire, and added how much Lord Barkley had surprised them all by his help. He had even dashed out the fire ablaze in Darcy's jacket. Charlotte listened to all, wide-eyed. She had not dreamed Darcy would do so much. And as for Lord Barkley, it was beyond her comprehension why he had troubled himself.

She said as much. Neville told her, "Dash it, he was enjoying himself! Oh, I know that sounds cold-blooded, but I don't mean that. He has the spirit, and he's game. When he saw something needed to be done, he threw himself into it. Lady Frances wasn't half tearful when he got home, black as a chimney-sweep, with his eyebrows singed!"

Before the Barkleys left, Charlotte was promoted to the chaise longue in her sitting room. She begged Neville to ask them to come up to her there before they departed.

The couple came, full of curiosity and concern. Lady Frances seemed somewhat subdued, Lord William Barkley was his usual red-faced, loud-voiced self—except for the singed eyebrows, which gave him a strange, babyish look.

Neville showed them in.

"We must not take your time and strength," said Lord Barkley at once. He bowed over her still-bandaged hand. "Wanted to tell you, you're a game one, all right! Haven't enjoyed myself so much in years—" His wife gave him a poke in the ribs. "Except for your injuries, my lady!" he quickly added with a boyish grin.

"I wanted to express to you, Lord Barkley, how much I appreciate your assistance in the fire. My brother has informed me that we must be grateful to you for your help in the directing of the water lines and for—for—dashing out the fire in Lord Arundell's coat." Her hoarse voice gave out on her, she coughed, and they both looked most anxious.

"No, no, you must not talk, my dear," said Lady Frances. "May I just say, you have been most gracious in your hospitality. I cannot understand why you think so much of those orphans, but it has endeared you to all the countryside. I shall have much to gossip about in London this season, all shall hear what a heroine you are!"

Lord Arundell came in the open door just then, looking grave to see Charlotte sitting up and trying to talk. He listened to what they said, then interrupted Charlotte as she tried to reply.

"No, no, you must not speak more, not today, Charlotte," he ordered, in the arrogant fashion she had once resented. "We shall have you sick once more."

"Wished to thank—Lord Barkley—" she whispered over the soreness.

"You have, you have, dear lady." Lord Barkley bowed

to her. "And we must take ourselves off. Any time you come to London, you must notify us, we will call upon you at once. Jolly times, what? Haven't enjoyed a season so much in years. Tell everyone what a jolly time we had here at Arundell."

Lady Frances repeated his pleasure, added her own rather cynical note, "And when you come, we must make sure you are well entertained, as we were here, my dear Lady Charlotte! I shall look out for some handsome young men for you in case Arundell is occupied—" And she laughed.

Darcy gave Charlotte a quick look. She managed not to appear displeased, and smiled faintly. They departed, to her relief. Lord Barkley was excellent in an emergency, but at close quarters he did not wear well. And Lady Frances was too catty for her taste.

A few days later she was promoted to the formal drawing room downstairs for a couple of hours in the afternoon. Mrs. Nettleton brought in several older children from the mills, who presented her with a crude bouquet of wild flowers which they themselves had picked. They were scrubbed clean, wore nice clothing and shoes, and were scared to pieces. She smiled at them, thanked them, enjoyed looking at them. They were looking so much better, filling out, losing that haunted, desperate look which had caught so at her heart.

Another day, three more children came, and Rockingham driving them in his carriage. He swept them in with him, announcing himself cheerfully as she sat before the glowing fire. She felt cold so much, she was thin still, and even her warm green velvet gown was not warm enough, she had a gold wool scarf about her shoulders.

"My dear Charlotte," he greeted her, with real emotion in his voice and in his handsome face. He kissed her hands, then stood back, to allow the children to see her. She was pleased to see small Susie looking none the worse for her terrible adventure, silent Jed with his cheeky smile, and her favorite, Peter, with a muffler about his neck.

Peter spoke for the children. "We was thanking you for saving Susie," he said in his surprisingly mature deep voice. He beamed up at her, frankly adoring her. "Ye be the finest lady we ever met, not that we meet many ladies, ye see."

Rockingham was frankly laughing, from his chair. Charlotte frowned him to silence, and took Peter's well-scrubbed hand in hers. The bandages had finally been removed, but the flesh was tender and pink.

"Peter, you are the one I should thank. You have been a real leader for the children. I hope you will continue to help them all," she told him earnestly. "My father, Mr. Gordon, is always looking for good workers, and I shall recommend you to him. One day, you might be a foreman yourself, and help everybody in the mill."

Peter looked impressed. Jed leaned on her knee and gazed steadily into her face, not saying a word. She reminded herself she must ask Miss Morris if the small boy ever spoke. Little Susie came forward, presented a formal little bouquet of fragrant hothouse violets, and said, "I wish to thank you, my lady, for a-saving my life."

"And for taking such a risk—" hissed Peter, prompting her.

"And for taking such a risk—uh—" She faltered into silence, pressed the flowers into Charlotte's lap, and retreated bashfully.

"There now, you have made fine speeches," interposed Rockingham. "Sit down and be quiet, and you shall have some tea and cakes. Charlotte, may I ring?"

"Yes, of course." She touched the flowers, realizing he had brought them for her, through the child. She gave him a smile, more warm than she realized.

Charlotte had tea with them. The children had never

seen such fine cups and saucers, but after they had over-
come their shyness somewhat, they made swift inroads on
the cream-filled cakes. After an hour, Rockingham took
them back to the orphanage.

The next day, he appeared with Margaret and three
other children, and the ceremony was repeated. Margaret
was touchingly overwhelming in her gratitude. "She be
all that's left of my family, Susie is, ye see," she explained. "If she be gone, I ain't none left."

Fergus wandered in while they were there, blinked at
seeing Rockingham, managed to make friends with the
children, watched them all. When Rockingham appeared
again the next day, Fergus was there.

Charlotte would have protested to Rockingham, but
he always brought more of the children, and she would
not insult them all. They sat, adoring her, sometimes
speechless, their great eyes watching her every move.
Rockingham, in leaving, bent to her. "You are their
Madonna, you know," he whispered, his eyes serious
instead of mocking.

"He coming every day?" inquired Fergus Gordon after
they had left.

"For several days, yes," she nodded. "He brings the
children, you see."

"Harrumph!" and he retreated to the comfort of his
pipe.

October was almost over. It had rained every day,
sometimes in great gray gusty downpours, sometimes in
a gentle continuous patter against the windows. When it
finally cleared, the sun shone on the remnants of the
gardens.

Charlotte was much stronger now and up for most of
the afternoon. She had to endure seeing Mrs. Holt enter
the drawing room for tea, in her misty black dresses,
shining with diamonds, fragile, beautiful. Charlotte wished
the woman would leave! But if she did not—

Charlotte was thinking about that as she slowly went out to the rose garden that afternoon. She sat in the rose garden, gazing at the tattered remnants of the roses, seeing a few fine specimens, but most of the roses were gone. If Mrs. Holt did not leave, what must she do? She could not endure it much longer.

Darcy had been sweet and attentive to her during her illness. Now that she was improving she scarcely saw him except in the company of Mrs. Holt. Did she imagine a greater tenderness when he spoke to herself? A real solicitude for her health? Probably, she decided drearily.

She was thinking, thinking. If Mrs. Holt did not go, Charlotte resolved to speak to her father, and ask him to take her away with him when he departed. She might go to Leeds for weeks or even months, make the break gradual, and then request from Darcy a divorce, or at least a separation. Pamela would be hurt, and she dreaded to think what would become of all the children in the mills. But the work would be carried on, it was well started in the orphanage.

Rockingham found her in the garden. She saw him coming, and smiled easily at him.

"What? No children clinging to your heels, Fitz?" she asked.

He grimaced. "No, not today. I think that's the lot. They have all had their carriage rides, and those who wished to come have come. I have done my duty—and seen my lady also." He seemed quite pleased with himself.

He seated himself next her on the white garden bench. He was abruptly more serious.

"Charlotte, I have remained long for a purpose. I have observed the relationship between yourself and your husband—and the not so fair Mrs. Iris Holt. Have you had enough, my dear?"

He said it so quietly, it took a moment to sink in.

"What—do you mean, Fitz? It is not your concern—"

"I love you. It is my concern. I wish to take you away from here. That—that iceberg of a man does not appreciate you. Why should he have you?'

"Fitz, we are married," she said gently, looking away from the intent blue eyes, so like Darcy's, yet not alike. Bold, inquisitive, yet strangely humble for Fitzhugh Rockingham. "I have married Lord Arundell, and you must not speak so to me."

"Marriages can be dissolved," he said. "You are not happy with him. Let me speak to your father—"

"No," she said sharply. "Never. Please, Fitz, it will do you no good." And it could wreck her own plea to her father, if he thought her about to choose Rockingham as her next husband. He still did not approve of the man.

"I love you. For the first time in my life, I love, deeply and truly," he said, so quietly she was forced to believe him. "And loving you, I can wait. I shall remain, and hope."

He lifted her hands, those pink-skinned, just-healing hands which had known the fire, and put his lips to them gently, one after the other, holding them very gently in his big hands.

She looked down at the handsome blond head, and had never liked him so well as now, seeing past his cynical manner, his brazen front, to the deep wells of a man who could be good and fine.

"I am sorry—" she was beginning, when a furious voice interrupted.

"What are you doing here, Rockingham? I have forbidden you to see my wife alone!" It was Darcy, and he had witnessed those kisses on her hands, and the intimate pose of the two in the rose garden.

Fitz Rockingham stood up, faced his host. "The world knows that I love her, why should not you?" he drawled, in his most insolent tone.

Darcy's blue eyes flamed, he took a step forward. Charlotte held up her hands, wearily.

"Enough, enough! No quarrels, please! I am tired, and want to go inside."

Rockingham was instantly offering his arm, Darcy stood back, furiously. So on Rockingham's arm she went into the castle, to the formal drawing room. Mrs. Holt was behind the tea tray, as though she belonged there, her misty black skirts spread on the blue sofa, pouring out tea for them all.

The others had gathered also, Fergus Gordon, Neville, Kenneth. None missed the sight of Rockingham entering with Charlotte leaning heavily on his arm, followed by Darcy, with a white taut line about his mouth, the blue eyes blazing.

Mrs. Holt smiled. "Darcy, you will have brandy, rather than tea?" she softly inquired.

He went to her side at once, and Fergus scowled at his daughter. Charlotte sank into the nearest chair. She was in despair. Nothing would help, nothing. She was in Arundell's bad books.

The remainder of the afternoon, Mrs. Holt monopolized the conversation. She spoke of friends of herself and Darcy, laughed about some amusing incidents of the old days, acted hostess for them all as Charlotte sat silent, staring into the fire. Darcy even laughed with Mrs. Holt, as he never laughed with her. No, it was no good, she must leave. She must persuade Fergus Gordon it was a disaster beyond redemption, this dreadful marriage.

And then she must leave—leave Arundell, her loyal staff, Mrs. Nettleton so kind and good, the villagers who were her friends now, and the children—and Pamela— and Darcy himself. She felt a pain in her chest when she thought of this. It would hurt horribly to leave him, never to see him again except at a distance. But more would be the pain of remaining, a stranger to him, the man she longed to love and adore. How odd was love, she mused, that one could love where it was not wanted, continuing when all one met was cold contempt and disbelief.

Pamela had not come down. Charlotte finally excused herself, and went up to the nursery, and had a little talk with Pamela. The children had occupied Pamela for a time, she sometimes went with Neville to play with them. But these past rainy days she had been alone, with her playhouse, her dolls, and her books.

Pamela rested her head against Charlotte. "You are better now, mama?" she asked hopefully. "I was not allowed to see you for so long. It will be better now, won't it?"

Charlotte finally left her, to return to her own sitting room. Oh, how could she leave Pamela, who had no one else? Her own father neglected her, the child would not come to tea when Mrs. Holt was there, she disliked her so much. They would become more and more alienated. She sank down on the chaise longue, to rest and try to think.

Fergus Gordon came in with only a brief knock and shut the door after himself. "Don't get up, Charlotte, don't get up. Won't stay long," he said, and flapped his coat-tails at the fire, scowling at his child. "What do ye mean by all this cavorting about with Rockingham? You have to watch your reputation, ye know! Can't encourage a rake like that, hanging about for months. Send him on his way with a flea in his ear!"

She managed a shrug. "Why should I? Darcy has his light o' love here," she said flippantly. "I must amuse myself, must I not?"

"Trying to make him jealous, eh?" said Fergus, wisely. "Won't work, me dear. Arundell is a man, he can do as he pleases. Restless eye, probably. Well, I won't say you don't have a complaint. Not many wives have to endure the mistress in the same house! But he calls the tune, me dear, because he pays the piper here. You can't do much about her. But that Rockingham—"

"I quite like him now," she said defiantly. "He has been the perfect gentleman."

"When it suits him," said Fergus. "You watch your step, me girl! That man will make trouble, if he pleases! And Darcy won't back you up if you play him false! A man thinks too much of his future heirs to allow any looseness."

She clenched her jaw. Yes, a man could do as he wished! A woman must be circumspect, for the sake of the children to come. The children—

"Father, I would speak frankly with you. What if I should leave Arundell?" she managed to say very quietly, the hoarseness of her voice, from the fire, giving emphasis to the words. "I do not believe our marriage will work at all. It has not, it does not improve. When you leave, will you take me with you?"

"Leave Arundell?" Fergus asked slowly, incredulously. "You would not leave—no, no, ye would not, me girl!" He eyed her nervously, knowing his daughter.

"Why should I not? He cares not a fig for me. And his devotion to—to Mrs. Holt—is obvious. She shows me the jewelry he gives her, all those diamonds, her very gowns are paid for by him," she said drearily, staring past her father into the fire. "Shall I remain, to be continually humiliated? All the village is gossiping. And the Barkleys will carry it all back to London, I am sure. Do you wish me a laughingstock?"

"No, no, demmit," said Fergus, growling. "Have done, my girl. You've been ill, you're weak yet. Don't make such decisions when you're weary. Think about it. I'll be around a time. Ye have not spoken to Arundell, have you?"

She shook her head. "Not yet," she said. "Shall I?"

"No, don't do that. Let me think on it," he said, and

he frowned down at her thoughtfully. She was putting him into a panic, being so quiet and determined. Arundell was humiliating her, he knew she resented the way Mrs. Holt was taking her place. And all those diamonds— "He gave her diamonds, you say?"

"All that she wears," said Charlotte.

"Harrumph!" He flipped his coattails again and again, thinking. His busy mind worked around and around the problem. And he thought of something. "Let me consider it, Charlotte," he said, briskly, a light of excitement in his eyes. "Yes, let me think on it."

Chapter 20

October turned into bright blue November, with brilliant skies, the stark black limbs of trees against it like silhouettes. Scarlet gladioli bloomed their last in the gardens, the vines against the gray-gold walls of Arundell flamed their reds and browns.

Charlotte continued to improve. On the first day she could, she decided to go to the orphanage to consult with Miss Morris and see the children. In the back of her mind was the resolution to leave her husband. First she must see that all plans were in working order, and caring for the children would continue after she left.

Kenneth and Neville rode with her, Kenneth in the carriage, Neville on his favorite gray. The coachman drove up with a flourish, to halt before the now lovely town house, before the wide green lawns where the laughter of children rang. Neville halted his stallion and slipped down deftly. Charlotte was happy that he was so much better also. Two of the boys came up shyly to take his horse, patting its neck bravely. Neville grinned at them, teasing them a little.

Miss Morris fluttered out to greet her former pupil,

and Charlotte greeted her with a kiss on each of her rosy cheeks. Miss Morris looked blooming, her eyes bright, her cheeks colored with health. This experience was good for her, decided Charlotte, gratefully. Some benefit had come from her marriage to Arundell.

She was escorted to the main lounge, and seated tenderly by Kenneth. Some of the children clustered about her, eying her with great wondering eyes. She smiled at them, beckoned to little Susie, who came to lean against her confidingly.

"How goes everything, Miss Morris?" she asked, and they began a comfortable conversation.

Margaret was one of the maids bringing in morning tea. A little fuss ensued when two of the boys wanted each to bring a cup to Charlotte. Miss Morris settled it deftly, easily, to Charlotte's hidden amusement. She touched the soft brown hair of Susie, and the child smiled up at her glowingly. Her face had filled out from the thin gray lines, her eyes were happy.

The children had tea with them, then ran out to play once more. No school lessons this morning, for my lady was here and it was a holiday. Kenneth went out to help Neville show the boys about harnessing a horse. Charlotte talked to Miss Morris at length, inquiring about the progress of the children.

Small Jed did not speak at all, Miss Morris told her sadly. "It was probably some shock when he was younger, some terrible event. He cannot speak. The doctor examined him, he made not a sound. Peter has appointed himself his guardian, and speaks for him. But I fear the children will think him very stupid. He can do sums, and he has begun to write out words. He does best at drawing some pictures, and seems to enjoy that. He is a good-natured child, and no trouble at all."

"Poor darling," murmured Charlotte, thinking of the cheeky grin. If she stayed, she might one day coax him from the shock, soothe him, make him feel secure. That might bring back his voice. Or Miss Morris might be encouraged to help him more. But if Charlotte must go—

She turned from that thought and finally took her departure. Neville was still absorbed in the two boys, learnedly discoursing about saddling a horse, but Kenneth came with her. Neville saw them off with a wave.

She talked of the children to Kenneth on the way home. He was as sympathetic as she was, as interested. They were still discussing small Jed as they walked into the Great Hall. The butler took her cloak and Kenneth's and said, "The company are gathered in the drawing room, my lady."

She sighed a little. She was weary, but she could not retreat forever into her own rooms. She nodded and turned toward the room, Kenneth close behind her.

Iris was seated behind the teatray, having been hostess again, thought Charlotte, irritated. Rockingham was seated opposite her in a great chair, looking at his ease. Darcy leaned on the mantel, Fergus Gordon was in a chair near Rockingham, looking furious and red about something.

All stared as Charlotte entered, followed by Kenneth.

"Ah, here are the truants," cried Iris, in her fluted voice. "And what have you done with poor Neville? Deserted him again, when Rockingham waits you here?"

Charlotte stiffened. She longed to turn about and leave, but that would be cowardly. She went to her favorite green chair, and sank down, her feet on the hassock before it.

"I have been at the orphanage," she said shortly, her voice still husky from the smoke damage.

Iris laughed. "Of course, my dear Lady Charlotte," she said, her eyes mocking.

Fergus sat up like an alert terrier, sharp to the smell of the hunt. "You like to make insinuations, Mrs. Holt," he said briskly. "Your favorite game, what? Suppose you come to the point. What do you mean about my daughter? Before she came, you implied that she was having an affair with Rockingham here. Now my daughter is here, you'll repeat what you said!"

Mrs. Holt leaned back, supremely confident in her blond beauty, her hard blue eyes fixed on the angry face of Fergus Gordon. "My dear Mr. Gordon," she said smoothly, "why stir up a hornet's nest? Everyone understands the situation, it is not unusual in our society. Only provincials do not comprehend."

"As I am a provincial—" began Fergus.

Darcy cut in, with a weary wave of his hand. "Let be, let be," he said curtly. "It is not a matter for discussion—"

"I mislike gossip and hints," Fergus flared up. "And me daughter is precious to me. I'll hear straight out what Mrs. Holt has to say, and we will have the truth before us. What do you mean, that she has an affair with Rockingham? Then you sneer when she comes in from an innocent trip with Kenneth, her cousin?"

"Mr. Gordon," said Mrs. Holt, sitting up straight, her cheeks flaming, "you are very innocent of the ton! A female may have an affair with whom she pleases, so long as she is discreet! However, your daughter flaunts her affairs in the faces of all!"

"And you state she has an affair with Kenneth?" insisted Fergus, grimly.

Kenneth stepped forward, his face white, his mouth set. Fergus gave him a fiery look, and a wave. "Be quiet, I will hear her!" said Fergus.

Charlotte leaned back in her turn, about to protest. If her father wished to hear and believe that female, then she was finished indeed! She had thought her father would protect and believe her when all else did not.

"Well?" barked Fergus Gordon.

"Of course," said Mrs. Holt. "It is obvious. She drives everywhere alone with him! The world knows of the time

she spends with him. They were devoted—until Rockingham arrived!"

Charlotte sent one look toward her husband. She was
amazed at the look on his face, the cold analytical look,
his eyes narrowed, as he looked down on Mrs. Holt. His
arm rested on the mantel, he seemed perfectly at ease,
though his fingers were clasped tightly about a small
ivory statuette on the mantel.

"And then?" asked Fergus. "You mean Charlotte
turned to Rockingham?"

"He is very charming," shrugged Mrs. Holt daintily.
She seemed a little more uneasy. "Your daughter encouraged him in London, we have all heard of the horse race,
the balls he gave for her. He was obviously furious when
she was married off to Darcy in such a hurry. I quite
expected to hear from Arundell that his wife expected a
child at once!"

Charlotte drew in a sharp gasp. Kenneth stepped forward again, his nostrils pinched, on a breath of outrage.
Darcy slowly stood up straight.

"But she is not with child," said Fergus gently, and his
fingers began to tap, tap on the arm of his chair. His
snapping green eyes glittered the way they did when he
spotted a business bargain. "Now, madam! What evidence
do you have that my daughter has ever played her husband
false? What clear facts, beyond insults and hints? I'll hear
your story patiently! But ye must have facts!"

"Nonsense!" said Mrs. Holt, angry now, red spots of
color on her pink cheeks. "What need of evidence? Poor
Darcy has been played false again! Like Lucille, his
second wife is mistress to a man, and ironically the same
man, Fitzhugh Rockingham!"

"You lie!" The quiet modulated tones of Rockingham
had turned sharp. He stood up, to take a tense pose before the mantel, unconsciously imitating Darcy at the
other end of the wide mantel. "You lie! As you have

before! You drove poor Lucille wild with your playing up to Saltash! Then you told her to make him jealous, to play about with men to attract him again! The poor innocent child, that gentle believing soul—you pretended to be her friend! Her friend! A snake in her bosom! She turned to me in distraction, and begged me to pretend to be in love with her!"

"What a likely story!" Mrs. Holt sneered, her color fading, to turn her white as death in her black garments. She shoved the tea trolley from her impatiently with her black-slippered foot. "No one believes that. You had her with you constantly. And the child was yours—all know it—"

Charlotte dared another look at Darcy. His eyes were narrowed to slits, he stared at Mrs. Holt as though seeing her for the first time. But he was silent.

"The child," said Rockingham. "God, the child. Even that, you would not spare your demon's tongue! The child was Rockingham's, you said. Well, I declare before you all, I had no affair with Lucille. I was sorry for her, pitied her with all my young heart. She glowed with hope over the child, hoped that Arundell would return to her. Instead you flaunted yourself before her, lied to her, as you have lied to Charlotte! And the child died, with its poor hopeless mother!"

"Is this true?" Darcy's ice cold tone interrupted the hot voice of Rockingham. "Is this true?"

"No, he lies!" cried Iris Holt shrilly.

Rockingham turned to Darcy directly. "On my honor as a gentleman, on the memory of my mother whom I adored, I tell you it is true! Lucille was never my mistress, nor is Charlotte. Charlotte never encouraged me. Lucille turned to me, begging for help as from a brother. That is all!"

"If you believe him, you are more a fool than I thought," sneered Iris Holt furiously. She stood up. "I am going to my room. I have a headache, from all this sound and fury over nothing! All to protect the reputation of his latest mistress!"

"Stay, woman," said Fergus. He too stood up. All stood now except Charlotte, who felt she could not. Her knees were too weak. "I asked you for facts, not tales. What facts have you? When ever has my daughter remained alone with Rockingham? You swore he encouraged her, she was with him alone. When, woman?"

She hesitated, then blurted out, "On their rides in the early morning! I looked out time and time again, to see her stealing out to meet her lover! She went to the stables alone, then rode out with him!"

Fergus leaned back with a sigh, his heels hitting the ground once more. He had been thrust forward, by some tremendous emotion. "Now I know you lie," he said grimly. "For my daughter went out with *me*—with me every morning. None but the groom Hobbs rode with us. We talked, or were silent. So you have lied—yet again. And I think you lied ever."

A great sigh came from Charlotte. Her father had done it again. She could have hugged him, but had not the strength to rise. He was beaming, his hands thrust into his pockets, rocking back and forth on his heels. He had pulled the coals from the fire, and they had not burned him. She loved him with all her heart, her dearest papa!

Darcy said quietly, "So this is the way of it. You will leave, Mrs. Holt. Never contact us again. I shall see to it that you are not received anywhere in society again. It is—unforgivable. And all because I believed your lying tales, gave you jewels for your help in dressing Pamela—though you did a damn poor job of it! I paid for your dressmaker, I asked you to come here—my stupid scheme for making my wife jealous—as you suggested! And it almost worked again."

Rockingham asked the question they all wanted to, but

did not dare. "You mean, Arundell, she was not your mistress either? All those diamonds, the dresses——"

Darcy nodded, grimly. "I asked her to play a part. She played it willingly, and too well. I ask your forgiveness, Charlotte. Mrs. Holt, why do you linger!" The tone sharpened, became a whip. "You will pack to leave!"

"I shall be leaving also, Mrs. Holt," said Rockingham, ironically. "We shall leave the young married couple to themselves, I believe. May I offer you a ride back to London? You have so besmeared both our reputations, it can do no damage!"

"Go to the devil!" she cried, and whirled from the room. He laughed aloud, and went over to Charlotte.

"I think she will not want my company," he said cheerfully, "and I am sure I do not care for hers. Charlotte, farewell. I shall return to London, and society. Thank you, my dear, for allowing me to know a truly lovely woman."

He lifted her hand, and pressed his lips to it.

"Thank you, Fitz," she said, in a low husky tone.

He lifted his head, retained her hand in his for a moment longer. "And am I forgiven—for the horse race—your brother, all?" he inquired in a soft tone.

She nodded. "Forgiven. Completely, forever."

"I thank you. It is more than I deserve. Farewell, my dear." He went to the door, lifted his hand to the company, his sardonic look on Darcy, still standing at the mantel as one in a daze. "Good-bye, all. I will look for you in London, on the season!" And he was gone.

Charlotte stirred, stood up. Darcy was so quiet. Did he regret his mistress? No, Mrs. Holt had not been—Charlotte dared not think what this meant to her. She dared not hope—

"I will see that a maid is sent to assist Mrs. Holt," she said and left the room.

Mrs. Holt was served a tray in her room before departure. Charlotte did not go to see her off. They sat at luncheon in virtual silence. Neville had returned and looked from one to the other in a puzzled manner. Kenneth seemed thoughtful, but happier. Darcy—she did not know. Fergus was beaming to himself smugly.

Charlotte longed to be alone, to think what this would mean. It seemed as though everything had exploded before her at once, and all the long waiting of days and months had climaxed in one sharp storm which had cleared the air like a summer shower.

What could it mean? Darcy had apologized before them all—but that did not mean that he loved her. He wanted to make her jealous—why? Did he still think to keep her, to have an heir from her? How he must have hated the humiliation, this public airing of the first marriage and its failure. Would he hate her for this, and hate her father as well? She had rejoiced when Darcy and Fergus had gotten along so well, would this destroy their friendship?

And what would become of her?

She went up to Pamela.

"I heard that dreadful woman left!" cried Pamela eagerly, as soon as she came into the schoolroom. "Oh, mama, what happened?"

"Well, everyone was angry with her, and she decided to return to London," said Charlotte, and decided that was as good a story as any.

"Is she coming back?"

"No—I believe she is never coming back. I don't think we shall see her again."

Pamela hugged her about her waist impulsively, her small sallow face beaming. "Then I shall come down to tea again," she offered, in somewhat of Darcy's grand manner, as one conferring a favor.

Charlotte laughed a little and sat down to talk to Pamela more comfortably. Pamela showed her some sums she had done, then discussed her reading. She really should have a governess, Charlotte thought, and one should be found for her. Perhaps Miss Morris could recommend someone, for Charlotte had not had time to spend hours with her.

But if she did not stay in Arundell—Charlotte pressed her forehead with her hand dubiously. Should she leave now? Or would it help anything to remain?

When she returned to her own pretty drawing room, beside her bedroom, she found Darcy there, pacing slowly back and forth before the round bay window, gazing out at the view. He turned when she entered and eyed her gravely. His face seemed more drawn and somber, and her heart sank.

"You must be seated, you look weary," he said at once. "Is this all too much for you? Do you wish to rest? I had wanted to have a talk with you, but it can wait."

She sank down on the blue sofa, her knees practically giving way. What would he say? "I am not too tired," she forced herself to say. "What do you wish to discuss?"

He looked oddly uncomfortable, and finally went to sit beside her on the sofa, only a few inches between them. But he did not touch her, his hands clasped on his knee, gazing into the fire.

"There is so much to say, I scarce know where to begin," he said finally. "I have had a short talk with your father. He urged me to be frank with you. And he assured me you are ever honest and forthright, no matter how impulsive you seem. So we must clear matters between us."

"Yes, I think we must," she agreed dully. Perhaps her father had suggested a separation, later a divorce! He might have revealed that Charlotte had suggested leaving.

"First, I must apologize for my stupid scheming with Mrs. Holt. I am dim-witted, Kenneth said so to my face, and I cannot deny it. Not to comprehend that the woman wanted more than money and jewels from me. She actually thought I would marry her—her!" And he looked angry and contemptuous. "But to bring her here, where you are mistress of my home, to flaunt her before you, in my idiotic plot to make you jealous—"

She interrupted softly, her voice huskier than ever. "Why—why did you wish to make me jealous?

He turned at last to face her. "Because I wanted all your attention," he said simply. "I wanted to make you admit that you—desired me at least, if you could not respect me. I lay awake nights, thinking of the contempt in your face as you flung the words at me, how you despised me. If I could get you to love and desire me, I thought you might one day come to—wish to respect and honor me, as I did you. I could not think what else to do. No matter how gentle I was with you, and how you submitted to me, when day came you turned from me in great contempt. You never confided willingly in me, you came for advice only as a last resort. I was in despair. It seemed—forgive me—my first marriage over again, when Lucille drifted from me, and I could not discover why. But you were so different, she was gentle and passive, and never spoke much. You are quick-witted, you are intelligent, you speak out—but you had contempt for me."

She clasped her hands together, her pink-skinned hands, just healing. "Darcy, I have a confession to make," she began haltingly. "I brought much on myself. I urged Kenneth and Neville to find out the truth of your relationship with Mrs. Holt. I—asked her to come and see me, we talked before the—the wedding. She said she was your mistress, and I believed her when she displayed the jewels you had given her. It was wrong of me. I should never have received her. If I had known more of the world, I should have known her dishonesty."

Darcy reached out and took her hands gently in his.

"You talked with her, and she lied about me? Was that what stood between us?"

"Partly. And you—you never said—you had anything but desire for me," she said faintly. His nearness made her feel weak. Was she going to be faint again?

"And I did desire you, my love," he said softly. "But it was more than that. I loved your high spirits, your gaiety. You made me feel young and happy again. I loved your gentle warmth with Pamela, and longed for it to warm me."

"Oh!" murmured Charlotte, not knowing which way to look. "And—and you did—not despise me for—for striking out at you? The night I flung water on you—at the ball—"

He laughed aloud. "I was furious! I longed to turn you over my knee and spank you! And then to kiss you again. I thought of your soft mouth under mine, your yielding body against mine—and the way your eyes sparkled when you were enraged— Oh, my dear, never did a man fall so quickly and so hard for a woman! I wanted you with coolness the first season, I thought you would make a fine wife and mother, but you were too young, I resolved to wait another season. And found you more beautiful and desirable than ever."

He had possession of her hands and was drawing her closer to him. "And you thought—I would be docile and obedient—a good wife—" She tried to mock, her spirits rising after long depression.

"Oh, never that! Never docile and obedient! I was never so foolish!" he whispered against her mouth. He kissed her gently, then with growing passion, drawing her more closely into his arms. "Oh, Charlotte, I love you, my red-haired girl, my fire opal! I thought of you at once, like one of my flaming opals, with heart of gold and all colors, sparkling for me—"

Then finally she dared to put her arms about his neck,

and draw herself closer to him, and yield to the passionate kisses on her mouth, her throat, her shoulder as he drew back the green muslin gown from her soft flesh. She felt the heat in him, the banked fire as he kissed her, and something was melting deep inside her—the ice that had frozen her for long.

"Oh—Darcy—I do love you," she whispered at last against his hard firm mouth. "I do—love you—so much—that I ached for you, and wept for you. It seemed so impossible that you could love me. And I would not settle for less than that. I could—could not endure it—if you did not love me."

"My precious, my dearest," he murmured, in such warm tones that she felt she had never known him. How delicious it would be, to come to know the real Darcy behind the stern face, to know him warm and human and loving and close. His hand caressed her thick red curls, stroked over her pink cheeks, circled her throat with gentle fingers.

"Darcy?" She drew back a little, on a thought. "I wish— oh, I wish that we might always be as frank with each other as today! I should hate it terribly if ever difficulties come between us, I could not endure it—"

He drew back, to gaze gravely into her eyes. And she knew at once he was thinking of that appalling first marriage of his, wrecked by that spiteful woman. Gentle Lucille, troubled, not knowing how to win back the love she had known, too timid to speak with him.

"Yes, we shall promise each other," he said at last, "that no matter how difficult it is, we shall always be frank with each other. We will trust each other, then no one can ever come between us again. Do you promise, Charlotte?"

"I promise," she said happily.

"And I promise, always to trust and believe in you, and to speak truly to you," said Darcy.

It was like the wedding ceremony all over again, with-